"Welb… …us [Bret Easton]

"Perfectly paced, hugely enjoyable, and not to be missed."

"Welbourn has managed to encapsulate a generation."

"Few of us can so eloquently paint a picture."

"There's a confronting honesty in the way Welbourn writes."

"Welbourn is a skilled writer."

"Bearing similarities to some of the best I've read."

"An exceptional piece of observational narrative."

"Genuinely gripping and heartbreaking."

"Welbourn portrays a realistic view of the world. It's raw, fresh, and intoxicating."

"Fast paced and easy to read."

The Ones We Fear

Robert Welbourn

SRL PUBLISHING

SRL Publishing Ltd
London

www.srlpublishing.co.uk

SRL PUBLISHING
THINKING DIFFERENTLY, DELIVERING CHANGE

Also by Robert Welbourn

Belonging
Ideal Angels
Great Romances of the 20th Century

Hannah,

Before we met my life was a series of loosely connected vignettes. You transformed it into a coherent narrative.

Chapter 1

'Freak!'

'Eww look at her!'

'What a stupid bitch!'

'Disgusting freak!'

'Stupid, poor loser!'

'Loser!'

Alex heard the cries before he saw the crowd; they rent the air, ripping the morning sky apart. What had been a perfectly normal, average day had taken a sinister turn; Alex could feel it in the atmosphere. A ring had formed in the middle of the playground, an undulating mass of students moving and swaying in kind, like seaweed being gently rocked by the tide, and without needing to see he knew exactly who was at the centre of it. Whenever a ring formed like this at Deerborn Secondary School, there was only ever one person at the centre of it.

The shouts grew louder, more and more voices joining in. It was a cacophony of sound, a mixture of hatred, excitement, glee; the voices were visceral, their feelings unbound. The sound of a group of children, teenagers mostly, reminding an outsider of their place. Reminding Janet of her place.

'Janet! Janet! Janet!'

The crowd started to chant her name, the many voices becoming one, but the noise was far from a celebration; if anything it was an incantation, as if to draw yet more spite towards the poor, innocent child at the centre of all the vitriol.

'What kind of name is Janet anyway, what are you, like 50?'

'My grandma is called Janet and she's nearly dead!'

'Why don't you just kill yourself, Janet?'

The voices separated into their component parts, and each line was delivered with such a mixture of sarcasm and disgust that Alex flinched. He'd been moving in the direction of the crowd, making his way slowly, reluctantly, towards it, like a moon pulled in by a planet's gravity, losing all control of itself and doing what it must, but he stopped at hearing these words. *Janet.* It wasn't exactly a cool name, a pretty name, a *young* name, but still, he thought, Janet couldn't help what her mum had decided to call her. Especially if what they said about Janet's mum was true, it wasn't Janet's fault. You don't choose your parents, a fact Alex knew all too well.

'Janet Janet, fatter than a planet!'

The crowd took up the chant, and soon the majority of the voices merged into one again, a monster's voice, loud, booming.

'Why are you so poor, Janet?'

'You're so dirty it's disgusting.'

'Why don't you ever wash your clothes?'

'Why don't you ever wash your hair?'

'Why don't you just fuck off?'

Alex reached the mass and began to push his way through. He manoeuvred bodies out of the way, using his shoulders and elbows to force a path through the wall of excitement, fear, exhilaration. The bodies were warm, alive, he could feel the anger emanating from them, it was palpable. He pushed harder, claustrophobia threatening to rise from within him.

He could also feel himself pushing through the air itself, so infused with the frothing and baying of a group of angry, taunting teenagers, a vicious mob of humans turned animals. It was almost electric, there was a heat to it that belied the overcast weather. The air was so heavy that Alex felt like if it was removed, if this had been taking place in a vacuum, it would have been easier to move. He thought to himself, actually it is a kind of vacuum. One with Janet at the centre.

Eventually Alex reached the front of the crowd, which had formed the shape of a doughnut, a doughy, circular collection of people with a clearing at the centre. Bursting out of the mass of bodies, like a freediver breaching the surface, desperately gulping air into his starved lungs, Alex was confronted with exactly the scene he expected.

On one side of the clearing, on her hands and knees, head hung down so her hair was hiding her face, was Janet. From where Alex stood she looked so helpless, so defeated. Her lank hair, long and greasy, probably a mousy brown but too dirty to be able to properly discern, swayed as Janet's body rocked slightly with each thudding impact. At the other side of the clearing stood Emma Sullivan, the usual suspect. The sun glinted off the golden crucifix she wore around her neck as she threw her head back in laughter. Behind her were her gang, Jenna Marsden, Aliyah Khan, and Francesca Lombardi, the new Italian girl in class. And behind them, Emma's boyfriend Jason Basely, a lumbering hulk of a boy too big to still be a child in anything but age. Luckily, Alex thought, *his* gang were nowhere to be seen. Alex dreaded to think what might have happened then.

The four girls laughed as they threw objects at Janet; at first Alex struggled to make out what, but after a couple of seconds he realised it was erasers. Francesca was holding a small, brown cardboard box in her left hand, and with her right was gleefully passing small pink and grey rubbers to Emma, Jenna, and Aliyah. They, in turn, were throwing them at Janet; as Alex stood, his feet rooted to the spot, the trio threw rubber after rubber at Janet, many of the small pieces of stationery missing her, many not. Each one that hit did so with the faintest of thumping noises, and coupled with the gentle swaying of Janet's body, Alex could imagine the impact. Being hit by one single eraser wouldn't do much damage; being hit by ten, twenty, god knew how many, the cumulative impact must have taken its toll. Especially in front of a mocking crowd.

Alex felt his temper begin to rise, and not just at

Emma and her gang. Those four were pieces of shit, Alex knew that, everyone in school knew that. The problem was, Emma Sullivan was both beautiful and intelligent, a devastating combination for anyone anywhere, but especially so for a 15-year-old girl still in high school. Not only did she get As in every subject, handing in all her homework on time, turning up to all their mock exams and passing easily, she was also easily the hottest girl at school.

With her long, straight blonde hair, her large green eyes, small button nose, and bright, glaring smile, everyone in school, at least all the boys anyway, and not a few of the girls, had crushes on her. Boys trailed after her wherever she went, like crowds of seagulls following a trawler, hoping she'd bestow on them a smile, a hello, anything at all. They basked in her attention, lived for it, some probably even willing to die for it. That she never gave her fans anything only seemed to make them want it more, and if her plan through her ignorance was to discourage them, it didn't work. The cross she wore coupled with her weekly church attendance meant the majority of teachers were in her thrall, too; whenever anyone had the temerity to tell on her – not Janet, never Janet, but the occasional other student who felt her wrath – the teachers would dismiss their complaints. "Not Emma Sullivan," they'd say, "it can't be Emma Sullivan, she's too good."

Jenna and Aliyah were pretty, too, tall and slim, with soft features and bright eyes; Jenna had violently red hair, Aliyah's a badly dyed blonde. She'd turned up to school with the bad dye job one Monday morning, and everyone has immediately assumed she was copying Emma. Whether it was true or not, such is high school, no one cared to find out. Rumour soon became fact.

No one had made up their mind about Francesca; she was new at the school, a transplant from elsewhere, an other, and her arrival was still too recent for anyone to have formed a firm opinion. She was pretty, probably, people said, but she was still too new for that opinion to be the prevailing one, and for her reputation to precede her. As well as this, people were suspicious of her; no one was quite sure how she'd ingratiated herself with Emma and her gang so quickly and it made them uneasy. The smart money would be on the fact that she'd joined in the othering of another to prevent being the other herself, but no one at Deerborn Secondary was that insightful, at least consciously. Between the four girls, however, there was enough beauty and intelligence to make them untouchable. Especially when they were juxtaposed with Janet; poor, dirty Janet.

Alex wrenched his eyes from Emma and her gang and rested them on Janet. Still on her hands and knees, Alex wanted to run over to her, grab her, shake her. It was at her that the majority of his anger was aimed. He didn't hate her, not like Emma and her gang and most of the school, teachers included, did. He didn't like her either, oh no, that was not the case at all. If anything he was wildly indifferent, he felt about Janet how he felt about most of his fellow students at Deerborn. They were just people he was forced to be with, forced to study with and learn with and eat with and play football with in PE until the school year ended a few months later. Then he'd finally be free to leave, would never see the majority of them again.

If it had been up to Alex, he wouldn't have had anything to do with anyone in the school; but he knew that wasn't possible, knew he needed to blend in to survive, knew, in his heart of hearts, that he did actually need his fellow students, he did actually need the people around him. And so he laughed with his friends, he listened to the teachers, he kept his head down and did his best to get by.

But right then, in that moment, he wanted to break from the crowd, storm over to Janet and grab her arms, drag her to her feet, brush the hair out of her face and shake her. He wanted to shake her as hard as he could, try and shake some sense into her, shake some willpower into her, shake some of the meekness out of her. He wanted to scream in her face that she should stand up for herself, she should fight back. She should, at least, stay on her feet, walk away, exit the situation. That was better than doing nothing at all, than simply accepting her place, surely? Alex wanted to tell her that she had to do *something, anything,* or the torment would never end. Because Alex had seen his father coming in dejectedly from work, had heard his mother console him, whisper in his ear that it would get better, she was sure of it, she promised. Alex knew that bullying didn't stop when you left school, and that some people, like his father, like Janet, like Billy Loomis who would eat anything for 50p, would be bullied forever.

It wasn't just Janet he wanted to grab and shake; he wanted to do the same to Emma, to walk over to her and shake her and slap her face, like he'd seen in films when people are hysterical. He wanted scream at her, "what gives you the right? Why do you get to decide who's popular and who gets bullied? Who put you in charge?"

He wanted to, but even over and above knowing he wouldn't, he knew it would be futile. No one had decided Emma was in charge; everyone had decided Emma was in charge. Her father was the local councillor for Deerborn, the village they called home; the public had voted him to be in charge, and this conferred a certain amount of status on Emma. Her father was in charge of his father's generation, therefore Emma was in charge of her own. But more than that, much more so, what really put Emma in charge was her beauty. She'd matured faster than other girls; she grew tall before them, starting shaving her legs (and talking loudly about it in the corridor between classes and in the dining hall at lunch) before them, grew breasts before them. If anything, that was what truly put her in charge. Not only was she beautiful, a girl slowly becoming a woman before everyone's eyes, but she had *breasts.* And not only had she grown them before most of the other girls, she'd never been ashamed or embarrassed by them. Where other girls tried to hide theirs, wearing baggy jumpers, constantly keeping their arms folded, Emma wore hers like a badge of honour. And for someone as beautiful and popular as Emma, a thing becomes what she wills it to be. So where other girls were taunted for their breasts, whether they were too small, too big, one slightly bigger than the other — for there's no winning for teenage girls, not when it comes to teenage boys — Emma displayed hers proudly. She started talking loudly about bras, about how her mum was taking her shopping, and not just for plain, boring bras, but cute ones, in pretty colours with patterns and designs. Emma had learned long ago that to master something you had to own it, and so she did.

Whilst the children wouldn't learn for many years, the adults knew it was this confidence that had really put Emma in charge, that made her leader not just of their year, but of the whole school. The year previous she'd been bold, brash, but there had been a holding back, a sense that she was capable of more. Only having been in year 10, not the top of the school, meant she was reserved, waiting, like a tiger in the bush, knowing its moment will come and so not rushing. When Alex and Janet and Emma and the rest of their year had come back that year, into their final year at the school, Emma had truly flourished. And that had been hell for Janet.

There was so much Alex had wanted to do, standing there surrounded by the baying crowd; he felt like he'd done the first time his dad allowed Alex to go with him to watch the annual boxing match at the Harvest Festival in Hagan's Field, the one with the stone circle children weren't supposed to go near any other time of the year. At first the crowd had been perfectly calm, perfectly reasonable, men and women sitting, standing, talking, drinking. And then two men had entered the ring, a bell had rung, and everything had changed. Those same people, some of whom Alex recognised, like kindly Mr Jones who ran the library, and his wife Mrs Jones, who Alex knew worked in Hull for the *Hull Daily Mail*, had ceased being people, and had become animals. Where a minute previously they'd been talking calmly, reasonably, discussing the weather or the local economy, suddenly they were screaming and shouting, egging on these two men to fight each other, to hurt each other. Blood was on the cards, blood was in the air, and when the crowd got a scent, they'd seemed to devolve to their basest animal selves. It was the same right there on the playground.

On the opposite side of the ring Alex had seen see his two best friends, Tom and Mo. Normally very calm boys, they were two people who were, like Alex, just happy to get by. They weren't popular, weren't unpopular, but simply blended in to the school's ecosystem. And like Alex, they were patiently waiting their freedom the following June after their GCSEs; however, unlike Alex, right then they were monsters. They were snarling, shouting, Mo was even moving his arm as if he had a box of erasers, too, as if he wanted to pelt them at Janet, increase her pain and suffering, become a part of it.

Alex could also see Lisa, Maria, and Dani, three of the swots who sat at the front of every class, answered every question, even sometimes asked for extra homework; they too were like bestial versions of themselves, they were no longer humans but Frankenstein's Adam, rejected by humanity and tearing it apart as a consequence.

The shouting had begun to hush; it was like a reverse ripple effect, starting from the back of the crowd, though it took its time to reach the centre. Alex noticed it before Emma and her gang, and turning he saw the crowd behind him part like the Red Sea before Moses as two teachers pushed through. Mr Barnett, the head of Maths, and Miss Aseen, the new Science teacher, eventually made their way to the centre of the doughnut; Francesca was the next to notice, and in a panic she dropped the box of erasers, spilling them through the clearing, small pieces of rubber bouncing in every direction. It would have been comedic if the situation wasn't so grave.

'For fuck's sake,' Emma said to Francesca as she bent down to pick up a handful of ammunition before she straightened back up and continued her aerial bombardment. Jenna spotted the teachers next and tried to quickly shove the erasers she was holding into her non-existent pockets; they too spilled onto the floor about her feet. Aliyah and Emma, however, were blissfully unaware of the impending end to their fun, and continued to lob the erasers at the prone Janet, who still was not moving, neither to defend herself nor flee.

Silence descended on the crowd until all that could be heard were the soft thumps of rubber hitting Janet. She was completely silent, any tears her hair might have been hiding without volume, until Emma caught her in the face, just under her left eye, and she finally cried out. The noise was sad, like a dog being whipped, and it broke Alex's heart even as his anger remained. Emma was delighted with the noise; she turned to face the crowd as if to soak up the praise she thought she was due, and that was when she spotted the two teachers. Rather than panic like her friends, she simply stood on the spot, putting one hand on her hip in a posture of utmost petulance.

'You four, here, now,' boomed Mr Barnett, his voice shocking its way through the fresh silence like thunder on a quiet summer night. Emma's underlings moved quickly to where he was pointing, to a spot just in front of him; Emma stood stationary for a few seconds, as if daring him to ask her again, before with an audible sigh she too moved to stand in front of him.

'Head's office, now,' he shouted, spittle flying from his lips, his fury palpable. As the girls trudged away, and Mr Barnett followed them, Miss Aseen moved over to Janet. Even though it had only been perhaps ten seconds since the teachers had arrived, the crowd had nearly vanished, everyone moving away to other forms of entertainment since the show had ended. Miss Aseen squatted on her haunches; Alex couldn't hear what she was saying, but her words appeared to have no effect on Janet whatsoever, who remained on her hands and knees, head hung low, unmoving. This continued for a minute before Miss Aseen stood up, putting one hand under Janet's left arm and lifting her. Janet stood reluctantly, and allowed Miss Aseen to steer her across the playground, in the opposite direction to Mr Barnett and the group of offenders.

Alex remained standing where he was, unsure of how

to proceed, until Tom and Mo appeared before him laughing.

'Did you see that?' Tom said, barely able to get his words out, his voice high pitched and utterly soaked through with delight.

'Yeah, I thought Barnett was going to shit himself,' Mo was bent over with laughter, he put one hand on Alex's shoulder to steady himself but stopped abruptly when Alex shrugged it off.

'That was shit.'

'Huh?' Mo said, standing up straight. Tom had stopped laughing, too, and was regarding Alex with half a suspicious look on his face.

'What you on about man?' Tom asked.

'What Emma and those bitches did to Janet, that was fully shit.'

Neither Tom nor Mo said anything for a moment, before Tom started smiling.

'Do you fancy Janet?' he said, laughter returning to his voice.

Mo started laughing, too, and soon they were both jumping and dancing round Alex, pointing and chanting at him.

'Alex and Janet sitting in a tree, K-I-S-S-I-N-G.'

'Fuck off,' Alex said, repressing his anger and trying to sound like he was joking.

'You fancy Janet, you freak,' Mo said, once again bent double with renewed laughter.

'Ew, no thanks,' Alex said, hating himself even as he said it. 'Who the fuck would fancy that dirty bitch?'

Tom and Mo roared with laughter at this, delighted to have their companion back from his odd behaviours. They didn't notice Alex flinching at the sound, didn't see the shadow that crossed his face, the darkness on his features. From across the playground came the sound of the bell clanging, summoning them back inside to begin afternoon lessons.

'Oh fuck,' Tom said. 'Double maths with hard-on Harden, we better get a move on.'

The trio stalked across the playground, the patches of sunlight poking out from behind the clouds feeling like taunts to Alex. It was a warm September afternoon, and Alex wondered to himself, as they made their way back into the bland brick school building, how something so awful could happen on such a beautiful day. Little did he know, there were so many more beautiful days to come, days that would feel without end, days that made him happy to be alive. And so many awful events he'd wish he weren't.

Chapter 2

Janet hadn't appeared in maths. Alex had thrown regular glances at the door, every slight noise from the quiet class making him jump and throw his head around, but as the first hour had ticked over into the second he'd realised she wasn't coming.

Alex normally liked maths; he was a bit of a prodigy when it came to mental arithmetic and enjoyed working out percentages. He found them satisfying, the way everything had to add up to 100, a nice, round, easy number. Numbers made sense to Alex in a way a lot of the world didn't; the world was messy, uncoordinated, surprising things could, and did, happen on a regular basis. But with numbers, everything stayed the same. Numbers obeyed rules and laws without rebelling; one plus one was two, it always had been and it always would be. Every percentage was out of 100, and always would be.

Although saying that, he'd been faltering a bit of late; once they'd started introducing letters into the equations he'd become confused, his brain hadn't been able to grasp it. Letters belonged in English, he thought, that was their home. In English things had different meanings, one sentence could be interpreted in a variety of ways by a variety of people. He didn't hate this, per se, in fact a lot of the time he enjoyed reading a book and then finding out other people had interpreted it completely differently than he had. He enjoyed hearing other perspectives, learning new ways of approaching things. But nothing, to Alex, was quite like the firmness and solidity of numbers, and he usually loved double maths, watching things neatly slot into their places. But he hadn't today.

Even as Mr Harden stood at the front of the class, textbook in one hand and marker pen in the other, explaining some equation as he drew it on the whiteboard, Alex couldn't stop thinking about Janet, and in particular her hair. He wondered if that was why Emma had latched on to Janet in the first place, had become her enemy. Emma's blonde hair was never not perfect; never was there so much as even a single strand astray, a single individual hair that didn't know and perform its role to perfection. It was as if they were as scared of Emma as the rest of the school were, aware they could be cut at any moment if they displeased her. Alex could imagine Emma sitting in front of her mirror each morning, her eyes fixed and focused, carefully and lovingly straightening her hair, pulling the hot irons down the length, stroking it, caressing it. One day the previous year, in Science, he'd found himself staring at Emma's hair, unable to stop. It was beautiful; even though he hated Emma for what she'd done to Janet earlier today, for what she'd been doing to Janet for the four going on five years they'd all been in high school, he wasn't going to sit there and pretend she wasn't beautiful. He, like everyone else, was drawn in to her gravity. He wasn't completely enmeshed; if Emma was the sun he was Neptune, still completely beholden to her but on the outskirts. If Jenna and the others were Mercury, then he was lightyears away, in her gravity but not in her aura, cold, distant, lifeless.

Alex had been staring at Emma's hair almost without realising; indeed, it was only when Emma shouted, in the middle of class, ever the attention seeker, 'Can I fucking help you?' that'd he'd been startled out of his reverie, had jumped at the sound and then blushed bright red upon the realisation that he was the target of Emma's vitriolic question.

Mr Buckingham, the science teacher before Miss Aseen, had sent Emma out of the class and given her detention, for a combination of interrupting his lesson and doing so with vulgar language, but that hadn't stopped people laughing at Alex, making fun of him for being obsessed with Emma's hair. Thankfully, a couple of weeks later, Sharon Beesting had fallen over in a puddle and arrived at school soaking wet and smelling like shit, and Alex's hair-related faux pas had been forgotten. There's a lot to be said, Alex always thought, for the shortness of teenage memories.

Alex wondered, his mind wandering as Mr Harden explained that $a^2 + b^2 = c^2$, if the fact that Janet never tended to her hair was why Emma picked on her with particular abandon. As much as he didn't want to admit it, Janet didn't help herself; school is like nature, Alex thought, like the things he'd seen on *Planet Earth*, the TV show with David Attenborough. It was a wilderness of wild animals, a mess of competing and warring factions. Everyone is constantly working to make sure they're not bottom of the food chain, not the victim of anyone else's misplaced hormonal teenage frustration. You had to be on your guard 24/7, and, as much as he was loathe to admit it, you had to fit in. And Janet didn't. But not only this, not only did Janet not fit in; she didn't seem to care either.

Like just now, Alex thought, the way she stayed perfectly still on her hands and knees, head hanging down, not moving, not defending herself, either with words or actions, not even simply standing up and walking away. Emma felt she had a divine right to punish Janet, and by acquiescing, by not fighting back, it almost seemed like Janet agreed.

And although they weren't friends, never would be, Alex knew, as did everyone else at school, that Emma's hair was her pride and joy. So for Janet to so neglect her own, Alex thought, was an affront to everything Emma stood for. By refusing to regularly wash or comb her hair, Janet was insulting the thing Emma held most dear. By not using shampoo and conditioner and blowdrying it and straightening it meticulously, carefully, and above all lovingly, Janet was effectively spitting on Emma's one true love. And Emma couldn't allow this.

Eventually Alex had been startled out of his mindless meanderings by the bell signalling the end of the day. He and his 30 fellow students gleefully stuffed their exercise and text books back into their bags, the noise level jumping from quiet to deafening as the ending of another day signalled free time, time away from the prison most regarded school as. The students proceeded to fight their way out of the classroom, out of the building, running off the school grounds with shouts of abandon.

Alex fell in step with Tom and Mo, the trio turning right out of the school gates and walking to their respective homes. The sun was still high in the sky, and they each carried their coats, jumpers shoved unceremoniously into their bags, basking in what little autumn sun the year still held. Winter would approach fast, it always did in Deerborn, and soon it would be all winter coats, hats, scarves, rushing from school to home to stay as warm and dry as possible. Though they were all only 15, the trio were mature enough to appreciate good weather whilst it lasted; in the darkest depths of winter Deerborn was known to become completely isolated from the outside world under a deluge of snow, and the boys had experienced this enough times for themselves to not wish it to hurry up.

'Did you hear, Janet got sent home?' Tom said, as the trio walked in a line, kicking an empty Coke can between them, the aluminium rattling loudly in the still afternoon air.

'Did you see her?' Mo asked.

'Nah, Dave Kidson told me.'

'Did he see her?'

The can bounced across the pavement, occasionally reflecting the brilliant sun. A sharp glinting flash caused Alex to cover his eyes and them rub them furiously, willing his vision to return.

'Nah, but he said that Sarah Bones saw her being walked out the gates by her mum.'

'Oh shit,' said Mo.

'Yeah, apparently she was in with the head for ages waiting for her mum to come, and then when she did they left like five minutes later.'

'I hope her mum gave Gullis what for, the stupid old dickhead.'

'I bet she did,' Tom laughed. 'I'd love to have seen it, I bet she had a proper go at him.'

They paused as they came to a road, Alex pressing the button and the three of them waiting patiently for the green man. In years gone by, they would have dashed across, regardless of the colour of the traffic light, regardless of the volume of traffic passing at 40mph. But since they'd discovered girls, they'd also discovered a distaste for running. It's impossible to look good when you run, and no one wants to look like an idiot in front of girls.

The green man came and they continued their journey, the can disappearing into a bush as Tom gave it a huge kick. They continued in silence for a moment before Tom went on.

'Her mum seems like a proper weirdo.'

'Well, yeah,' Mo said, in a very reasonable tone. 'What

do you expect? No one is that weird by themselves, they have weird parents too, or a weird older brother or sister or something.'

'Does Janet have any brothers or sisters?' Tom asked.

'No,' Alex said, his voice breaking slightly from lack of use as he did. 'She's an only child.'

'Oh, hello, nice of you to join the conversation,' Tom laughed.

'How do you know?' Mo asked, cocking his head to one side like a spaniel, half suspicious and half amused.

'I dunno,' Alex said quietly, lamely. 'I just do.'

'Is it 'cos you fancy her?' Tom said, laughter in his voice which Mo joined in with.

Silence fell upon the boys again, and they walked for a few minutes without speaking. Alex couldn't get Janet out of his mind; she disgusted him, as she did everyone else, but he couldn't help but feel sorry for her. Alex had been the subject of Emma Sullivan's ire for one sentence, nearly a year ago, and it still stung. He couldn't imagine being a perennial target, never knowing peace or freedom.

'She doesn't help herself,' Tom said.

'Who?' Mo asked, as if they hadn't been talking about Janet for their entire walk.

'Janet, you idiot,' Tom said, pushing Mo with both his hands, trying to knock him off his feet.

'Oi, fuck off,' Mo said indignantly, remaining upright and proceeding to do his best to push Tom over. The pair stopped walking and began to scuffle, each trying to get the other in a headlock. Alex continued walking, leaving them behind. He couldn't stop thinking about Janet, no matter how hard he tried. And he was trying harder than he'd tried at anything recently, harder than he would have cared to admit.

Soon Tom and Mo caught up with Alex, both out of breath. They turned a corner and were at the top of Alex's street. They all stopped, stood in a triangle facing each other.

'You wanna go to the field and play football?' Mo asked them both.

'Let's do it,' Tom responded louder than was necessary. His scuffle with Mo had brought his adrenaline to the fore and he was bouncing on the balls of his feet, clearly keen to expend some energy.

'Alex?' Mo asked him.

'I can't,' he responded. 'I've gotta go out for dinner tonight, my uncle's birthday or something.' It was a lie, he didn't even have any uncles, but Alex didn't feel bad in the telling. He didn't want to play football, to hang out with Tom and Mo. No, he wanted to go home and shut himself in his room and not think about anything, especially not Janet.

'You didn't mentioned anything before?' Tom said, far closer to Alex than Alex was comfortable with. Alex could feel Tom's hot breath of his face and took a step back, but Tom only moved a step closer.

'I didn't know, my mum text me at lunch.'

'But you said this morning you forgot your phone at home,' Mo said, also moving close to Alex, sounding suspicious. 'What's really going on?'

'It's... I mean... I... erm...' Alex sputtered, annoyed at himself for having been caught in his lie so easily.

'I know what it is,' Tom said, drawing up to his full height, a huge grin taking over his face. 'He's going home to cry over Janet.'

Tom burst out laughing as he said it, and Mo joined in immediately. The pair started pointing at and taunting Alex, dancing around him and jumping and laughing once again.

'Alex fancies Janet,' they half shouted, half sang. 'Alex fancies Janet, Alex fancies Janet.'

For the second time that day Alex's face went a deep shade of burnt red, and he felt the heat on his cheeks. He tried to start walking down his street but Tom and Mo stopped him, pushing him back, not allowing him to pass.

'Are you going to your girlfriend's house?' Mo said, pursing his lips in a mock kissing face.

'Oh Janet, I love you,' Tom said, shaping his face the same way. The pair began to pretend to kiss each other passionately, being careful to leave a foot of space between them. Alex started tapping his foot in frustration, and, having had enough of Janet and mocking in general for one day, shoved the pair aside and stormed off down his street without looking back.

He heard Tom shout, 'See you tomorrow, Loverboy!' but kept walking, his head down, his frustration beginning to get the better of him. The reason he'd stalked so suddenly off was the tears brimming in his eyes; apropos of nothing, Alex had found himself about to cry. Whether it was Janet, Emma, Tom and Mo, the heat, being caught in the lie, or simply the ever-bubbling cauldron of hormones that was his brain, he didn't know. All he knew was that he had to get home before he started crying in earnest; if Tom and Mo saw that he'd never live it down, it'd be all over school the next day and then he'd be in the same boat as Janet. That boat was the Titanic, and he had no intention of going down with it.

Reaching his house he opened the small white gate, slamming it shut behind him, and stalked up the short garden path. He opened the bright red front door, the colour eerily similar to his cheeks, and threw his bag and coat to the hall floor in frustration. He kicked off his shoes and was about to stomp upstairs when he heard voices from the living room.

Curiosity getting the better of him, he took his hand off the newel post, his foot off the first stair, and quietly padded down the hall instead. He moved slowly past the deer antlers displayed on the wall, the paintings of woodland scenes, careful to make as little noise as possible. The only person in the house at that time of day should have been his mum; his dad was at work, and his mum never had anyone over. As he moved closer to the living room, where the voices slowly drifted from, he realised it was in fact his dad to whom his mum was talking.

Without listening to the words, without knocking on the closed door, another fact that struck Alex as odd – this door was never closed – he walked in to see his parents sitting on the couch, arms around each other.

They were both crying, and seeing them set Alex off; he burst into tears himself.

Chapter 3

'Come here, love, oh come here.' Alex's mum patted the seat next to hear, the empty end of the grey three-seater couch on which Alex's parents were sitting. It was an old thing, sagging in the middle, threads fraying along the arms, stuffing showing when you moved the cushions. It had been sitting in that exact spot in the living room since before Alex was born; he knew his parents wanted to replace it, but simply hadn't been able to afford to.

Alex stayed where he was standing in the doorway, one hand on the door handle, reluctant to move. He'd never seen his parents cry before, and didn't know what to do with it. He was old enough to know intellectually that his parents were flawed creatures, fallible; he was 15, not a child, he didn't think they were invincible. Still, it was one thing to know something in your mind, to understand it, and another entirely to see it play out in front of your eyes. He wanted his mum to comfort him and his tears, but he didn't think he had the strength to do so for her.

Alex's dad wasn't looking at him; his eyes were on the

floor, searching the carpet as if searching for a clue to a murder, looking first this way, then that, his pupils searing into the worn material. Alex watched him for a moment; the two looked so alike even Alex could see it, and sometimes when he looked at his dad's curly black hair and warm blue eyes he felt like he could have been looking in a mirror. The longer Alex studied his father, the more he could feel an awkwardness rising in him. He realised he needed to move so his dad could raise his head, could look from the floor to somewhere else. Alex's mum continued to pat the couch, desperate for her son to join her so she could cling on to him, hold him and feel him and remember he was real. Slowly, with all the sureness of foot of Bambi on ice, Alex strode across the living room carpet, feeling its thinness beneath his socked feet, and sat down next to his mum.

The living room was small and dark, the carpet a deep forest green. The wallpaper was also like that of a forest, thin trees reached from the floor to the ceiling, between them birds and flashes of other animals. More deer antlers hung here, and to Alex it had always felt as much like the outside as the inside could possibly be. Now, sitting next to his upset parents, the air in the room was heavy with emotion. The atmosphere was tense, fragile, and Alex was scared to move too quickly in case he fractured it. Things felt on a knife edge, and Alex didn't want to be responsible for them tipping one way or the other. He wanted to be looked after, not have to look after anyone.

The three of them barely fit on the couch – the fact it

was a three-seater didn't mean it could actually hold three people, that was surely just a marketing term – and Alex felt uncomfortable. He was wedged in, half his bum on the couch, the other half kind of resting halfway up the arm. His spine called out in pain but he ignored it; he was young, not a child but years from being an adult, and his spine still had plenty of give in it.

As he sat down his mum took his hand, and Alex let her. Her hand was soft and warm, reassuring, and Alex immediately felt better for having his hand resting in it. Now it was his turn to sit with his eyes on the floor, he joined his father in the search for the clue, the something that might provide an answer. After a minute or so he stole a glance at his father and saw his mother was holding one of his hands, too; she was spread between them, the two men in her life, father and son. She was clinging on to them.

Alex wanted desperately to ask what was going on, why his dad was home in the middle of the afternoon, if everything was okay. He wondered if Aunty Jean had finally died; not finally as in he was glad of it, but because she was so old and had been sick for a long time. She wasn't his actual aunt, but his dad's, and had been diagnosed with cancer when Alex was just a baby. She'd been fighting and fighting all these years, seeming only to get stronger whenever the doctors pronounced her moments away from death. He was finally summoning up the courage to ask when his mother broke the silence, saved him from having to be the one to do so.

'Your dad,' she said, her voice breaking as she looked

at Alex. Even with his head down he could feel her eyes on his scalp and he wanted to look up, look at her, but he was unable. He knew his tears would come afresh when he did. His mum faltered, coughed, sniffed, before continuing.

'Your dad has lost his job I'm afraid, Alex.'

Alex finally looked up, looked at his father, as if he needed his dad to say it to know it was true. His dad didn't say anything, merely grunted in confirmation. Alex wondered if his dad was scared of opening his mouth for fear of the tears returning, too.

'What,' Alex began, stopped, continued. 'What do you mean?'

'That bast–' His mum caught herself before swearing. 'That horrible man, Mr Sullivan, fired your father today.'

The room was quiet. For a moment the only sound came from the old clock ticking away the seconds on the mantel piece, before Alex spoke.

'I don't understand,' Alex said, his voice no longer that of a 15-year-old but of a child, he'd reverted back to almost his infant self, sitting there clutching his mother's hand, not knowing the ways of adults.

His mum started to speak again but his dad touched her knee, finally looked away from the floor and at her, shook his head. Alex knew they'd exchanged something then without words, the way only people who know each other well can. He did it sometimes with Mo and Tom, a look or a nod or a small smile exchanging more information than words ever could.

His mum fell silent, and finally his dad began to

speak.

'Unfortunately, son,' he said, his voice cracking, 'Mr Sullivan has let me go.'

'But why?' Alex asked, still not understanding. 'You've worked there for ages, I thought you were good at it?'

Alex's father blanched then, as if stung by his son's words.

'He told me it's because I hadn't met my targets, but I know that was just an excuse. I know why he really did it.'

Alex still didn't understand; he knew his dad, in his job for the building society in Hull, had targets to meet each month, but he didn't really know what that meant. What did his dad actually have to do? And why hadn't he done it? Alex wanted to ask his dad so many questions, but he stayed quiet, said nothing. There was nothing to say.

'That bastard,' his mum said, completing the word this time, and Alex was shocked. He'd never heard his mum swear before; if it hadn't been such a sombre atmosphere he would have been impressed, he would have laughed and given her a high five and told her to do it again. But as it was, he merely let the word fall between them, remained silent, waited for someone to speak.

'The real reason I got fired, son, is because I didn't turn old Mrs Willerby out of her home. Mr Sullivan told me this morning to visit her, and if she didn't have any money to evict her there and then.'

'Is that even legal?' his mum asked.

'Technically no, but you know what people are like around here,' Alex's dad said, and Alex could almost feel the hatred he spat out with every word. 'You can't legally just kick someone out of their house there and then, you have to go to court, get an order, hire bailiffs to do it. But around here, what Mr Sullivan says goes. He has everyone in his pocket, even the police–'

'–come on dear,' Alex's mum said interrupting him, glancing at Alex as she did so. 'I don't think Alex needs to hear all that now.'

'You're right, love, you're right.' He sat up a little straighter, cleared his throat, before looking at Alex once more. 'I knew Mrs Willerby wouldn't have any money, she hardly ever does, but I wasn't going to turn her out in the street. She's lived in that house all her life, was born in it and grew up in it. That daughter of hers, what's her name–'

'–Janet,' Alex said in a monotone, continuing to stare at the carpet. In doing so, he didn't see his parents quickly glance at each other before his dad carried on. The clock continued to tick, puncturing the momentary silence.

'Janet, that's right, she was born there, too. In fact, the women of that family have given birth within those walls for generations, hundreds of years if you believe the stories.' He coughed, cleared his throat. 'Who am I to kick them out? With the Harvest Festival coming up, it's crappy timing. And on purpose, I just know it. Just because times are hard, well they're hard for everyone!' He yelled, and Alex jumped a little as he felt the air change, could once again feel his father's anger like a tangible thing. He wanted to grab it and smash it, to make his dad okay.

'It's okay, dear, it's okay,' Alex's mum said to his dad, patting his hand.

'I'm sorry, love, I don't mean to get upset, it's just–'

'I know dear, but not in front of Alex, okay?'

'You're right, you're right. Sorry, darling.'

They fell silent, and Alex waited a moment before he spoke, finally finding the courage to use his voice. It came out incredibly quietly when he did, barely above a whisper.

'What's going to happen to Janet?' he asked, before quickly adding, 'and her mum, Mrs Willerby. What's going to happen to them?'

His dad sighed, looked at his mum, sighed again.

'I don't know, son, I just don't know.'

Alex thought about the Harvest Festival, about the upcoming school trip, he looked around the room at the worn and tatty furnishings, and asked another question, his voice even quieter this time; if the house hadn't been near complete silence his parents wouldn't have been able to hear him.

'What's going to happen to us?'

Chapter 4

Alex was laying on his bed with the radio quietly playing some pop song or other when he heard the knock at the front door. He didn't move at first; he wasn't doing anything, simply lying stretched taut on his bed, half listening to the music, hands behind his head as if he were on a sun lounger on the beach in Cornwall like he had been over the summer.

He was staring at – without actually seeing – the poster directly opposite his bed, which was the Hull City football team official squad photo for that season. The 30 or so men, most wearing kits, the backroom staff wearing tracksuits, and the manager wearing a suit, were all staring intently into the camera; some of them, if you truly studied their faces, looked like they might be trying to intimidate the photographer, or maybe even the camera itself. Others looked in turns happy, content, bored, and restless. All feelings Alex knew well.

His room was much like that of any other 15-year-old boy; there were various other pictures of Hull City players, mostly of his favourite, the midfielder Jean

Michaël Seri, as well as posters for some of his favourite films. There were a couple of posters of women, all fully dressed – his parents had allowed him to display them with this proviso. Initially, Alex had wanted to pin up some posters of bikini-clad women, but his parents had quickly nixed that idea. Alex hadn't been happy, even if he'd understood. He wouldn't want to go into his parents' room and see his mum showing posters of men in their underwear, so why should she have to see women in their underwear in his? Amongst the posters were a couple of pairs of deer antlers; Alex didn't like them, couldn't understand why his parents did, but was happy to live with them there. They took up such little space he just ignored them most of the time.

The floor, more threadbare carpeting, though this time a rich blue like the ocean, was littered with clothes in varying forms of cleanliness, various school textbooks, a whole host of Lego, some builds fully completed, others half done, yet more just piles of bricks and tyres and various human parts. His small wardrobe displayed more posters, Scarface and Goodfellas, movies he was probably too young to have seen and be celebrating, but did so anyway. There was a small desk underneath the window which overlooked the back garden. This was where Alex did his homework, although he'd be lying if he said he didn't spend more time looking out the window than down at the books in front of him.

The radio quietly played music as Alex's mind drifted. A song by a popstar who pretended to be a witch was playing, it was that summer's number one hit. Alex was sick to death of it. But not sick enough to get up and change the station; he knew it'd be over in a few minutes and so he let it play, tried to ignore it. Behind the music he could hear the sounds of kids playing across the village, their shouts and screams drifting through the open window. He envied them their ease.

Alex's mind ran with thoughts of his parents, and thoughts of Janet. The Harvest Festival was coming up, the biggest event in Deerborn. What if his parents said he couldn't go because his dad had lost his job? What if they said he could, but couldn't afford to give him any money so he couldn't go on any of the rides or play games on any of the stalls or even just buy some candyfloss? And similarly, what if his parents couldn't afford to pay for him to go on the school trip? He dreaded to think how much of a target that would make him, being left behind at school while everyone else piled onto the coaches, their laughter a mockery of his sadness.

Shaking his head, trying to clear it of the depressing thoughts, Alex stood up and moved over to his bedroom window. Though their garden was only small, barely more than a yard really, living in the small village of Deerborn meant that beyond their fence were endless fields. They stretched across the land, all the way to the horizon, and Alex would alternate between feelings of complete and utter freedom at the lack of fences and boundaries, and being completely overwhelmed by the endless space, the vastness of it, the fields moving away as if to infinity, grass and crops continuing forever. At 15, Alex had recently become aware not just of his own mortality, but his own place on the planet, a vast sphere moving through an unknowably large universe. Sometimes Alex was comforted to be such a small cog in such a gigantic machine; others, he felt so small as to be buried under an avalanche of insignificance.

Through his window he could just see the edge of Hagan's Field, and he shuddered at it, without knowing why. The sun was beginning its slow descent, the nearby church just finishing gonging the passing hour, when the soft rapping bounded off the front door. Alex didn't move at first; Tom and Mo were off playing football, and no one else had text him, so he wasn't expecting anyone. Besides, the door was never for him anyway; since his parents had let him have his first mobile the previous year on his 14th birthday, no one ever called for him any more. Why would they? Tom and Mo both had phones, as did everyone else he knew, and so they'd simply decide where to meet in their group chat, and all proceed there individually.

Alex heard one of his parents shuffle down the hallway and open the front door. Even though he was in his bedroom at the back of the house with his door closed, their house was so small he could hear everything as if he was standing on the doorstep taking part in the conversation himself.

'Oh, hello,' his father said, somewhat surprised.

'Hi,' he heard his mum say; she must have joined her husband on the step.

'I just wanted to give you this by way of thanks,' came a soft yet rasping voice, though it belonged to a woman it was deep and gravelly, but at the same time incredibly powerful. Alex thought whoever it was needed to have a good cough to clear their throat; the more they talked and didn't, the more he found his own itching. He took a sip of water from the glass sitting on his desk, the effort nearly more than it was worth. He swallowed before moving back to his bed and laying back down again.

'And I just wanted to say thank you again, for what you did today,' the voice said, sounding vaguely familiar to Alex, though he struggled to place it.

'No, that's… it's no problem,' his father said, sounding unsure how to proceed.

'Go on then, Janet,' the rasping voice said, 'hand it over.'

Alex sat up upon hearing this sentence. Janet? Could it be? Surely not? He got off the bed again, this time moving quietly to his bedroom door and, turning the handle as softly and gently as he could, slowly eased it open. When it was wide enough he slipped through the gap like a shadow, perching at the top of the stairs where he could look down, but if anyone looked up they wouldn't have been able to see him. It was indeed *the* Janet, her of the eraser pummelling earlier that day.

Alex saw Janet slowly, almost reluctantly, pass his mum a small, light brown wicker basket with a dishtowel draped over the top of it.

'Thank you so much,' Alex's mum said. 'You didn't have to.'

'It's my pleasure,' the rasping voice, which Alex now

knew belonged to Mrs Willerby, replied. 'Your husband did a wonderful thing today, he's a good man.'

Alex saw his father look down, putting his hands in his pockets and looking embarrassed.

Alex's mum had removed the towel and was looking into the basket. From his vantage point Alex could see what looked like plants, brightly coloured red and blue and purple things, and small glass bottles, brown and dull, their necks stoppered with small corks.

'This is so wonderful,' Alex's mum said, her voice wavering slightly as she said it. 'You needn't have.'

'It's nothing too fancy,' Mrs Willerby said. 'Just some jams and ointments and plants and things, things to help you get by day to day.'

'You didn't have to go to all this effort,' Alex's mum said.

'Really,' replied Mrs Willerby, 'it's nothing. I grow them all myself in the garden anyway, so it's no extra effort.' Alex could see Janet squirming on the doorstep; her head was down once again, her lank hair hiding her face. She looked very uncomfortable in her body language, one of her feet twisting back and forth, her hands worrying at each other. 'Like I say, I just wanted to say thank you again. You have a wonderful husband, and we're very grateful, aren't we, Janet?'

Janet didn't say anything, but her head moved ever so slightly in what might have been a nod. No one said anything for another moment, a blanket of quiet descending on the group of people, before Mrs Willerby brought the conversation to a close.

'Well, we must be getting on.' She looked at Alex's dad, who still looked uncomfortable, almost nervous, Alex thought. 'Thank you again, Jack, truly.'

'It's no problem,' Alex's dad said. He thought the news of his dad being fired by Mr Sullivan must not have made its way around the village just yet; he hoped Mrs Willerby might have brought more than a basket of jam if she knew the real price his dad had paid for helping her.

'Bye now,' Mrs Willerby said, and nudged Janet again.

'Bye,' Alex heard her say in the faintest whisper. Her voice was like that of a ghost, a delicate thing that felt powerful even as it sounded hollow. Had the house not been absolutely silent, he wouldn't have heard a thing.

Janet and Mrs Willerby turned and began to walk away. Alex stood up and quickly moved into his parents' bedroom; he knew he shouldn't go in, but it was the only room that overlooked the front of the house. He got to the large picture window just in time to see Mrs Willerby open the garden gate, and holding it open let Janet pass through before doing so herself.

'We're not keeping it,' he heard his mum say, but he ignored this, as well as his dad's reply. His attention was fixed firmly elsewhere.

As Alex watched them walk away, he realised Mrs Willerby reminded him of Janet; her hair was long and lank, dirty and in need of a wash. Like Janet's, he thought it might be mousy brown, but it was impossible to tell under all the grease. And...were those leaves? Did Mrs Willerby have leaves in her hair? It was hard to tell from where Alex stood, but he thought yes, she might have leaves in her hair. Even as he watched, Mrs Willerby stopped at the large bush that ran around his neighbour's front garden; she looked at the bush with curiosity for a moment, before reaching out and taking a handful of leaves, putting them in her pocket and continuing her journey.

Everyone in Deerborn thought she was weird – Alex included. What kind of grown woman had leaves in her hair? Sure, they lived in a rural village and nature was everywhere; on more than one occasion Alex had passed through a bush or under a low hanging tree and leaves had fallen into his hair, but he'd removed them immediately like any normal person would. He hadn't put them in his pocket, either.

Mrs Willerby also had the same slightly worn, patchy clothing her daughter wore. Although where Janet was wearing her school uniform; black jumper fading in colour and slightly frayed, skirt a little frayed, tights with runs in, Mrs Willerby wore what looked like a tent. It was one big piece of material, with a hole for her head, two holes for her arms, and then one big hole at the bottom her legs stuck out of. It was a faded brown, the colour of old mud, with large black patches sewn on. Whether she did that for fashion or necessity Alex didn't know, but he thought it was probably the latter. She didn't look like a woman who concerned herself with fashion.

The Willerbys were known to be poor; it was just Mrs Willerby and Janet living in the small, ugly house right on the edge of the village, at the bottom of the rough track road that didn't even have a name. The house did, however; it was called Dark Wood Manor, which Alex had always thought odd because it was nearly as small as his house. He thought manors were grand houses, huge buildings with many rooms in different wings and with big, loping grounds. A bit like the house Mr Sullivan, dad's boss – former boss, Alex thought with a lurch in his stomach – and Emma Sullivan, his daughter and Janet's tormentor in chief, lived in.

No one knew who Janet's dad was; there were rumours about the village, but Alex thought them stupid. It was 2024, who believed in love potions? But still, that was what the villagers whispered to each other behind cupped hands whenever Mrs Willerby left a shop; she'd used a love potion to ensnare a rich businessman, used him to have Janet, and continued to use him to pay for her house and for Janet's clothes and books and things. Although, if Mr Sullivan wanted Mrs Willerby and Janet kicked out of their house because they weren't paying, didn't this prove these rumours were ridiculous?

Alex didn't know, and really he didn't care either way. He was just about to go back into his bedroom when he froze; his movement must have caught Janet's attention, because she looked up at him. Their eyes met for a brief moment and Alex suddenly felt warm, very very warm. Granted, his parents' bedroom wasn't exactly cold, facing the sun as it went down and retaining the heat, but still, this was more than that. Alex felt hot, both on his face but inside too, in his heart. It was a good heat though, a reassuring one. He wanted to smile at Janet, to tell her things would be okay, but he couldn't. He wanted to shout at her, tell her things would only be okay if she made them that way. But to do either he was simply unable, and so he stared at her for a second, seeing her stare back at him. He felt trapped in her gaze, held on the spot. He was feeling warmer by the second, just verging on becoming uncomfortable, and then the spell was broken; Janet looked down once more and followed her mother up the street. The pair soon passed behind Mr and Mrs Mayberry's large bushes next door, and were gone from sight.

With a sigh Alex went back to his bedroom and lay down on his bed once more. The music on the radio had changed, the wannabe witch replaced by the latest manufactured boy band. He'd been thinking about Janet before they knocked on his front door; now he couldn't get her out of his head.

Chapter 5

Janet hadn't been in school the rest of the week; however, when Monday came around as it inevitably does, the weekend once again passing far too quickly for Alex's liking, and Alex made his way to History with Tom and Mo, she was sitting in her seat in the middle of the classroom. Other than her, the trio were the first students in the class; they took their seats too, Tom and Mo at a double table a couple of rows behind Janet, Alex to their left at a single desk.

The class slowly began to file in. History was a widely disliked subject; it wasn't the material that turned people off, but the teacher. Mr Farridge was a grumpy old man, quick to anger; he had a mess of grey hair that was always unkempt, and he ran his classroom like the Nazi army he so often railed against. The school had a dress code, both for uniform but also for make up and jewellery. Whilst students were supposed to be banned from wearing make up, only allowed to wear small earrings, and only one ring on each hand, most teachers didn't care. Most teachers knew enough about children to know when to pick their battles, and they realised if the children were in the classroom, and learning – or at least pretending to – then it didn't really matter all that much what they wore.

The same could not be said for Mr Farridge.

There had been a memorable lesson the previous year; it had been a cold, wet, miserable Tuesday afternoon in the run up to Christmas. The classroom had been decorated for the season, though only starkly, and the class had been giddy; Christmas break started on the Friday, and the whole school was in holiday mode. Except, of course, Mr Farridge. Where all the other teachers were playing games or activities or just wheeling in the TV to watch a film, Mr Farridge had been teaching the class about Tudor England, determined not to let something so pithy as Christmas get in the way.

He'd tried several times to get the class to be quiet, but upon yet another unsuccessful attempt, he lost his temper. He'd drawn up to his full height and shouted at Emma to stand up and come forward. The whole class had gone silent when they realised who he'd chosen; it wasn't just the pupils that were afraid of Emma, lots of the staff were too. Luckily she was generally well behaved in class, it was only outside she tended to act up, and most teachers ignored that, for fear both of her wrath, and the wrath of her father. As well as being the local councillor and manager of the building society in Hull, Mr Sullivan also sat on the school's board of governors. There was little in Deerborn his greedy fingers didn't extend to.

The classroom had remained silent, the lack of noise

like a physical presence, as Emma slowly stood up, and languidly walked to the front of the classroom. She had a smirk on her face; she was far from stupid, she knew her place very near to the top of the school, and so had been cocksure that nothing was going to happen.

When she'd eventually reached the front of the class – as 30 other pupils held their collective breath – Mr Farridge had grabbed her roughly by the shoulders and turned her to face her fellow students. Emma's smirk had vanished immediately at this, and shock reigned over every teenager. Mr Farridge had then loudly begun to count the number of ear rings and rings Emma wore.

'Sullivan, what does the dress code say?' he'd barked at her upon completion.

'It says–' Emma had begun meekly, a state most of her contemporaries had never seen her in, before Mr Farridge had loudly cut her off.

'–it says one pair of small ear rings, and one small ring per hand.' His voice had boomed through the small, silent room, making the windows rattle in their panes. No one dared move, Alex had barely dared to breathe for fear of making a sound and drawing the teacher's wrath upon him.

'How many pieces of jewellery is that?'

'Three,' Emma had said, her voice containing a small amount of defiance.

'And how many are you wearing?'

Emma didn't answer; she knew she was caught in a trap, and to answer would be to betray herself, so she remained silent. Mr Farridge answered for her.

'Eight. Eight!' he thundered. 'I know you're a smart girl, Emma, so you must know that eight is greater than three.'

He'd turned to the class himself, an immense smirk on his face; it was so similar to the one Emma had worn a few minutes earlier he might have stolen it from right off her face.

'Take five of them off and go to Mr Gullis' office.'

Emma had done so, but she was muttering about her father all the time she did. She stomped to her desk and grabbed her coat and bag with such venom that her chair fell into Jenna, who was cowering in the desk next to hers. Leaving, Emma slammed the classroom door behind her, and when the sound died the classroom was silent as the grave.

No one had seen Emma at school until after Christmas; no one knew what had happened to Mr Farridge, either from the head or the board of governors, but he hadn't changed a bit. Any reprimand he might have suffered hadn't altered his teaching methods, and for a few weeks this had gained him some begrudging respect from the students. They all envied his standing up to Emma, and wished they were able to themselves. Unfortunately, as time passed the incident was slowly forgotten, and everyone grew wary and scared of Mr Farridge again. Old patterns reasserted themselves, as they so often do; events regressed back to the mean.

Now, with the classroom full, nary a Christmas decoration in sight, everyone seated quietly with their books out, Mr Farridge entered from the back of the room.

'Good morning class,' he boomed, and the class returned a practiced 'good morning Mr Farridge,' without a single drop of enthusiasm. Mr Farridge, unperturbed, strolled to the front of the classroom and, picking up a marker pen, scrawled with venom on the whiteboard a single word.

'Today,' he announced, 'we're going to study witches.'

Alex couldn't help it; he glanced over at Janet, and saw most of the other students doing the same. Everyone knew the rumours about her mother, and though no one ever said anything about Janet herself, most people's parents, if not their children, believed that apples don't often fall too far from trees. Besides, they'd noted her dirty clothes and hair, the fact she rarely spoke – unless to a plant or animal – and didn't seem to have any friends. Their suspicions didn't allow them to whisper that she was like her mother, but they thought there was *something* there.

As Mr Farridge began to lecture in earnest, speaking of Salem in the late 1600s before moving the topic closer to home, talking about women turning on women, men thirsty for blood, giving a long anecdote about Matthew Hopkins, the Witchfinder General, the class opened their exercise books and wrote down what Mr Farridge told them to. Alex alternated between looking at his book and glancing at Janet; she was sitting stiff as a rusty nail, her spine straighter than he'd ever seen it, not taking any notes. Alex could feel the tension emanating from her every pore, and he pulled at his collar uncomfortably.

In the row behind her sat Emma and Jenna, with Aliyah and Francesca to their right. Alex thought he could hear Emma whispering to Janet, hear her murmuring away to her. The incident the previous year hadn't dented Emma's confidence at all; no one else would have dared speak at the same time as Mr Farridge. No one but Emma.

Alex tried to hear what she was saying, but she was speaking so quietly that over the sound of 30 pens and pencils scribbling across paper, and Mr Farridge's voice booming, he couldn't make anything out.

He leaned in their direction as far as he could without being too conspicuous, but jumped when Emma's hand shot up.

'Mr Farridge?'

Mr Farridge stopped, looking confused. He wasn't used to being interrupted, and seemed about to carry on regardless before he stopped himself and responded.

'Yes, Sullivan?'

No other teacher would have dared call Emma by her surname; Alex thought there was a grudging respect between the pair, that their encounter the previous year had formed a camaraderie of sorts between them. Two strong, terrifying people who, if they didn't like each other, respected what they saw of each other mirrored back at them.

'Are there still witches now?'

'Well,' Mr Farridge said, putting the piece of chalk on his desk and turning to face the class. 'Some people believe there are. Others believe there aren't, and have never been. There's a lot of evidence–'

'–how would you know if someone's a witch?'

If the interruption affected Mr Farridge he didn't let it show.

'Well there are a number of ways one might–'

'–are they dirty?'

This time Mr Farridge hesitated. The class was silently watching the interaction between the pair, their eyes moving from one to the other like a crowd at a tennis match. At this last, a few people, Alex included, glanced at Janet. What Emma was doing wasn't in any way subtle, even by the standards of teenagers.

Alex couldn't be sure, but he felt the classroom was warmer than it had been a minute before. He was only wearing a shirt, the later September warmth still hanging in the air rendering his jumper superfluous, but still, he was beginning to sweat. He could see a few other people shifting in their seats uncomfortably, though that might have been more due to the tension than the temperature.

'I mean,' Mr Farridge said, slightly wrong footed. 'There isn't any lore or hasn't–'

'–I think they're dirty, horrible creatures, that's how you spot them,' Emma declared, looking around the class as she did so with a huge, smug smile on her face. Alex thought he could see her father's political genes reflected in that smile. It was a smile for the crowd, not for herself. It didn't reach her eyes.

'I think witches are smelly, disgusting, foul creatures, and we should round them up and burn them at the stake.'

'Shut up.'

A low murmur had been building throughout the class, but it stopped at these words. Everyone looked around to try and find their source, but this was only made clear when Emma spoke again.

'What did you say?'

She was staring at Janet's back, her eyes boring into her. Janet remained stock still, but Alex could see she was shaking ever so slightly. Her body was trembling a tiny amount, and Alex unbuttoned the top of his shirt as he felt the temperature rise a little more.

Janet remained silent, and this only seemed to goad Emma more.

'What did you say to me you stupid bitch?'

A shock ran through the class; whilst everyone was happy swearing at each other at break time and lunch, no one swore audibly in front of teachers. For one very good reason.

'That's enough, Sullivan, let's carry on.'

'Oi,' Emma said, ignoring Mr Farridge and raising her voice at Janet. 'What the fuck did you say to me?'

'Sullivan, detention!' Mr Farridge boomed, but Emma continued to ignore him. She picked up one of Jenna's pens and threw it at Janet; it landed in her messy hair and stayed nestled in the clumps, much to Emma's delight.

'That's fucking disgusting,' Emma said with a sneer on her face. Alex couldn't help but think how quickly her face could go from supermodel beautiful to incredibly ugly. She was snarling like a cornered animal.

'Leave me alone,' Janet whispered.

'Oh, it finally speaks!' Emma said, and, clearly linking Janet's reaction with the pen in her hair, grabbed Jenna's pencil case and threw more items at her.

Janet remained unmoved by the assault; it was only when Emma threw an eraser, which bounced off Janet's head with an audible bonk that cause the entire class, Alex included, to burst into laughter, that Janet moved.

She turned in her chair, her legs facing forward but her shoulders and back aimed at Emma.

'Leave me alone,' she said, this time slightly above a whisper, and Alex could feel the anger in her voice as if it were a physical thing. The classroom was really starting to heat up; Alex glanced around and saw people taking off their jumpers, unbuttoning their shirts, shifting uncomfortably in their seats.

'Why don't you ever wash?' Emma said, and her gang giggled.

Mr Farridge wasn't doing anything, seemingly as trapped in Emma's aura as everyone else was. Alex willed him to say something, to do something, to stop Emma, but he simply remained where he was and let it happen.

'Why don't you have a shower or a bath or something, you disgusting freak?'

Suddenly the classroom lights went out with a pop; one of the bulbs had exploded, raining glass onto the classroom floor, and a small scream ran throughout the classroom. Neither Emma nor Janet seemed to notice.

'Why don't you fuck off?' Janet said, and that moved Mr Farridge to action.

'Willerby, watch your language, that's detention for

you too.'

Before he knew what he was doing, Alex was speaking.

'That's not fair, sir.'

Now that Mr Farridge had found his voice, he seemed to have snapped out of his trance enough to realise that actually, this was his classroom, and actually, he needed to take some kind of control.

'What did you say, Butler?'

Alex froze, knowing he'd gone too far. Mr Farridge took his silence as encouragement, and with a sneer creasing his face seemed to return fully to his usual self.

'I guess you'd like a detention too, Butler,' he said, glee filling his voice. 'Be my guest.'

He picked up his chalk, seeming to think this was the end of things, but Emma wasn't done. Holding Jenna's now empty pencil case, she threw it at Janet, who was still facing her. It hit Janet square in the face, and this caused the class to roar with laughter. The noise was deafening, and even though he'd just been chastised, even though he felt sorry for Janet, Alex couldn't help but laugh along with them, swept up in the moment.

However, the noise immediately caught in this throat as he saw Janet look at him. They made eye contact again, and what Alex saw there made his heart break.

There was such pain in Janet's eyes, such sadness, that whatever laughter Alex had been about to continue emitting died within him. His heart shattered into a thousand tiny pieces, like the fragments of the lightbulb only moments before, and he wanted the ground to open up and swallow him.

'That's enough,' Mr Farridge shouted, and something like order reasserted itself. Mr Farridge glanced at the clock; it was 9:50, and with the lesson due to end at 9:55 he cut his losses.

'Right, class dismissed. Sullivan, clean up this mess. And you, Butler, and Willerby see me after school tomorrow for detention.'

Alex slowly shoved his books back into his bag and, slinging it over one shoulder, pushed through the crowd and out into the corridor. He could hear Tom and Mo calling his name through peals of laughter but he ignored them. He ran down the corridor and into the boys' toilets, locking himself in a cubicle and, before he knew what was happening, burst into tears.

Chapter 6

The end of day bell rang shrilly through Miss Klein's English classroom. Normally it would have sparked joy in Alex; freedom, sought after ever since his alarm rang to wake him from his slumber, was finally achieved. He'd done the part of the day that belonged to others, and now his time was his own, to spend as he pleased until it was time to go to bed, go to sleep, and upon waking begin the whole charade again.

Normally that would have been the case, but not so this day; no, this day saw Alex stand up slowly, reluctantly, without a single shred of his being wanting to. Because once his bag was packed, rather than home, or the park, or Tom or Mo's house, instead he'd be making his way to Mr Farridge's classroom for detention.

His parents had been furious when he told them; whilst he was far from a straight A student, he also rarely got in trouble. Alex could count on one hand the number of detentions he'd received since joining Deerborn Secondary School aged 11; not only that, but the other three had all been in the first two years, when he was -

and he'd happily admit this to anyone who asked – very small, very young, and very stupid.

This was his first detention for three years, but it was less about that and more about the cause of it. He'd admitted to his parents as soon as he arrived home, his father still there in the afternoons whilst he looked for a new job, why he got the detention. And whilst ostensibly it was for swearing, he knew that really, actually, the detention was punishment for laughing at Janet. When she was being picked on by Emma, made a spectacle of, instead of defending her, he'd joined in with the crowd baying for her blood. He'd been a willing participant; he hadn't thrown anything at her, or said anything to her, but he was complicit. And sometimes that's worse; attacking someone, in its own twisted way, he thought, shows a kind of bravery. Standing back and watching someone attack someone weak is cowardice, which in many ways is much more debilitating. Alex hated himself for it, and so as soon as he walked into the living room he told his parents about the detention and the reason, and burst into tears.

After comforting him for a few minutes until his tears had stopped flowing, the three members of the family once again crowded onto the faded, worn grey couch, deer antlers regarding them from the walls, his mum had sent him to his room for the rest of the evening. He'd happily accepted his punishment, knowing how much he deserved it.

He was saved from Mr Farridge, however, by Miss Klein calling out to him as he slowly placed his items into his backpack.

'Alex, Janet, there's been a change of plan. You two are in here with me for your detention. Emma,' she'd said, Emma's head whipping round, her blonde hair flying outwards in a wave, 'you're with Mr Barnett in his classroom. He's expecting you imminently.'

Alex had to suppress a smile at his double good luck; he didn't have to face Mr Farridge, and he didn't have to face Emma. He stopped packing up, instead sitting back down. Tom and Mo each gave him a sympathetic look as they left, but he simply shrugged, a "what can you do?" gesture. 'I'll text you' he mouthed to them, fully knowing he wouldn't. Because even as he celebrated his good luck, a dawning realisation hit him. He wouldn't have to face Mr Farridge, and he wouldn't have to face Emma Sullivan, but he would have to face Janet. And in facing Janet, he'd have to face himself.

The classroom quickly emptied, its quietness a stark contrast to the furore of excited students only a moment before, leaving the three of them behind. Miss Klein waited for the last of the students to leave before pushing her chair back with a scraping sound and walking over and closing the classroom door with an ominous thunk. She returned to her chair behind her large wooden desk and suddenly the classroom felt very small to Alex. Where moments before the room had held thirty students besides the teacher, it now held two, and seemed barely big enough for that. Alex glanced at Janet; she was sitting at her desk, in the same row as Alex but two aisles to his left. As usual her head was down, her hair hiding her face.

'Right you two, why don't you come sit up front here. No point in you being all the way back there,' said Miss Klein.

Alex, eager to be as obedient as possible, immediately stood up and, moving to the front of the room, sat at the desk directly in front of Miss Klein's. A second later, he heard the soft scrape of Janet's chair being moved and she sat down in the desk next to him. He didn't dare look at her but glanced out of the corner of his eye; her head remained angled down, no part of her face visible.

When they were both seated Miss Klein stood up, the scraping of her chair legs on the floor cutting through Alex like the knife he felt he deserved, and moved around her desk to perch on the front of it. She moved aside a couple of small objects, a replica deer skull and a small wooden figurine, perhaps five inches tall, of a person with no discernible features, to make room for her half sitting, half standing position; to Alex she looked very uncomfortable, but he didn't say anything. His plan was to be as small and quiet as possible, to get through detention without further harming Janet or himself.

'Well, you two. What am I to do with you?'

She looked at them both; Alex met her eye for a second but couldn't hold her glance, and looked away in shame; a set of deer antlers was mounted on the wall above the whiteboard and he focused on these. Out of the corner of his eye he saw Janet look up for a moment too, before her head fell back down to its original position. Its default position, Alex thought with another pang of shame.

'Mr Farridge of course told me what happened. He forgot when he gave you detention today that he had a dentist appointment, which is why you're here with me.' She looked at Alex and Janet in turn, half a smile on her face, one hand playing with a small wooden crucifix she wore around her neck. 'Emma is having her detention separately for obvious reasons. I know I'm not supposed to say this, but good riddance to her. There's no helping that girl, the sooner we get her out of here the better. Calls herself a Christian, too, I don't think so.'

Alex was shocked to hear Miss Klein talk so brazenly about Emma; he'd been going to school with Emma for four years, he knew all about what a nightmare she could be. But he'd always assumed it was different with teachers, that they just thought she was some silly girl to be easily managed. Evidently this was not the case.

'Janet, I'm sorry you're here.'

Alex was shocked for the second time in a few moments. He'd never heard a teacher apologise to a pupil before. Janet must have been shocked too, because her head shot up, quickly enough that her hair flew backwards and out of her face. For a brief moment Alex could see her face, and he looked into her deep, brown eyes. They were very pretty, he thought, deep and soulful. He felt funny inside, in a way he couldn't quite pinpoint, some of the warmth of a couple of days previously when they'd made eye contact at his house appeared again. He was transfixed, as if a power held his gaze. However, as soon as Janet's eyes surfaced they were gone, Janet obviously realising what had happened and quickly smoothing her hair back down. She glanced at Alex to see if he'd seen and he tried to smile at her but nothing showed on his face.

'I'm sorry you have to be here now, Janet. From what Mr Farridge told me you did nothing wrong. Still,' Miss Klein said with a sigh, standing up and smoothing her long pale green skirt before perching back on the desk, 'rules are rules, and I'm not allowed to send you home when another teacher has given you a detention.'

Janet's head, whilst not completely up, was no longer completely down either. Alex could see a bit of her face, her left cheek, a hint of her lips. Her skin looked smooth, a light shade of brown, the skin of a person who spends a lot of time outdoors. Her lips were full and red, they looked soft and plump, and Alex found himself wondering what it would be like to kiss them. Miss Klein's continued monologue snapped him from his reverie.

'You on the other hand,' she said, now facing Alex. 'I'm very disappointed in you, Alex Butler.'

Now his head fell, it was his turn to cement his eyes to the floor, his turn to avoid any and all gazes in case of hostility. He could feel his cheeks turning red, his neck too, and suddenly his white school shirt – as well as the skin beneath it – felt several sizes too small.

'Emma is the way Emma is, for better or – realistically – worse. I always thought better of you, however.'

Alex could feel the sting of tears behind his eyes, and

frantically swallowed back the sobs threatening to leak from his mouth. He had no idea why he was crying so easily at the moment, especially around the school. He also didn't want to know.

'But,' Miss Klein said with a sigh. 'What's done is done. Alex, I want you to spend the next 30 minutes doing homework. Janet,' she said, standing up and once again flattening her skirt, moving back around and sitting behind her desk. 'You're free to do as you wish. Do you have a book or something you can read? Or you can do your homework, I don't mind. As long as you're quiet, so I can get on with this marking,' she indicated a pile of red exercise books sitting on her desk. 'Also, so if anyone happens to glance in, it looks and sounds like you're being punished.'

She said this with a smile, and Alex, sneaking a glance at Janet, saw she was smiling, too. He'd never seen her smile, and the change that came over her was incredible; Alex thought she looked like a different person. For one thing, she looked 15, which Alex only then realised she never usually did. Thinking about it, Alex realised she usually looked older. In fact, she looked like his dad had been looking the last couple of days: bent, not broken but not far from it, almost defeated. A pang hit Alex in his chest, not quite in his heart but in that region, and, swallowing, he took his French book out of his bag and began to try and write out the correct verbs based on the pictures that accompanied them.

Janet took from her small, tatty backpack, one that looked older than Alex, Janet, and Miss Klein combined, an equally small, tatty book. The cover was purple, with pictures of flowers on it. Alex couldn't make out the cover, but he could just see the words 'Nature's Apothecary' on the battered and frayed spine. A series of small bangles sat upon Janet's wrist; they looked like they were made from string or twine or something, with small tokens - of what Alex couldn't quite make out - dangling from them. The tokens danced as Janet's arm moved, and Alex was once again entranced.

A small cough made Alex jump, and he realised Miss Klein was staring at him as he watched Janet. Janet seemed not to have noticed, so absorbed was she in her book. Alex quickly returned to his French homework, knowing he was probably getting at least half the answers wrong but not caring. His mind refused to focus, and he didn't try too hard to make it do so. He was never going to France, especially now that his dad had lost his job and they had no money, so what was the point?

The afternoon passed in near silence, the only sounds those of Miss Klein's and Alex's pens whispering across paper, and the tokens on Janet's wrist quietly clinking together as she turned the pages of her book. What felt like an eternity later Miss Klein broke the silence by saying, 'right, that's four o'clock, you can both go.'

Alex quickly shoved his half completed, half correct French homework back into his bag and virtually ran out of the door without looking at either Miss Klein or Janet. He wanted to get home as soon as possible, get to the privacy of his bedroom, think about Janet's eyes, her lips, her skin. He threw open the classroom door, careful to catch it just before it slammed – another detention was not what he needed – and was about to take off down the corridor when he stopped himself, an idea suddenly occurring to him.

He stood outside Miss Klein's room, waiting. From inside he could hear Miss Klein and Janet talking; they were both speaking quietly, so he could only hear snippets of what they said, but certain words jumped out to him. Wyrmwood, calendula, aloe vera. The last one he recognised from his mum's shampoo in the bathroom at home, but the other two meant nothing to him. He heard Miss Klein say something about electricity and dirt, and Janet replying about spiders, but then the janitor turned on the vacuum in a classroom down the hall and what little Alex could hear was lost to the noise.

He stayed where he was, shaking slightly with nervous anticipation; a moment later the reason for this appeared. Janet left the classroom and moved into the hallway.

She started when she saw Alex, jumping ever so slightly. Alex's heart darkened for a moment at once more upsetting her, but he quickly quashed the feeling as he psyched himself up to speak. As well as the sound of the janitor's vacuum he could hear other kids running and shouting and laughing; summer was slowly turning into autumn, and he knew the days of playing outside were numbered. He wished he could still focus on such unimportant things.

'I'm,' he started, before stopping. His mouth was dry and he coughed, tried to make some words come. They did eventually, but only as a small, quiet squeak.

'I'm sorry. About yesterday.'

He wanted to say more but his tongue and lips weren't obeying his brain. Instead he stood looking at Janet; he was only a couple of inches taller than her, and part of him – whether his heart, brain, or something else he didn't know – longed to wrap his arms around her and hold her. He waited for her to speak, but when she didn't he found words himself.

'In Farridge's History lesson. I'm sorry I laughed at you.'

Now Janet looked at him; she turned her head up and her eyes found his. Alex took a step back; he'd been right before, her eyes were indeed brown, but looking at them properly now, there was a fierceness, a power he hadn't been able to see before. He felt seen, truly seen, but he couldn't put his finger on whether this was good or bad. He felt warm too, the skin on the back of his neck began to itch. He wanted to run, to drop his bag and sprint home as fast as he could; at the same time he wanted to stand there forever, to let Janet look into the deepest parts of him, to learn things about him he didn't even know about himself.

He felt the warmth increase, like it'd done the day before in History. He wanted to unbutton his top button, loosen his tie, but his arms, like his mouth, didn't belong to him. He was stuck where he was, unmoving, unable to do anything, as if caught in a spell. *Her* spell. *Janet's spell.*

He jumped a little when Janet quickly said, 'I don't forgive you,' and then abruptly turned and walked away, leaving him standing there. And stand there was just what he did, watching the space Janet had occupied, until Miss Klein came out of her room, arms full of books, and said, 'are you still here, Alex?'

This startled him from his reverie, and he said a garbled goodbye to Miss Klein before turning and walking in the opposite direction to Janet. He wanted to see her; he wanted to hide from her. His shoes squeaked and the sound echoed back to him in the empty corridor. He'd never felt more alone in his life.

Chapter Seven

Alex didn't see anyone on the journey from school to his house, and he was relieved. The moment he'd left the building, the late September sun caressing his bare arms, a light breeze carrying the smells and sounds of summer, the tears had come anew.

He wasn't crying per se; if he had seen anyone, he could have said the breeze was making his eyes water or was irritating his hayfever and he'd probably have gotten away with it, but he was glad he hadn't needed to. He ran home, the normally pleasant route seeming like a curse to him. The sunshine, green grass, bright flowers on the verges and in people's gardens, it all felt like a taunt. The easy way in which nature asserted itself during the summer months, the plants taking control over the world, flourishing in the sun, felt like it was making a mockery of everything Alex was feeling. Because he was feeling a lot, so many things he wasn't even sure what half of them were. He felt bad towards Janet, he felt anger towards Emma, but there was so much more, so many deeper and more complicated feelings. He was still disgusted by Janet and the state she kept herself in, but he felt this had softened slightly. He still felt sorry for her, all the while feeling like she wasn't helping herself, but there were new feelings, confusing ones.

He felt longing for her eyes, he wanted to look into them again. But he was also scared of them, the way they held him, pierced him, the way they made him feel exposed. He felt hot, too hot, like he always seemed to when Janet was around. He was scared of her whole, but curious about her parts. In short, he was 15, lost, confused, and upset. He needed his mum.

The sun beat down as he made his way through the streets, the glory of it not reflected within Alex. Lots of houses had open windows and doors and he could hear snippets of sound, not just conversation but laughter, music. Alex ran past the church, it's brown bricks standing high above him, steadfast in their silence, foreboding in their presence. The air felt cooler around the church, and a small part of Alex thought it had to do with more than just the shade it created. The tree-lined streets were still green, but the faintest hints of yellow were beginning to appear. Some branches hung down and seemed to reach for Alex as he passed, and in quieter moments when the road was as clear as the pavement, he thought he heard leaves whispering.

Upon reaching home he threw open the gate and it banged off the fence on the other side with a small crash. Alex ignored it and ran up the short path to his front door, also ignoring the plants either side which had joined in the village's taunting. He pushed open the front door but was saved a telling off when it hit the coat rack with a soft thump and rebounded. He moved out of the way just in time for it to shut itself with a soft clunk, the hallway falling into darkness, the deer antlers looking ominous in the low light, in his low mood, and he kicked off his shoes, dropped his bag, and listened. He could hear his parents talking in the kitchen, the room directly opposite the front door, and he started walking towards it with purpose, slowing the closer he got. His parents were talking about Janet's mum, and he stopped outside the half-closed white door, trying his hardest not to make a sound, just listening.

'I don't know what she plans to do,' his dad was saying. 'If she works, I don't know where, or even if she gets paid.'

'But hasn't she always paid her bills on time?' his mum asked, hesitation evident in her voice. 'I'm no fan of the woman, but you can't fault her for that, at least so you've always told me.'

Alex's dad sighed before continuing. 'I don't know why you still…' he stopped, sighed again. 'Yes, she's always paid. Her entire family has, I looked before I went to see her last week. Ever since the house was remortgaged back in the 80s, every payment has been made full and on time. This is the first that's ever been missed.'

'And Mr Sullivan wanted to–'

There was a loud bang which made Alex jump, before his dad started speaking again.

'Exactly! Every payment made in full and on time for

nearly 40 years. Then one missed…'

He trailed off, and for a moment there was quiet. Alex could hear the sounds of kids playing in the field behind their small garden, a car drove past the front of their house and continued down the road. His mum broke the silence.

'She's a horrible woman, but that's no reason to make her homeless. Think of her poor daughter, she's done nothing wrong.'

'Neither has–' Alex's dad began, before stopping and clearly deciding to change tactic.

'That man goes to church every Sunday in his best suit, wife, son and daughter in their Sunday best,' Alex's dad said. 'He sits there in the front row looking like the kindest, most open-hearted man in the world, but this is the reality.' Alex heard his dad sigh once again, and Alex thought he sounded tired.

'One missed payment!' he barked. 'That's why I didn't do anything. The house has been in the family for hundreds of years, if you believe the rumours.'

'Problem is,' his mother said, 'lots of people do believe the rumours. *I* believe the rumours.'

'I know you do, and I wish you wouldn't. It's ridiculous.'

'I know dear,' his mum cooed, seemingly ignoring her husband's scorn at her. Alex imagined his mum with her hand on his dad's arm, rubbing it. He longed to be comforted by her, but he needed to hear as much as he could about Mrs Willerby. It might help him understand Janet better.

'That's half the problem, that people just believe what they hear. That bollocks about Janet's dad; I bet he was just some lazy git who got Mrs Willerby pregnant, couldn't handle the responsibility, then legged it when he found out she was pregnant. Happens all the time, every day, and I bet 99 times out of 100, no one starts rumours about… well… about, you know.'

'You know what they say, though, all rumours have some basis in fact. There's something wrong with her, look at the state of that house of hers. And Janet.' Alex, hearing her name again, swallowed his breath.

'So what about the state of her house?' his dad asked. 'It's her house, she owns it, she can keep it how she likes.'

'I just wish she'd take better care of that daughter of hers.'

Alex started at yet another mention of Janet. He moved a step closer, leaning as far into the door as he could without moving it.

'I know, love, I know; that we can agree on. She's 15, and going to school looking like that, she deserves better.'

'I don't know why she allows it, Mrs Willerby. For all her faults she loves that girl, you can see it in the way she looks at her. To let her go to school that filthy, with her hair and uniform looking like that, I can't believe it. Especially when she's always been in the same class as–'

Another bang, and this time Alex jumped off the ground, nearly banging his head on the low hallway ceiling. He wasn't a tall child by any stretch, but their home was small and old, low ceilinged; quaint would have been a nice, polite way of putting it.

'As that… *man's* daughter. Like father like daughter I've heard.'

'It's a shame, Janet, that's her name,' Alex's mum said with triumph in her voice, as if she'd been trying to remember and finally had. Alex's head started pounding hearing her name. Janet. Janet. Janet. 'It's a shame Janet doesn't have a better role model, someone to really take care of her.'

His dad laughed, a short barking sound entirely lacking in humour. Alex's mum continued.

'Do you know, just the other day I bumped into Mrs Billings when I was going to get some milk, and she told me she'd just seen Janet. She said Janet was talking to her hand, just standing there in the street.'

'That's strange. Was she on her phone, maybe?'

'Oh, come on now, you know she doesn't have a phone. Mrs Willerby doesn't allow anything like that in her house, you know that, Jack.'

'So Janet was, what, just talking to her hand? Maybe she was pretending to have a phone, trying to fit in?'

Alex's heart, previously still pounding, slowed right down and dropped when he heard this. He barely used his phone, but still, at least he had one. He couldn't imagine not; Janet was outcast enough, not having a phone didn't help anything. Imagining her pretending to have one broke his heart anew.

'If you stop interrupting me I'll tell you!'

'Sorry, dear.'

'So Janet was talking into her hand, it was closed up like a fist, and Mrs Billings was about to walk away when Janet opened her hand, and a bloody great big spider ran down her arm and away.'

'A spider?' Alex's dad sounded incredulous; whether he didn't believe Mrs Billings or he did and was shocked by the spider, Alex couldn't tell.

Alex wasn't sure what to think. He knew Mrs Billings, everyone did; she was the woman in the village who never let you get your ball from her garden. If it landed in there it was gone, and all the kids avoided her because of this. Alex might have assumed she was wrong, or mistaken, or even lying, wanting to say bad things about Janet to make herself seem more interesting, but somehow, Alex thought she was telling the truth. There was something different about Janet, everyone knew that. But Alex felt, having looked into those eyes, he'd seen part of her no one else had. He hated spiders himself, wouldn't be seen dead near one, but he could imagine Janet liking them.

But talking to them?

He braced himself to continue listening to his parents but he accidentally slipped, knocking the door slightly.

'Alex, dear, is that you?' his mum shouted down the hall.

Alex padded back up to the front door and, picking up his bag, shouted 'yeah, Mum, it's me' before running up the stairs and shutting himself in his room. He had a lot he wanted to think about.

Chapter Eight

The morning was cooler than the days that preceded it; autumn was winning its annual fight with summer, seeing off the previous season with callous disregard to the opinions of the humans who had to live under it.

For the first time since March or April, Alex's mum forced him to wear his winter coat. She ignored his pleas, pretty reasonable in his eyes, that it wasn't actually *that* cold. Sure, it was cooler than it had been for months, and it felt like the coming of winter was much more proximate than the fading of summer, but it was still sunny, it was still fairly warm. Alex's mum wouldn't hear it, and Alex, realising he'd be late for school if he didn't give in, did so. The second he was out of the gate, hidden by the Mayberry's bushes, he took it off and shoved it unceremoniously into his backpack.

Walking up his street, feet dragging on the hard black concrete, he couldn't get Janet from his mind. The thing his mum had said the day before, about Mrs Billings seeing her with a spider, didn't make sense to him. Why on earth would Janet be talking to a spider? The more he thought about it, the more it confused him.

The loud honking of a car's horn made him jump, and suddenly a memory came to him, as if in jumping he'd knocked a book off a mental shelf which had then fallen into his lap, open at just the right page.

It had taken place the previous summer; he was with Mo and Tom, they were walking through Deerborn, down the main street that ran from one end of the village to the other. Alex had brought his football and the three of them were kicking it as they walked, passing it between themselves, minding their own business. They'd reached the large field that made up Deerborn's park; it was completely plain apart from a small playground in one corner, and Alex had been wondering what constituted a park and what just a field when Mo suddenly stopped, his foot on top of the ball. Alex and Tom kept walking, only stopping when they realised they were just a pair, no longer a trio. Stopping and turning, Alex had seen Mo staring across the road.

Following Mo's gaze, Alex had seen Janet. This had been some time in July, and the sun had been beating down; Alex remembered he had only been wearing shorts and a t-shirt, and the sweat had been pooling under his arms. Despite having been 14 he was still relatively new on his journey into adulthood, and hadn't discovered, much to his parents' chagrin, deodorant. He'd stopped, his pose mimicking Mo's, except without the football under one foot.

Across the road had been Janet, standing next to a bush. At first, it had simply looked like she was just standing there not doing anything; in spite of the July heat Janet had been covered from head to toe as usual, her arms covered to the wrist and legs to the ankle, her top right up under her chin. Her clothes were brown, though whether by design or by dirt Alex couldn't work out. Her hair, ever unruly, had been less lank than it usually was. Tom had made a joke about it being the day after her monthly bath and all three had laughed, though stopped suddenly when Janet seemed to stiffen, worrying she might have heard them. They stood still, silent, and when Janet slouched once more they knew they were in the clear.

Janet had had her hands cupped together, held up to her mouth; Mo made a joke about her eating leaves due to poverty and Tom laughed, but Alex hadn't paid too much attention. He was fascinated by her, by trying to figure out what she was doing. Mo had gestured for them to leave, and Tom had followed, but Alex had waited a minute; he was certain that Janet's lips were moving, that she was speaking.

Alex watched for another moment or so, waiting for confirmation, but none came; the ball, kicked by one of his friends, had shot across the road, causing a car to brake abruptly and slam on its horn. The noise had made Alex jump and look around; by the time he'd placed the noise, had watched Tom retrieve the ball, shouting a half-hearted apology to the driver, and had his eyes turned back to where Janet had been standing, she was gone. He looked around to see if he could see her, but she was nowhere to be seen. Alex had crossed the road, waiting a moment for the angry driver to move on, and had stood where Janet had been standing only moments before. He looked at the bush, at the floor, all around him. There was nothing unusual; in fact, there was no sign Janet had even been there to begin with.

Alex had been perplexed, his face scrunched up in confusion, but when the football came flying at him, and he had to duck to avoid being hit in the face, he was snapped out of whatever curiosity he'd been in. He kicked the ball across the road, shouting at Tom and Mo how they were crap at football, always had been and always would be, and had carried on with his day, living a glorious summer afternoon as a 14-year-old without a problem in the entire world. He'd forgotten all about seeing Janet until just now.

As he turned the corner and joined the main road, he saw Tom and Mo waiting for him a little way up the street. Jogging, he joined up with them and fell in step with the pair, the conversation soon turning to the previous night's football matches. Hull had drawn at home to Plymouth, a game they should have won easily, and none of the boys were impressed by the performance or the result. Alex joined in the conversation but only fleetingly; he couldn't get Janet out of his mind. The memory of that summer afternoon had come back so strongly, so suddenly, that it had taken over his being. He only stopped thinking about past Janet when they arrived at the large sign reading *Deerborn Secondary School* with the school's emblem, a large stag with gigantic antlers beneath it, just in time to see present Janet enter the building.

Another memory hit him, this one much more recent; after detention the previous afternoon, Janet telling him she didn't forgive him. Just thinking about it stung and he tried to push it away, tried to replace it with the memory of Janet's face, but his mind wasn't playing along. It wouldn't let him forget her words, the way they'd hurt him, left him feeling lost, confused, unmoored. Feelings he didn't understand but felt all the same.

'You coming, mate?'

Tom's words snapped Alex back to reality and he joined his best friends in the mass of young bodies making their way into the building. The trio fought their way through the crowd to the stairs and, making their way up one flight and turning left down the hallway, arrived at and entered Miss Naveed's room, their form room.

'Ah, boys,' Miss Naveed said, seeing them enter, 'nice of you to join us.'

'Sorry, miss,' Tom said, quickly taking his seat.

Alex hadn't even noticed they were late, so lost was he in thoughts of Janet. Sitting down, his mind immediately tried to vanish into her orbit again, and it was only Miss Naveed speaking that stopped him.

'I've had a note from Miss Klein saying some of you still haven't paid for the school trip. It's next week, so make sure you get your money in as soon as possible so you can go. Janet, Alex, Michael, Stephen, Mohammad, Sierra, I'm talking specifically to you.'

'Here you go, Miss,' Mo said, standing up and

walking to her desk, handing her a small slip of white paper along with a £10 note. 'My mum gave it to me this morning.'

'Thank you, Mohammad,' Miss Naveed said, putting the slip and the paper in her top drawer, picking up her pen and marking his name off the note in front of her. 'The rest of you have until Friday, but please try and get it sooner. The trip is Monday, and the sooner we know you're definitely coming, the better.'

The bell clanged throughout the room, making Alex jump; he'd drifted away again, and coming back to himself was alarmed at how much he seemed to be doing so lately. The previous silence was replaced by the sound of 30 chairs scraping back, voices shouting over each other, fighting for airspace. Alex slowly stood up and joined the throng of bodies; as he left the room he saw Janet approaching Miss Naveed's desk. He longed to hang back, to hear what Janet was going to say, to hear her voice give life to words, words he could treasure in his heart, but he could think of no excuse and so simply left the room.

As he walked with Tom to History – Mo had Geography, the trio not sharing all their lessons – he found his mind drifting again, but for a different reason. Now he was thinking about the school trip, and more importantly, whether he'd be able to go. It was a trip to something called Brontë Country, a couple of hours away by coach to just outside of Bradford. He wasn't bothered about the trip itself, didn't care if he missed it. But he didn't want to be the only one not going.

His worries stemmed from the fact his dad had lost his job; they'd never been a rich family, his mum working part time in the local supermarket, his dad full time at the building society, but they'd always got by just fine. Alex had never been abroad, never been on a plane, but they went away every summer, even if only for a week, to somewhere nice by the sea. Last year they'd packed their things into the small family car and driven nearly 10 hours down to Cornwall; Alex had complained most of the way there, but upon arrival had stopped immediately. The blue of the sea, the white of the sand, the rushing of the waves; he'd had the best week of his life.

But he worried, now that his dad wasn't working, whether his parents would be able to spare the money. It was only a tenner, nothing major, but he also knew his dad wasn't having much luck finding a job. Alex may only have been 15, but he was old enough to know some adult things, and one of those was that Mr Sullivan had a lot of influence in Deerborn and the surrounding villages. He even had a little in Hull, and when you got on Mr Sullivan's bad side, things became difficult. He had no doubt his dad, under any other circumstances, would get a new job easily. But as things were, he wasn't so sure.

If Alex couldn't go on the trip, and had to stay behind in school, spending the day with one of the teachers, or even, god forbid, in the teacher's lounge, he'd never live it down. He'd been putting off asking his parents for fear of them confirming what he suspected, but following Miss Naveed's announcement in form he steeled himself. He'd do it that night, he told himself, the second he walked through the door he'd march into the living room or kitchen or wherever his parents were and ask them. He hoped things would be fine; he feared they wouldn't be; he wanted to know either way for sure, sooner rather than later.

Chapter Nine

The rest of the day passed without incident and soon the bell sounded, releasing the pupils, granting them their freedom once again. Though it happened every day, to Alex it sometimes felt as if it was the very first time. Some days the torture of school felt like it'd never end, that it may just go on forever until he was dead, and that would have been his life.

Tom and Mo both had detention; Tom hadn't done his History homework and Mo had accidentally sworn in front of Mr Gullis, the headteacher, so Alex walked home alone. He didn't mind; he knew he had to ask his parents about the school trip, it was now or never, and so his walk home was slow, reluctant. He was like a number halving; if zero was his home, the gap from he to it would shrink and shrink, but never quite disappear. Unfortunately, neither he nor his home were numbers, and he did eventually arrive at his house, at the sight of his – so it felt – near-Sisyphean task.

He arrived home in spite of his best efforts; he'd taken the long route, not walking down the main street but loping through adjacent ones, walking up streets that were actually the opposite way to his house. These streets would all eventually bend in U-turns, however, and set him back on course. His house was fate; it was inevitable. Though not without trying; he even stopped by the duck pond to watch a mother and her two young children throw bread into the water. They looked so peaceful, so happy, the children smiling and laughing as their mother handed them pieces of bread and they threw them into the water, the animals splashing and scrambling, going wild for the free food. Alex wanted to tell the family to stop, tell them that bread was bad for ducks; Alex had learned in Geography that instead of bread the kids should have been throwing grapes or nuts. But he said nothing, as always, simply watched the family until he noticed the mother looking at him, suspicion etched across her face, and he quickly looked away before turning around and leaving the pond, continuing his journey.

He noticed lots of birds in the sky above him, huge clouds of black shapes that moved as a singular mass for a time before suddenly changing direction, breaking down into their component parts before finding each other once again. They were too high up for Alex to tell what birds they were; but honestly, if they'd been right in front of him wearing a label he'd still have struggled. He thought they might have been crows, but why he thought this he wouldn't have been able to explain had anyone asked. He watched them from the corner of his eye, nervous without knowing why.

As he travelled he passed the small supermarket, the one his mum worked at, and was nearly knocked off his feet when blurred shapes came flying out in a cacophony of shouts and excited screams. They passed in a second, Alex flattening himself against the supermarket's wall to avoid being knocked off his feet, and a moment later a man followed, yelling as he ran.

'Oi,' he shouted, his volume affected by his panting, 'get back here and pay for those.'

Following the man's gaze, Alex had seen Emma Sullivan and her gang, Jenna, Aliyah and Francesca, run down the street. He heard Emma shout, 'fuck you' and then they were gone.

The man looked at Alex, a dirty look that seemed to pin the blame for the apparent theft squarely on him, as if by being the same age and in the same location as the actual thieves, he was equally to blame. Alex heard the man mutter 'bloody kids' under his voice as he headed back into the shop, and once he was gone from view Alex quickly peeled himself off the wall and half-walked half-jogged down the street, took the first right and turned up the street that ran parallel to his own.

About half way, a snicket cut through to his street. The passage was narrow, deep green hedges taller than Alex lined both sides, hemming him in, their branches like arms reaching towards him. A few paces along he stopped; ahead of him, though seeing the figure only from behind and at a distance he couldn't be sure, he thought was Janet. She was squatted on her haunches, and it looked like she was poking something with her finger. Alex wasn't sure what she was doing there and so he watched her for a moment, tried to see if he could discern. As usual her head hung low, her hair shielding her face, and all he could see was her index finger going backwards and forwards. He looked, but Alex couldn't see what she might have been poking, if that was indeed what she was even doing. Suddenly, moving so quickly Alex was startled, she stood up and threw her head around, looking directly at him. The pair made eye contact, though the distance between them was too great for Alex to be able to properly see Janet's face. He was about to start walking towards her when there was a loud bang from behind him and he whirled around instinctively, trying to find the source of the noise.

After scanning for a moment, the quiet residential street offering no clues, Alex turned back around and his breath caught in his throat as he did: Janet was gone.

He quickly ran the thirty or so feet of the snicket, emerging onto his own street, but looking left and right he couldn't see Janet anywhere. He saw a couple of kids from his year at school talking to his right, standing outside what he knew to be one of their houses. To his left he saw the mum from the duck pond and her two children, and quickly averted his eyes so as to avoid being spotted again. But there was absolutely no sign of Janet; it was as if she'd vanished into thin air, or had never even been there in the first place.

Accepting she must have just gone faster than him, or maybe gone into a house down the street, a friend (though Alex knew she had none) or a relative (Alex thought he'd heard his dad tell his mum the same, that there were none), he sighed and trudged home. The snicket was three doors from his house, and he realised he couldn't put off arriving there any longer.

He gently pushed open the small white gate before softly closing it behind him. Once again his mum's carefully tended front garden felt like a taunt, like it was mocking him for having such bad feelings on such a beautiful day. When he felt like this nature felt sinister to him, like it was something that wanted bad things for him. It confused and hurt Alex a little; even though the temperature had dropped even more from when his mum had forced him to take his coat that morning, the sun was still shining, the sky was still a sea of blue, only occasionally broken up by islands of white clouds. He didn't want such beauty to dislike him.

Opening the front door, he bent down, unzipped his bag, and retrieved the crumpled permission form for the school trip. He pushed it against his chest and did his best to smooth it with his hands; after a minute or so he thought he might have made 1% of a difference, and he walked down the hall.

The house was quiet; there were no voices to indicate who might be home, and where they might be, so Alex headed to the living room. Moving down the hall, glancing at the various sets of deer antlers as he went, wondering if they, like the outside nature, seemed to hate him, he stopped and pushed open the door to his right. He was pleased to see his mum, who looked up with a smile when she saw him. Alex thought there was something lacking in the smile, something missing, that perhaps it didn't quite reach her eyes like it usually did, but he ignored the thought. He had to talk about the school trip, had to ask about it, and didn't want to be distracted with thoughts of questions whose answers he'd never reach.

Looking around the living room, Alex saw his mum was alone. He thought this was perhaps a good thing; he knew his dad could be an emotional man, and Alex worried that if his parents had to say no, his dad might worry he was letting Alex down. Part of Alex thought this was true, and hated him for it even before he had an answer. Another part knew his dad had done the right thing and that was all that really mattered; he just wished he hadn't done it right before Alex had a school trip that had to be paid for.

'Hi, love, how was school?' his mum asked him.

She was sitting in the single arm chair opposite the couch, the lamp on next to her, the paper in her lap. She closed and folded it in half with a rustle as Alex sat on the couch, sinking into the decades-old cushions.

'Fine. Where's Dad?'

'He's... erm... well he's...' his mum hesitated, stuttered, stumbled. 'He's just nipped out for a bit.'

Alex wanted to know more but stopped himself from asking; he'd finally built up his nerve enough to ask, and wanted to do it before he chickened out.

'Mum, listen, there's this school trip next week...'

He trailed off as he saw his mum's face immediately drop. There was a soft scrunching sound, and Alex saw her hands crunching the newspaper, pushing and pulling it. Alex thought she looked scared, and it scared him. He forced himself to keep talking.

'It's for English, to go to Bradford or somewhere near there, anyway,' he glanced at the permission slip, 'Haworth, just outside Bradford. Something called Brontë Country, I dunno…'

He trailed off again, losing his nerve, and was glad when his mum spoke.

'Brontë Country, oh lovely, it's a beautiful part of the world. The Brontës were sisters, authors, all three of them, although they had to publish their books under fake names, men's names, because women weren't allowed to write then, or at least they were but no one would read their books, women were supposed to cook and clean and–'

'Mum!' Alex said, interrupting her. She was rambling, nervous, and Alex thought if he didn't stop her she'd talk all night, and then his dad would come home, then he'd be too embarrassed to ask again.

'Sorry, love, go on.'

'So there's a school trip there, and I just need you to sign this.'

He reached over and handed his mum the piece of paper, feeling relieved to be unburdened of it. His mum looked relieved too, her features softening, her face uncreasing itself, but only for a moment. As she looked down to read it, Alex looked down too, and blurted the next sentence out quickly, the words forming one mass of linguistics.

'I also need a tenner to go on it too, if that's okay?'

There, it was out. He felt a huge sense of relief; whether he could go or not was almost irrelevant then, the main thing was that he'd asked. He'd done his part, what came next was out of his hands.

The feeling only lasted a moment, however. In a matter of seconds, he got over his excitement at having asked and the dread at being denied flooded back in. And moments after this, Alex learned his dread was appropriate.

'Oh, love, I'm so sorry.'

Alex kept looking at the floor, at his socks, the carpet, the bottom of the chair; anywhere but his mum.

'I'm really sorry, love, but I don't think we can afford this.'

'But Mum, it's only a tenner!' Alex pleaded, still not looking at her.

'I know, love, but with your dad losing his job and all…'

She trailed off, and they both sat in silence, both willing the other to speak first.

'If it was any other time…' his mum said, trying to comfort Alex. He almost believed her.

'Mum,' he said suddenly, with such vehemence that he saw his mum jump. 'It's only a tenner, and I need to go, I can't be the only one in the year not going, they'll all laugh at me.'

'I know, love, I under–'

'You don't understand!' Alex jumped to his feet, looked down at his mum, his anger starting to rise. 'It's

£10 Mum, how can we not afford it?'

'Well your dad–'

'Yeah I know, Dad lost his job. Why did he have to go and do that?'

'He didn't mean to!' Alex's mum was still sitting down but she was looking up at him now, her face pleading with him. 'He did what he felt was right, he wanted to help that Mrs–'

'He wanted to help that *freak*!' Alex shouted, and then his mum stood up too.

'What did you say?' she shouted back, anger permeating her voice.

'If dad hadn't helped that freak he'd still have a job and I could go on this trip.'

'Alex Butler, how dare you–'

'I know you think they're freaks too, Mum!'

'Go to your room!' It was his mum's turn to roar; she'd drawn herself up to her full height, and though she was several inches shorter than Alex, he cowered before her.

He knew he'd gone too far, and he felt bad for calling Mrs Willerby a freak, but neither fact lessened his anger at all. His stupid dad had lost his stupid job because of that stupid woman and now Alex couldn't go on the school trip. He'd never live it down. Tom and Mo would be alright about it, would make fun of him a bit but not loads, but the rest of the school? Especially Emma. Emma was rich, she got whatever she wanted, and she had no mercy for those who couldn't afford things. Just look at the way she treated Janet, as if she were scum from the bottom of the pond. Alex felt hot in the face, he was angry but he wanted to cry.

'I hate this family!' he shouted, suddenly running out of the room and up the stairs, slamming his bedroom door behind him.

'What the hell was that?' said his shocked father, who'd just that moment returned home. His mother said nothing, too stunned by her son's actions to reply.

'Darling,' he said a little louder. 'What's wrong with Alex?'

'Don't ask,' Alex's mum's voice floated out of the living room in response. 'How did it go? How'd you get on?'

'Okay, I think. They don't tell you there and then what benefits you get, but I seemed to fit all the criteria. They said they'll write to me in a few days and let me know.'

'That's good,' Alex's mum said, moving into the hallway and giving her husband a hug. As he wrapped his arms around her, Alex's mum felt comforted even above all of her worries. It was one thing to be worried about paying bills, but then to have school things on top; she hated to let Alex down. Before she realised what was happening she started crying; up in his room Alex heard her snivel and it set him off. He cried until there were no more tears left in him, then he fell asleep, fully clothed, on top of his duvet.

Chapter Ten

'What you got today?' Mo asked, cocking his head to one side and looking a little like a curious and confused dog.

'The usual,' Tom replied, lifting his squashed sandwiches out of his small, transparent plastic lunchbox. 'You?'

'Same,' Mo said with a sigh. 'Same stupid lunch every day. I can't wait 'til I'm grown up so I can have whatever I want every day, instead of just cheese bloody sandwiches.'

'What have you got, Alex?' Tom asked, shifting his body to face his friend.

The trio were sitting at the back of the playground, on a low wall that separated the concrete from the playing field. Behind them the grass stretched out forever, impossibly green; the blades fluttered and danced in the soft late-summer breeze, each time they bent they soon straightened again, as if they too knew the year wasn't going to offer much more sun and they wanted to claim as much of it as they could before it was gone.

Ahead of them was grey; the grey of the concrete

playground, the grey of the breeze blocks that formed the school building itself stretching up above them, looming over them in imitation of the teachers it housed. The pupils were grey too: grey trousers, grey shirts, grey jumpers. It was a sea of monotony, greatly in contrast to the bright colours behind them; the boys focused on their lunches, however, and paid little attention to such grand but ultimately worthless ideas.

Alex opened his lunchbox to find the answer to Tom's question.

'I have,' he said, speaking slowly as the secret was revealed, 'corned beef on, yuck, *brown* bread.'

'Aww, mate, unlucky!' Mo laughed.

'Brown bread,' Tom began, before Mo and Alex joined in and they all said with a chorus, 'sucks.'

'Must have been on offer,' Alex said glumly, trying to explain away his foul lunch. 'My dad still hasn't got a job, so Mum is mostly getting whatever's on sale at work. It's fucking shit.'

Alex put his sandwiches back in his own plastic tub, his appetite suddenly diminished. He looked at his two friends, both sitting to his left, but neither were looking at him. They were looking at their lunches, focusing intently on them, as if by staring into the souls of their food they could avoid any awkwardness that would arise by making eye contact with their friend and having to acknowledge what he'd said.

Mo and Tom ate in silence, the only sounds coming from their crisp packets being opened, chocolate wrappers being torn, bottles opened and slurped from. If anyone had been sitting close to them they'd have been disgusted by the noises; they'd have been fools though, what more can one expect from three 15-year-olds?

All three looked up simultaneously when they realised it wasn't just them that were silent; the rest of the playground was, too. Alex saw a crowd forming on the other side of the playground and his heart dropped. There was a fight, or someone was beating someone up, or something of that ilk. He prayed that Janet wasn't involved, although he knew she would be. It was ever thus. He placed a bet with himself that Emma was picking on her, and then cursed himself for thinking about the situation so flippantly.

A younger child walked past singing the current number one, a bland – or so Alex thought – pop song from the pop witch, as she'd taken to calling herself. Alex was momentarily distracted, began to have a thought linking the singer with Janet and her mum, before his eyes and mind wandered back to the forming mass of students.

'What's going on do you reckon?' Tom asked, nodding in the direction of the crowd.

'Dunno, mate,' Mo replied. 'Who cares?'

'Yeah, for real,' Tom nodded his agreement, apparently speaking in concurrent words and nods.

Alex stood up without realising what he was doing, his body moving on autopilot, and started to walk across the playground. It was mostly empty; the pupils were crowded into the small section of it where the unknown events were taking place.

The crowd hadn't stayed silent for long; once the initial shock had passed, the gathered pupils started shouting and cheering and goading and encouraging whoever was in the middle. Their words formed a mass Alex couldn't pinpoint any part of specifically, so despite the noise swelling the closer he got to it, understanding didn't follow.

Alex soon reached the crowd and, much like the previous week, pushed his way through to the front. It was easier this time than last, and when he got to the front he knew why; once again it was Emma and her gang bullying Janet, but they weren't alone; standing just behind Jenna, Aliyah, and Francesca, who stood a foot or so behind Emma, was Jason Basely and his own gang of hanger-oners, the twins Michael and Tim Ricketts, and Brian Sond.

Where Emma was just a playground bully, Jason Basely was another animal altogether. There were rumours he'd actually been arrested once; no one seemed to be able to agree on what he'd actually done to occasion being taken away by the police, but everyone agreed he had. Some people said he'd beaten up a kid in Hull one Saturday, beaten him so badly he'd broken the kid's arm; others said he'd stolen a car and led five police cars on a chase all over Hull; yet more said he'd broken into a Currys and stolen a load of iPhones and then sold them in the local CEX and made thousands of pounds. Whatever the reason, his arrest seemed to be a known fact; and because of this, where people were scared of Emma, wary in her presence, they were actively terrified of Jason.

Alex found it easier to push through the crowd today because they were hanging back, more cautious; it was widely known that Jason was permanently on the edge, like a fragile bomb, and all it took was one knock to set him off. Just last year, a kid from the year below had bumped into him in the corridor; it hadn't been hard, Jason hadn't even moved, it was actually the kid himself who bounced off Jason and hit the floor. But none of this mattered to Jason; what mattered was that the kid, whether intentionally or not, had bumped into him. Jason waited for him after school and beat him up. Jason was suspended for a week, but he didn't care; such was his violent streak that he spent more time out of school than in it. Further rumours abounded that the headteacher, Mr Gullis, wanted to exclude him, but Emma's father had stepped in to prevent this. The rumours continued to say he'd done so because he didn't think his daughter's boyfriend being excluded from school would reflect well on him in the local community. He didn't seem to realise that being associated with Jason Basely, no matter how remotely, had just that effect, and nothing Jason said or did could possibly make it any worse.

Reaching the front of the crowd and seeing that, once again, Emma was picking on Janet, Alex felt something snap inside himself. He could see the cross Emma wore around her neck dancing as she moved. As well as this, his feelings for Janet made his head spin; he was confused and frustrated. Seeing her face properly, seeing how pretty she might be, made him feel attracted to her.

The fact she never washed that same face, or combed her hair, or washed her clothes, still disgusted him. The fact she seemed to talk to spiders freaked him out, but also at the same time he didn't really believe it, despite what others, or even he himself, had supposedly seen. The fact she didn't stand up for herself, just let Emma attack her, whether it was throwing erasers, or like right now, punches, made him want to scream and hit her himself. He wanted to slap her out of her passivity, like you see people do in films. Sometimes people need a quick shock, that's what the films said, and sometimes a slap was the only way. She wasn't hysterical, in fact quite the opposite, but Alex still thought a slap would work.

But why wasn't she hysterical? Anyone else would be if they found themselves in this situation; on the floor, being attacked yet again by the same culprits. The attacker's friends jeering and mocking, and her boyfriend and his friends waiting for a reason to beat up anyone who tried to stop it. The rest of the school forming an audience to watch her humiliation, jeering and mocking themselves; and perhaps most importantly, no one doing anything to stop the assault. Alex wondered how someone could suffer such a thing, repeatedly, and not lose it.

All of these feelings constantly rattling around in his head, his stomach, moving up and down his arms and legs, threatened to take over Alex. Combined with his dad losing his job which meant he wasn't able to go on the school trip and the fact that he had to eat brown bread, it was all too much. He wanted to scream; he wanted to scream all the time, at school, at home, in the village, everywhere he went. He wanted to scream at the trees and the bushes and the sky, ask them why they'd turned against him. He thought if he could just scream, some of the feelings might leave him, or he might even shock the others, and as a by product himself, into some kind of action. He thought screaming might achieve *something,* and that that something, no matter what it was, would be better than the nothing which surrounded him.

He looked at Emma pummelling Janet; Janet was on her hands and knees once again, her head down, most of her lank hair hanging limply over her face. Emma was standing above her, the hair that wasn't hanging down grasped in one hand, raining punches with the other. The three girls of Emma's gang stood behind her, laughing, pointing, clearly thrilled by the spectacle. Jason was laughing too, shouting encouragement to his girlfriend, probably wishing he could join in. Alex watched all of this occur, standing silent and still, or so he thought. He slowly became aware that people were looking at him; faces in the crowd were turning towards him, looks of confusion painted on them. Aliyah was looking at him, surprised etched on her features, and he saw the Ricketts twins slowly turn their heads and focus on him, confusion covering theirs.

It took Alex a moment to realise why, but understanding came suddenly; he wasn't just thinking about screaming, he actually *was* screaming. Standing there on the playground, watching Janet being hurt again for what he could only assume was no reason; without even realising it, at some point he'd opened his mouth, drawn in his breath, and begun to yell at the top of his voice, expending all the air in his lungs until he could scream no more, and repeating the process.

He realised he didn't care about the fact he was screaming, didn't care people were looking at him, confusion morphing into disgust. People were now pointing and laughing at him but none of it meant anything. Feeling spurred on by his own screams, he moved forward, stepped from out of the crowd and into the circle.

'Stop it,' he said to Emma, almost mesmerised by the gold cross bouncing up and down with her arm. She continued as if she hadn't heard him.

'Stop it!' he said, louder, more firmly. His throat was scratchy and dry but he persevered regardless.

His words clearly had an effect eventually because Emma's fist, raised and poised to strike, remained where it was. Her head slowly turned, moving at approximately the pace of a container ship, the speed reflecting the temerity she felt, as if she was looking for whoever had dared interrupt her sacred ritual, dared to break her spell. She looked at Alex, disgust written on her face as if he were a worm or a piece of dirt, as if he were so pathetic he had no right to even be in her presence, let alone speak to her, let alone tell her what to do.

'What did you say?'

The crowd had fallen silent; the air was tense, fragile like a pane of glass just waiting for a reason to shatter. Everyone was looking at Alex and Emma, looking from one to the other like they were watching a tennis match. Even Janet flicked her eyes upwards, the best she could manage as her movement was restricted by the fact Emma still had a handful of her hair. Alex thought he could smell Janet, and mixed in with the smells of blood and sweat he could smell earth, air, nature; things that were not unpleasant. He found his mind beginning to drift, the scents carrying his thoughts away, until he suddenly snapped back to the present.

Alex's voice momentarily fled him, but he soon found it and put it back to use, clearing his throat as he did so.

'I said stop it. Let her go.'

Emma laughed, a reaction Alex hadn't expected.

'Says who?' she said, still tittering; behind her, her three gang members were laughing too. Behind them, Jason was rubbing his hands together ominously.

'Says me. Let her go and leave her alone.'

'Or what?'

'Or I'll...' Alex trailed off. Emma was right; what would he do if she didn't leave Janet alone? He couldn't hit her, she was a girl. Besides, her boyfriend, the strongest kid in school, was a matter of feet away. Alex might have been brave and reckless, but he wasn't stupid.

'Exactly!' Emma said, laughing once again. Turning back to Janet, Emma's fist, which had stayed raised throughout the whole interaction with Alex, came crashing down upon Janet's head.

Alex heard a soft thump of connection, which made him pause. Then he heard something which spurred him back into action: after the thump was the faintest whimper. Looking at Janet, Alex saw a small pool of blood on the floor, the liquid shimmering in the midday sun, rippling as small drops continued to fall into it. Alex traced the flow of blood and saw it was coming from a cut on Janet's face, just visible through a small gap in her hair.

The day was already warm, at least it was in the middle of the mass of bodies, but even so Alex felt the temperature in his body rise. Before he knew what he was doing, as Emma's arm began to fall once more, he stuck out his hand and caught her wrist. Her arm continued on its trajectory, Emma's momentum threatening to get the better of Alex, before it shuddered to a halt with a violent shake. For a brief moment they both stood perfectly still as if completely confused as to what was actually happening. And then a lot of things happened very quickly.

With a start Alex let go of Emma's wrist; he tried to run away, his legs working on instinct where his brain had betrayed him, but he felt a tug on his collar and suddenly he was laying on his back on the playground. The ground was hard, he could feel a stone pressing on his spine, but he was unable to move.

Despite her arm being released, Emma didn't bring it down; seemingly still somewhat shocked by Alex's grabbing her, she let go of Janet and used her now-free hand to rub at the wrist, looking like a criminal on a cop show who'd just had their handcuffs removed.

Janet, sensing an opportunity, jumped to her feet and

ran, pushing her way through the crowd who moved aside to let her pass. Janet fled, not looking back, not running in the direction of the school but to the gates, through them. She ran all the way to the edge of the village and the small, dilapidated house she shared with her mother.

Jason stood over Alex, looming ominously, a devil holding court over a hopeless sinner.

'Did you just touch my fucking girlfriend?' he said, real vitriol in his voice.

'He did, babe, he–' Emma started, but Jason interrupted her.

'Shut up,' he said, glancing over his shoulder for a moment before turning back to Alex. 'Answer me: did you just touch my girlfriend?'

Alex, laying on the floor, too scared to move, too scared to do anything other than focus on not wetting himself, remained silent. Although, even if he had had the wherewithal to answer, he still most likely wouldn't have. When he got like this, Alex knew, Jason was going to hurt someone. Saying anything, anything at all, no matter how reasonable or excusable, would only make things worse.

Becoming increasingly frustrated by Alex's silence Jason bent down, grabbed the front of Alex's jumper in two hands, and dragged him to his feet. Alex swayed slightly, blood rushing to his head with the sudden movement, and would have fallen back down had the twins not quickly moved forward and grabbed an arm each, keeping him upright. The twins were nothing if not opportunistic; it was the basis for their entire relationship with Jason. They were small, weedy, generally disliked, and they knew it, hence glomming on to him. What Jason got from their relationship Alex didn't know, from the outside it certainly didn't seem symbiotic, but Alex did know that Tim and Michael Ricketts were untouchable. That was what they got from it.

Alex wanted to imitate Janet and run away; his strength was slowly returning, and he thought he had enough to run home. The only issue was his still being held. He tried to wriggle out of the hands of the brothers, but despite their small stature they were stocky and strong and he was unable to move more than a few centimetres. Alex slowly began to accept his fate.

In a way he felt he deserved it; yes, he'd had detention the other day, after he'd joined in laughing at Janet, but that hadn't felt like enough penance. He'd been feeling lost ever since and now he realised why: it was because he hadn't paid for his crime. Standing here, with Jason Basely about to do god knew what to him, he knew it was time to pay. And a small part of him was happy to. The majority of him was terrified and still focusing entirely on not wetting himself, however, and he began to shake all over.

'My wrist really hurts, babe,' Emma whined from behind Jason, all her malice gone. She was suddenly doing the perfect impression of a lost and scared little girl, all traces of the violent monster she'd been only moments before thoroughly vanished.

'I'm taking care of it,' Jason barked without looking at

her. His eyes never left Alex. 'No one, and I mean no one, touches my girlfriend.'

Alex felt a sudden flash of pain in his nose, unlike anything he'd ever felt, and then the world went black.

Chapter Eleven

Alex knew he was in the midst of a dream but that didn't make it feel any less real. He was walking down a narrow path; leaves crunched softly under his bare feet with each step he took, and a feeling of guilt pervaded him with each crushing. To either side of him were hedges, rising high above his head and bending to meet in the middle, forming a tunnel he was walking through. The hedges were so thick as to not let in any light, and so in the dark tunnel Alex had no idea whether it was day or night. But he also knew it didn't matter.

Ahead of him he could see a light, far in the distance. It wasn't white or yellow but orange, and it slowly flickered. As Alex cautiously moved towards it, feeling compelled to approach without knowing why, a figure slowly started to materialise in front of the light. From where Alex was the figure appeared as a silhouette and he was unable to discern any distinguishing features. As he grew closer he realised it was probably a woman, due to her diminished size. She was hunched over, and had what looked like a bird on her shoulder. The closer Alex got to the light the brighter it burned, leaving the silhouette even darker in comparison.

Realisation slowly dawned on Alex: the light was a fire. That was why it was orange and almost seemed to dance in his eyes, the light flickering upwards, licking the top of the tunnel, swiping at the overgrown hedges. Though he knew he should have done, Alex felt no fear that the fire would set the bushes alight. He simply continued to walk, waiting for the figure to become clearer.

He took step after step but the distance hardly seemed to close at all. And then with a sudden rushing noise in his ears, the fire and the figure were right in front of him. He could feel the flames licking at him, even with the person between he and they. The person was so small they did nothing to block the heat, and Alex could feel his face getting warmer and warmer. Alex still couldn't make out any features of the woman, so he looked past her at the fire; now that he was close he saw it was coming from a miniature house, like a dolls house.

Looking closer still, he realised he recognised that house. It wasn't his, he was relieved to see, it was much bigger, much grander. Despite how familiar it looked he couldn't quite place it, but he *knew* it, of that much he was certain.

He continued to stare at it until a quiet *cawing* noise interrupted him, and turning his gaze back to the figure he jumped; despite nothing changing in the tunnel, he could now make out the figure perfectly. It was Mrs Willerby, and on her shoulder was perched a crow, black as the night except for small white spots circling its eyes, almost like make up, which emphasised the eyes to the point Alex felt them boring into him. Alex thought it was the most beautiful animal he'd ever seen and he gazed at it, enraptured.

He was only pulled from his reverie when Mrs Willerby spoke in her unmistakable gravelly voice. It almost sounded like she was chanting:

Belenus I come to thee
Wander in of will freely
Offer all the names of he
Send them back unhappily

When she finished she lapsed back into silence, but the flames behind her danced with renewed vigour. Without knowing how he knew, Alex became aware that Mrs Willerby, with her song, had created the flames, and had power over them. He watched her but she wasn't looking at him, she was facing the flames. They lit her face and he saw malice there, as well as hunger. The image scared him.

Looking at the crow perched on her shoulder he saw it was still watching him. It cocked its head to one side, peering at him with one glassy eye, black surrounded by white surrounded by black in turn. Alex was just beginning to feel incredibly uncomfortable when the crow opened its beak, and Alex could have sworn it started speaking.

'Janet, Janet,' it cawed softly, the only other sound the

flames licking at the hedges now that Mrs Willerby's incantation had ceased. 'Janet, Janet,' it repeated, as if it were now completing an incantation itself. 'Janet, Janet,' the crow continued, flicking its wings and making the flames continue to dance before Alex's eyes.

The crow continued to repeat Janet's name, and wrenching his eyes from it Alex saw Mrs Willerby was looking at him. He looked into her eyes but they were black as the night; he couldn't so much as make out her pupils. They were ringed with white, as the crow. She opened her mouth and Alex began to feel very nervous; whatever she was going to say, he realised he didn't want to hear it. She began to chant again.

Camulus I offer you
This youngling of a beast so true
It wanders not through morning dew
But through the night and darkness blue
Release it from its prison do
Unbound, unbidden, unloved, unknew

Though again he didn't understand the words, Alex began to feel very afraid. He couldn't have said why, but he was warm, warmer than he'd been though he was no closer to the flames. Even as he continued to stand there he could feel himself getting hotter, his skin felt like it was on fire. He itched all over but when he tried to scratch himself he found he couldn't move his arms. He tried to take a step but couldn't move his feet, either.

The fear in him began to rise and he was on the verge

of panic when Mrs Willerby said, 'you are not him.' The crow turned its gaze back on him and cawed one final, 'Janet!' before standing up to its full height, stretching its wings to their full span, and saying, 'wake up!'

Soft voices filtered into Alex's ears as he slowly came to; his eyes remained closed for a moment, sunlight filtering through his lids and into his pupils. The afterimage of a fire burned behind his eyelids, but he had no idea why. Had he been dreaming? He tried to think but couldn't; if he had been having a dream it was long gone, not even so much as a whisper remained.

He moved his hands to wipe his eyes, wanting to thoroughly scratch them before opening, and his arms moved slowly at first, reluctantly, before acquiescing and doing what his brain commanded.

After rubbing them for a moment, he did indeed open his eyes, but only for a split second; the sun was shining directly in through his bedroom window, and he was momentarily blinded. Using his now fully able hands he shaded himself from the sun and opened his eyes a second time, this time finding the partially blocked light much more palatable.

He was alone in his bedroom; he had no memory of how he'd gotten there. The last thing he remembered was Janet on the playground, blood pooling under her face, and then he woke up. He thought maybe there had been a bird, a crow or raven or something, but he couldn't hold onto the thought, it slipped through him like grains of sand in a sieve. With a start he threw back the duvet and was mortified to find he was wearing pyjamas; someone, most likely his mother, must have changed him at some point. He put his hands down his pyjama bottoms and was relieved to find he was wearing underwear. Perhaps a portion of his modesty had been spared.

There was a glass of water on his bedside table and with no little effort, using two hands for security, Alex picked it up and took a sip. He hadn't realised how dry his mouth and throat were until he felt the water on them, and he greedily gulped down more, spilling some on himself but not caring. The water was the nectar of the gods, and Alex felt it a pleasure to be blessed.

Putting the half empty glass back down, Alex realised he had no idea what time it was, or even what day; he scanned his room for his phone but didn't see it. Sitting up, he winced at the pain in his chest. Slowly, cautiously, he unbuttoned his pyjama top; he winced again when he saw his skin.

Bruises, a sea of black and blue and dirty yellow, littered his chest like lily pads on a pond. The small gaps where there were no bruises showed painfully white in contrast, his skin seeming to shine in all places, where he was injured and where he wasn't. He took off his top and looked at his arms: no marks, they were clear. Taking a moment to compose himself, recovering from both the pain and the shock, he got out of bed. His legs seemed fine, they carried his weight with no complaints, other than a slight stiffness; he rolled his pyjama legs up one at a time, but his legs, much like his arms, were clear. His chest had clearly taken the brunt of the damage.

He spotted his backpack on the floor and was just bending over to reach for it, to see if his phone was held within, when he stopped. He'd seen a flash of something in the mirror attached to his wardrobe door, something he didn't recognise; he straightened up again, once more wincing at the pain inflicted on his chest by his movements, and who knew what else, and froze, three quarters erect.

The thing he'd seen in the mirror was himself, though not himself as he'd ever seen.

The reason he'd not made the connection between himself and the reflection in the mirror was due to the colour of his face; where his chest was a mix of colours, a painter's pallet of bruising, his face was a dark blue mess. And it wasn't just the colour, but the shape too; his face was so swollen that not only did he not look like Alex, indeed he barely looked like a human. His cheeks rose both upwards and outwards, no longer smooth and flat but spherical, like two dark plums under his eyes.

And his eyes! Alex hadn't noticed until he'd seen himself, but he was looking at this room, looking for his phone, looking for himself, through slits. For a brief second he thought his eyes were surrounded by bright white paint, but after blinking a couple of times he realised his eyes were simply two dark circles. He thought he looked a bit like Bruce Wayne when he'd applied the face paint but before he'd put the Batman mask on. Alex quickly scoffed at this idea, though. Based on the way he looked he was very far from Bruce Wayne; at best, he was one of the bad guys Batman beats up.

But was he one of the bad guys? What had happened? Why had he been beaten up? Alex didn't know for sure he had actually been beaten up, but the evidence all seemed to be pointing in that direction. As he was looking at himself in the mirror, wanting to touch his face to see if it hurt as much as his chest but reluctant to do so, he remembered the voices that had woken him. He stood perfectly still, silent, and listened hard. By really focusing his every sinew on hearing he was able to pick up the voices once again, like a radio finding a far away signal. They were soft but clear; he recognised those of his mum and dad, but wasn't able to place the third one. He thought he saw a flash of black and white behind him in the mirror, but when he whirled round, the sudden movement causing a bolt of pain to shoot through him, there was nothing there.

'Thank you so much,' his mum said, and it sounded like she'd been crying.

'It's no problem, my dears,' the mystery voice replied, sounding very pleased with itself. 'Just have the boy drink this, and he'll be right as rain by the morning.'

'Sure, of course,' Alex's mum said, sounding dubious. 'What is it?'

'Oh, you know, a bit of this and a bit of that. Mugwort, yarrow, some anise. Never you worry what's in it.' Alex thought it was female but it was gravelly, harsh, and he couldn't be sure. 'Just mind what it does. All good, all good, I promise.'

'Thank you, Ann, we, erm,' his dad said, hesitating.

'We appreciate it. Don't we, dear?'

Alex could picture his dad elbowing his mum, wanting her to agree. The name rang a bell in his head. Ann; he knew that name but couldn't place it. He didn't think too hard, however; the more he thought, the more his head hurt.

'That we do, yes, that we do,' his mum said, sounding even more dubious somehow. 'And thanks for stopping by and checking on him, we do appreciate it.'

'It's my pleasure,' the voice said. Alex was now certain it was female, and not just because it came with the name Ann. He knew the voice, much like he knew the name, but he was starting to get a headache so sat back down on his bed, tried not to think about it. Alex thought it would come back to him whenever it came back to him; as he'd been standing up pain had started to rise in his chest and he wanted to lay back down, try and get some sleep. He wanted to pass out and wake up when he both felt and looked less awful.

He closed his eyes, was just drifting off when the front door closing, being knocked on, and then immediately reopening snapped him back to reality. He wished whoever it was, Ann or whoever, would go away so he could get some sleep. He still wondered what day it was, but was too tired and in too much pain to really care. He once again closed his eyes, and once again was just drifting off when there was another knock, this time on his bedroom door.

Without opening his eyes he said 'What?', trying to sound as grumpy as he felt. He heard the latch on his door click and opened his eyes slightly; he was expecting his mum or dad, and was incredibly surprised to see Tom poking his head in the room.

'You alright, mate?' Tom asked, his voice softer than Alex had ever heard it. If he hadn't have been able to see his friend he wouldn't have known the voice belonged to him.

'Alright,' Alex said, once again sitting up and trying, but failing, to hide the pain.

'Fuck, mate, you okay?' Tom took Alex's greeting as permission and moved fully into the room, closing the door behind him and looking around.

Tom had been in Alex's room a billion times; the pair had known each other since they were four, their mums working together at the supermarket. But each time Tom entered, it was like his first time; he'd look around, as if in the Natural History Museum, taking it all in, awed. Perhaps he was seeing if anything had changed, seeing if Alex had changed his posters, seeing if Tom needed to change his to keep up with what was popular.

Alex propped himself up with his pillows, his chest in pain but doing his best to hide it in front of his oldest and best friend.

'I'm okay, mate. Listen, Tom, can I ask you something?'

'Yeah, sure,' Tom answered immediately, but didn't look convinced. Alex briefly wondered if Tom worried he was going to get emotional, something that, despite their having been friends for over a decade, they never did.

'What,' Alex began, faltering and having to steel himself before continuing. 'What the fuck happened to me?'

A broad grin broke out on Tom's face; his fears dissipated in an instant, and he looked like he was ready to laugh.

'Oh, man, it was epic!'

'What was?'

'You were!'

'Was I? What did I do?'

'Well,' Tom said, looking down, his cheeks turning a very slight shade of pink; he had a handsome face, a vivid jawline and a strong nose. Sheepishness became him. 'To be honest, mate, you didn't really do anything. But you did it brilliantly!'

'What do you mean?' Far from being sated, Alex's curiosity was only increasing. He thought Tom would make a good host on a TV gameshow, leaving the audience waiting on tenterhooks to know if they'd won the jackpot or not.

'What do you remember? You tell me and I'll fill you in on the rest.'

'The last thing I remember,' Alex said, screwing up his eyes as he concentrated, 'is Janet being beaten up by Emma. When I got to the front of the crowd, I saw she was bleeding, and I think I wanted to stop Emma from hitting her any more. But honestly,' he said, breathing out hard and then inhaling sharply at the pain, 'I have no idea.'

'Okay, mate. Well,' Tom said, sitting on the edge of

Alex's bed, filling him in on what had happened earlier that day. Because much to Alex's surprise, it had happened only that lunch time, just a few hours prior. After Jason had punched him in the face, Tom said, knocking him out immediately, Jason had punched him a couple more times before proceeded to kick him in the ribs repeatedly. Tim, Michael, and Brian had all joined in, getting a few kicks in each, but it was Jason, Tom said, who'd done the majority of the damage.

'You were actually pretty awake this afternoon, you even walked home.'

'What?' Alex said in disbelief, a grin on his face that soon became a grimace. 'Really?'

'Really. Gullis eventually broke up the fight, if you could call it that, and he wanted to call an ambulance with you lying there passed out, but before he could you came round and just, like, stood up. He wanted to send you to the nurse but you said you'd go home, and just kinda walked off. He sent me and Mo after you, and we walked you home.'

'Thanks, mate,' Alex said.

'It's all good, mate,' Tom said, waving away Alex's thanks with one hand. 'Your mum fucking *freaked* when we brought you inside,' Tom said with a grin. Alex couldn't help but grin back, this one sticking.

'Really?'

'Yeah, mate, she bugged out. She burst into tears, like, right away. I dunno if you used up all your energy walking home, but the second you got through the door you collapsed. Me, Mo and your dad carried you up here and put you to bed, and then me and Mo left your parents to it and went back to school.'

'Seriously?' Alex couldn't believe it, he assumed Tom and Mo would at least be allowed to go home.

'Seriously! Gullis made sure to tell us as we were leaving with you that he expected me and Mo back in like half an hour or something. So stupid.'

'What time is it?' Alex asked. Tom took his phone from his pocket and checked.

'It's nearly four. I came here straight from school; Mo had to go home, something to do with his dad needing help or something. He told me to tell you he'll come tomorrow.'

'What happened to Jason?'

'Oh, you know,' Tom said with a weariness that belied his youth. 'The usual. Gullis suspended him on the spot, and his gang too, but that's it. They'll be back in a week like nothing's happened.'

'And…' Alex started, hesitating, before forcing himself to go on, to ask. 'What about Janet?'

Tom looked at Alex before he answered; it was a sly look, a knowing look, as if Tom was aware of facts about Alex that Alex didn't even know himself.

'Do you fancy Janet?' Tom asked, ignoring Alex's question.

'Fuck no!' Alex said, the vehemence of his words both surprising and hurting him. He adjusted his position on the bed, feeling every millimetre he moved, before deciding to be honest with his best friend. 'Honestly, mate, I don't know.'

'What do you mean you don't know?'

'I dunno! It's like…' Alex said, before pausing, trying to order his thoughts. He explained to Tom his mixed feelings, hoping he was conveying his meaning well enough. Tom looked confused, but whether by what Alex was saying, or the way he was saying it, he didn't know.

'Well whatever you feel, mate, what you did was incredible. People were talking about you all afternoon.'

'Really?' Alex said, pleased to hear it.

'Of course! You're a hero, man!'

Alex didn't say anything; he certainly didn't feel like a hero. He wished he could have done more, could have stood up to Jason; standing up to Emma was one thing, but she was a girl. It was Jason he needed to stop, although he knew he never would, never could. No matter how much he needed to.

'Oh, shit, I almost forgot.' Tom reached into his pocket and pulled out a small wooden figurine, no more than five inches tall. Reaching over, he handed it to Alex.

'What's this?'

'I have no idea! It was sitting on the pavement outside your house, on top of a piece of paper that had your name on it.'

Alex sat up, his heart racing. It couldn't be…?

'Do you have the paper? Did it say anything else?'

'Sorry, mate, I don't know. When I picked up the doll the paper blew away. I tried to grab it but I wasn't fast enough. Sorry.'

'That's okay,' Alex said, not looking at him. He was

looking intently at the small wooden figurine; it was hard to be sure, but it looked like a person. The wood was light, both in colour and weight, and the figure had a human-esque shape but was carved roughly, as if it'd been done in a rush.

'Was there anything else?'

'Nope, just that and the note. But, oh yeah,' Tom said, sitting up straight once again. 'I did see Janet's mum when I was walking here.'

Janet's mum! A lightbulb lit inside Alex's head. That was the voice he'd heard, that's where he knew the name Ann from; it was Mrs Willerby, Janet's mum, who'd been talking to his parents.

'Yeah, she was here talking to my mum and dad.'

'What about?' Tom asked, leaning forward.

'I'm not sure, I was up here and half asleep, I couldn't tell.'

'I wonder if she brought it?'

'If she did, why would she leave it on the pavement? Why wouldn't she give it to my parents to give to me?'

'Oh, yeah,' Tom said, leaning back deep in thought. 'Who knows then.'

'Yeah, who knows,' Alex echoed, although he thought he did. The figurine, although hard to distinguish in its entirety, did have one very visible feature. On the base, which was a small circle a little more than four and a half inches in diameter, was carved what Alex thought was initials.

JW.

Chapter Twelve

As time tends to have a habit of doing, the slower Alex willed it to pass, the faster it did. He spent the rest of the week off school recovering, at first laying in his bed, watching the TV his dad lugged up and perched somewhat precariously on his desk. When he began to feel better, his bruises fading, life infecting his body once again, Alex followed the TV back into the small living room and spent another day or two laying on the old grey couch. It was lumpy and uncomfortable, the stuffing uneven after years of use, but he was just glad to be out of his room. Laying in his bed, the only view of the outside world he had was of a small patch of sky, which was either cloudy and uninteresting to look at, or a deep, clear blue, and felt like it was taunting him.

The living room was also small, not much bigger than his bedroom, but just having a change of scenery was nice. Both metaphorically and literally; the living room had a picture window looking out into the front garden, and the street beyond, and even though it was a view Alex had seen nearly every day for the 15 years of his life, it was that much better than the small square of sky he saw from his bedroom that he was completely enamoured with it.

At first he felt like the pictures on the walls were staring at him; pictures of his mum and dad, pictures of the three of them; pictures of old relatives, brothers and sisters and aunts and uncles of his parents, people he vaguely recognised. There were also pictures of Alex's grandparents, both his mum's and dad's parents, but they'd all died before he'd been born so he had no memories of them whatsoever. He sometimes wished he'd had a granddad; when other kids at school spoke about theirs, the cool things they did like giving them BB guns or sneaking them a beer when their parents weren't looking at a family meal, he felt pangs of jealousy. Although he wasn't old enough to understand, Alex felt left out; a feeling, sadly, he'd only go on to feel more and more as he grew up. He wasn't going to grow up to be particularly alone, but he'd feel left out as often as anyone does. As we all do sometimes.

There were also paintings amongst the pictures, landscapes of beautiful countryside scenes, fields and farms and greens and yellows stretching as far as the eye could see. Deer walked among the frames, sometimes a single one, other times a handful. In some there were birds too, crows, and Alex studied them, looking for something he wasn't quite sure what.

Soon the pictures faded from his vision, as did the TV. The weekend was a brief Indian summer, and he longed to be enjoying it. Tom and Mo had called for him on Saturday morning but, though he was well enough to be sitting up by then, it still hurt to move too much. So Alex had to watch them walk away from the house, see them respectfully remain at walking pace until they were through the gate, heads down, not saying anything. The moment the gate closed behind them they started shouting and laughing, running away down the street. Whether they thought Alex couldn't see them, thought they were okay once they were off his property, or something else, Alex didn't know; what he did know was he longed to be with them, to be feeling so good with so few cares.

The reason Alex dreaded the coming Monday, over and above his usual dread for the end of the weekend and the start of another school week, was that Monday would bring with it the fated school trip to Brontë Country; the trip he was not a part of. He'd sheepishly told Tom and Mo when they'd called for him, finally admitting it to someone other than himself – he'd been meaning to tell Miss Naveed on Friday but hadn't been in school; his mum had phoned up and explained on his behalf – and making it feel much more real. Tom and Mo had offered as much sympathy as any pair of 15-year-olds could, quickly changing the subject back to football and Hull's chances of reaching the playoffs when the conversation allowed.

It wasn't missing the trip he was sad about; he liked English, but this term they were reading Jane Eyre, and whilst he could kind of understand why Miss Naveed, and some of the girls in the class, liked it, he thought it was boring. Miss Naveed kept saying 'reader, I married him!' to delighted squeals from the girls in the front row, the ones who loved Downton Abbey and Bridgerton, but the sentence meant nothing to him. He knew it was from the book, towards the end, and was supposed to be the ushering in of the happy ending, but he just wasn't bothered by it. He'd much rather read John Grisham or Lee Child, kick ass books where strong, brave men beat up the bad guys, kissed the girls, and everyone was happy. Plus, Jane Eyre was written really weirdly; Miss Naveed said that's how people spoke back then, but it didn't make any sense to him.

No, it wasn't missing the trip itself. It was what missing the trip would signify to the other kids that made him sad: he'd be marked out as one of the poor kids. Theirs was an odd school; everyone knew and was scared of Jason Basely, but he wasn't really a bully per se. He beat kids up, sure, and didn't do his homework, was generally a menace to students and teachers alike, but mostly left kids alone; he had his sights set higher than terrorising a bunch of harmless children. It was Emma that was the real bully, not just of Janet but of everyone. Whilst most of the boys in his year, and to be honest a lot of the girls, probably could have beaten her in a fight, the ever-looming presence of Jason behind her, whether he was actually there physically or just in spirit, stopped them. He supposed this was why Janet didn't fight back; Jason had no shame when it came to hitting women, if anything he was an equal opportunity beater-upper. He loved to punch, and had no qualms about his target.

What made Emma much worse of a bully was that she didn't come from a broken home. Mr Sullivan was very wealthy; he managed the building society, got money from being a councillor, and Alex was also sure he'd heard his dad say once that Mr Sullivan owned half of Deerborn and the surrounding countryside. Alex wasn't entirely sure what this meant, but he assumed it did mean Mr Sullivan had a lot of money. If Emma had been from a broken home, Alex might have understood some of her behaviour. The fact she was wealthy made it, to Alex, infinitely more cruel; he felt she attacked people because she wanted to, not because she was sad or poor or was being attacked herself. She wasn't an abused person, just an abuser. And because she was wealthy, she thought poorness a flaw in a person. If she'd been poor herself, she might have seen something of a kindred spirit in Janet; Emma would no doubt still beat her up regularly, but at least she wouldn't beat her up because she was poor.

But life didn't work like that, a fact of which Alex was aware even at 15 years old. Emma was beautiful, well groomed, and wealthy. Janet was ugly – at least so people said, Alex thought it might not be entirely true – not well groomed, and poor. And Emma loved to beat up people different from her.

Alex had thought for a time he might be able to get away with not going on the school trip because Jason had beaten him up so badly. He thought he might be able to convince his mum and dad to let him stay off school one more day, stay in front of the TV, hide. But no such luck;

when he'd mentioned it to his mum she'd scoffed at him, telling him people wouldn't care he couldn't afford it, that people would probably be even nicer to him if they knew his dad had lost his job and was struggling. Alex thought his mum didn't know a single thing about what it was like to be a kid.

And so, despite his best efforts, it was soon Sunday night, and Alex was going to bed. He'd tried one last time, pleading with his dad as he went to say goodnight, but he was as unmoved as his wife.

'It'll be okay, son,' his dad had said. 'Just go to school like normal, no one will even notice.'

'Yeah, right,' Alex had said. 'Everyone will notice.'

'They won't.' By this point Alex was already heading towards the living room door, his hand reaching out for the handle.

'If I get beaten up again on Tuesday don't be surprised.'

'Oh, Alex,' his mum had sighed, joining in the conversation. 'Don't be so silly.'

'Whatever,' Alex had said, quickly turning his face away as a smile broke out on it.

The reason he was smiling was because he'd remembered something; he'd been so caught up in his own missing of the school trip, he hadn't thought who else would be missing it. There were always two or three kids who missed each school trip, and every time, without fail, Janet was one of them. He smiled because, by missing the school trip himself, he'd be with her all day.

He ran up the stairs two at a time, stumbling at the top and using the banister to pull himself upright. He burst into his room and, opening his desk drawer, took out the small wooden figure he was by that point certain had been left by Janet.

'Tomorrow,' he whispered to himself, clutching the figurine in both hands, holding it close to his chest. 'Tomorrow.'

Chapter Thirteen

Form on Monday morning was like a carnival; the pupils were so excited by the prospect of a day away from the classroom they were untameable. The noise was raucous, with kids laughing and shouting both to and at each other. There were kids running around the room, climbing to stand on their chairs, some even threatening – but not quite daring – to stand on their desks. After several valiant attempts to calm them, Miss Naveed simply completed the register by scanning the room and then left them to it. They were loud and excited, but they were harmless; not a single one of them wanted to risk a last-minute halt at their breaking out of the confines of the school, so even though they were rowdy, they behaved themselves.

The only two not joining in the whooping and shouting were Janet and Alex, the only two not going on the trip. Where Alex was subdued precisely for this reason, Janet was just being her usual quiet, withdrawn-within-herself self. Alex glanced at her a couple of times but as usual she sat with her head down, ignoring those around her. Alex briefly wondered whether she'd notice a bomb going off right next to her; and if she did, would she even react, or simply continue to sit still, silent and unmoving, whilst the world around her collapsed?

Mo and Tom had filled Alex in on their walk to school that morning; Janet had been off the rest of the week as well. Emma, much like her star cross'd lover Jason, had been suspended; they each had been banished from school for a fortnight, although most expected at least Emma, if not Jason too, to return sooner, once Mr Sullivan had met with Mr Gullis, a habit he had each time Emma was in trouble over and above simple detention.

Janet had been off school the same days as Alex; he longed for her to look up so he could see her face, not just to see it because he liked it, but to see what damage she'd sustained. Alex couldn't get the image of that pool of blood from his mind. He'd never seen so much blood before, not even when he'd run into a lamp post nose-first when he was ten and had bled for what felt like hours, though his parents later told him was no more than five minutes.

He could still see it, shining brightly in the fading summer sunshine, the deep maroon colour contrasting with the dull grey of the playground. He'd expected it to be lighter, a much more vibrant red, like the colour of Man Utd's football kit. The darkness had surprised him, and he'd nearly asked his mum about it over the weekend, but had held back. He wasn't certain why, but he was afraid his mum would confirm something that he'd never be able to move past. He didn't need the darkness to be a certainty.

His own bruising was largely gone: on Saturday morning Alex's dad had come into his room and handed him a small glass with some brown liquid inside. It had looked like pond water, and smelled not too dissimilar. After much pleading from his dad, Alex had forced himself to drink it, gagging as he did so, barely keeping it down. Upon waking on Sunday morning, however, his chest and face had been almost completely healed, hardly any traces of what had befallen them the previous week remained.

Eventually the bell rang, and with even louder screams of excitement – something Alex hadn't thought was possible – the class grabbed their bags and coats and pushed each other out of the way to be the first from the room. Alex felt continual pangs of jealousy in his chest – his card wasn't completely, utterly, inescapably marked until the buses left for Haworth without him on one of them. If by some miracle he could make money appear, find £10 in a pocket he didn't know existed, buried in the bottom of his bag, slipped into his lunchbox by his mum as a secret or elaborate joke, then he'd still be able to be one of the regular kids. Once the buses left, he'd be one of them, the others. The *poor* kids.

Tom and Mo got up at a normal pace, putting on their coats and bags with no more urgency than if they were off to French as normal. Alex appreciated this show of solidarity from them, but really he just wanted them gone. The buses leaving would mark him, but also allow him some peace and quiet. He hadn't expected that, on top of the usual dread of Mondays, and the added dread of being left behind, he'd also be scared at what others would think and say of him after what he'd done to Emma. Even though he'd been right, he was sure of it, he still thought people didn't like it.

Emma was pretty, Emma was popular, Emma had clean straight blonde hair; Janet wasn't pretty (so people believed, regardless of the truth), Janet wasn't popular, Janet had dirty, lank, limp mousy brown hair. Emma, no matter her actions, was on the right side, and Janet the wrong. School life was as straight forward yet confusing as that. In addition to this, Emma was a girl, and Alex had put his hand on her. No matter the circumstances, that was a huge no. You didn't do anything violent to a girl if you were a boy, that was a fact known by everyone. Alex had violated it.

Another thing the empty class meant was an end to the whispers, the looks, the people talking behind their hands, clearly about him. He didn't like the spotlight at any time, let alone when it was shining on him in such a nakedly negative way. At least when the class slowly emptied, leaving just he, Janet, and Miss Naveed, he had some peace.

'See you later, mate,' Tom said, almost shyly, like he was embarrassed to be showing feelings, even for his oldest friend.

'Yeah, mate,' Mo added. 'Have a good day, yeah?'

'Thanks,' Alex responded glumly, unable to keep the emotion out of his voice. 'Enjoy the trip, I'll see you tomorrow.'

Because of the distance from Deerborn to Haworth the pupils wouldn't be returning to the school until 6pm; at least Alex would be spared the morning's spectacle played in reverse. As he thought this, Miss Klein entered the room.

'Right then, you two,' Miss Naveed said when the rest of the class had finally left, and it was just the four of them in the now quiet room. 'I'm heading off. You'll be with Miss Klein in here all day. You obviously still get morning break and your lunch, but other than that you'll be in here.'

Miss Naveed stood up, nodding at Miss Klein who smiled at her. Alex had been watching Miss Naveed as she spoke, but looked at Janet when, to his incredulity, she put up her hand.

'I'll leave this one to you,' Miss Naveed said to Miss Klein, picking up a pile of brown exercise books and leaving the room. Miss Klein sat behind Miss Naveed's vacated desk and looked at Janet.

'Yes, Janet?' Miss Klein said, the astonishment plain in her voice.

'How come you're not going, Miss? It's an English trip, isn't it?'

Her voice was small, soft; it was like she was speaking from a great distance, though Alex was only two rows behind her, maybe five feet away at the most.

'Well, Janet,' Miss Klein began, before stopping abruptly, as if only then realising it was just Alex and Janet as well as her. 'Alex,' she said, making him jump slightly. 'Why don't you come sit up the front here with

Janet, save me raising my voice? It'll be nice to give it a rest today, unless you two plan to cause a scene?'

Janet shook her head violently, her hair flying in chunks, the strands matted together. Alex couldn't help but shudder at the sight; as much as he longed to see her face, her lips and her eyes, he wished he didn't have to see her dirty hair as well, it ruined the image for him. Why couldn't she just wash it?

In spite of this revulsion, Alex's heart was pounding. Janet was sitting at a table for two, right in front of Miss Klein's desk, alone. *Alone.* Scarlett Blakeley was the unlucky – so the other kids said, and Alex, up until the last couple of weeks, would have agreed – kid who was assigned to sit next to her in registration. Scarlett was on the trip, meaning Janet sat alone. Meaning Miss Klein meant for Alex to sit next to her.

He slowly stood up, unsure if his legs would properly carry his weight, and after busying himself for a moment picking up his bag and coat, making sure his legs wouldn't betray him, he walked the few short paces to the desk.

He pulled the chair out with a loud scraping noise, the ancient legs scratching across the ancient tiles, and winced an apology to Miss Klein as her face grimaced at the sound. Janet didn't move; she was sitting stiff as a board, and Alex was careful as he sat down not to so much as even graze her, for fear she might shatter like a pane of glass. Janet didn't move the whole time he sat, opened his bag, took his pencil case out. Her own singular pencil was on the table in front of her, and Alex looked at it; it was nibbled at the end, small chunks of the wood missing, and Alex was fascinated. That pencil had been in Janet's mouth. He only looked away when Miss Klein started speaking again.

'Good boy, Alex,' she began, before finally answering Janet's question. 'Unfortunately, Janet, because there are two of us teaching English we take it in turns to go on trips, and this one is Mr Barnett's. I tried to get him to swap but he wasn't having it; I love the Brontës, their work is incredible. I particularly love Anne, who I think gets a bit of a short shrift. Everyone always talks about Emily and Charlotte, but I personally think *Agnes Grey* and *The Tenant of Wildfell Hall* are the best of the sisters' books. Although I do love *Jane Eyre* of course, but who doesn't?' she added quickly.

Janet didn't say anything; she remained still, seemingly absorbing the knowledge without feeling any need to reply. After a moment Miss Klein spoke again.

'So today is yours to do as you wish. I'll be tackling this giant pile of marking,' she said, patting a stack of dark blue exercise books on the desk in front of her. 'You two feel free to do as you wish. If you have any homework, now might be a good time to do it. If you've brought a book, feel free to read it. If you have neither let me know, and I'll find something for you to do.'

With this she picked the top book from the pile, opened it, and with a frown began to make marks Alex couldn't discern with a red pen. Janet was finally released from her spell as well; she pulled a forest green maths book, the cover replete with the school's name and stag's head emblem, as if from nowhere and, opening it and unfolding an A4 sheet of paper which Alex recognised as homework from the previous week, began to write the answers down.

Alex, his memory sparked by Janet, pulled from his bag the same colour book containing the same photocopied A4 sheet, and began to attack it himself. Glancing out the window at a nearby tree he saw a large black bird perched on a branch. He thought, though couldn't have said why, that it was watching him. Its head was cocked to one side, and one beady eye, completely black but surrounded by white, seemed to be piercing into him. He looked at Miss Klein and Janet but both were absorbed in what they were doing and were paying the bird no regard. Looking back, Alex was both disappointed and relieved to see the bird stretch its wings and take flight. For a brief moment, Alex had an odd sense of deja vu, the white around the bird's eyes almost triggering a memory from within him, but then the bird was gone and he couldn't say for sure either way.

The morning passed in near silence; the only sounds were the bell informing the rest of the school of lesson changes, the accompanying noises of pupils moving around, and the various pens and pencils of the three in the classroom doing their respective work. A couple of times Miss Klein had left the room, telling the pair she was just nipping to the staff room; Alex had been desperate to speak to Janet, when it was just the pair of them alone, but he hadn't dared. Each time his mouth had gone dry, his hands had become moist, and his frozen tongue had betrayed him.

Lunch came and went; Alex ate his packed lunch in silence, whilst Miss Klein and Janet went to the cafeteria to get their school lunches. When they were both gone, and Alex was alone in the room, he looked at the space Janet had vacated.

There was absolutely no trace of her at the desk or in her seat, no evidence she'd occupied the space all morning. Janet had taken her green book, sheet of paper, and pencil with her. There was nothing more on the desk, and ducking under it, Alex saw no bag, and sitting up again, no coat on the chair. He still couldn't work out where she'd produced the book from, and the more he thought about it the more his head hurt. It was as if she'd just pulled it from thin air.

Towards the end of lunch, Alex needed the toilet; he stood up, stretching as he did so, raising his arms to the ceiling and rocking back and forth on the balls of his feet, legs stiff, and walked out of the classroom, down a flight of stairs, and into the boys room.

When he returned to the classroom Miss Klein and Janet were back; Miss Klein looked up as he came in, but seeing it was Alex simply nodded at him before returned to her marking. Alex felt sorry for her; she'd been doing it all day but the pile didn't look any smaller than it had when she started.

Alex returned to his desk and was about to sit down when he froze; on top of his open book, filled with what he thought were probably completely incorrect maths answers, was a chocolate bar.

Sitting there all alone, surrounded by fractions and decimals, it looked out of place. The wrapping was a deep, dark blue, contrasting with the whiteness of the paper in his book and the very light, very pale brown wood of the desk. He looked at it for a moment, then looked at Miss Klein and Janet in turn. Both were absorbed in their own work and didn't notice him looking at them.

Alex sat down slowly, suspiciously; the chocolate bar felt like a trap, he felt like a mouse in a cartoon. If he took it a box or cage or something would fall down, and he'd be trapped. That's what Janet and Miss Klein had been talking about as they went to get their lunches, a way to get back at Alex for the last detention. The chocolate bar, though only a normal sized one, suddenly seemed gigantic to Alex. He wanted to ignore it, continue with his homework, but he couldn't unless he moved it.

Reaching his hand out slowly he touched it with his index finger, gently, as if to test that it was actually real. It was; it was firm, the wrapping was smooth, and there was a very quiet crinkling sound. He withdrew his hand quickly as if he'd been scolded, and again looked at Miss Klein and then Janet. Miss Klein was still frowning, making marks with her red pen, slowly turning pages, closing one book and picking up the next. Janet was reading a book, absorbed in its contents, her face a blank slate, completely still except for when she turned a page every few moments. For a second Alex panicked, wondering if he wasn't a ghost, the complete lack of impact his presence made scaring him a little.

Alex, dismissing the thought, reached out the same index finger and touched the chocolate bar again. Finding it still to be real, he quickly picked it up and put it in his bag, as if hiding the evidence of a great crime. The wrapper crinkled fairly loudly in the quiet of the room, but still Miss Klein and Janet continued with their own work. Alex might as well have been alone.

He was just about to return to his homework when Miss Klein stood up.

'I just have to go and talk to Miss Aseen about something, I'll be back soon.'

She swiftly exited, her skirt flaring out behind her as she walked, leaving Alex and Janet alone in the room. Alex decided to throw caution to the wind and was about to speak to Janet, ask her if she'd bought him the chocolate bar, when he was shocked to hear her speak.

'Thank you,' she said, her voice so quiet as to almost be a whisper. If there had been a single other noise in the room, even the sound of a pin dropping, Alex doubted he would have heard her. But he did, and her words took him completely by surprise.

'What?' he blurted out loudly, regretting it the moment he did.

'Thank you,' Janet said again, a little louder but still deathly quiet.

'What for?' Alex said, so dumbfounded by her speaking at all that he wasn't properly grasping her words or parsing her meaning.

'For last week, what you did with Emma.' Janet's voice was louder still with this sentence. Alex's brain finally engaged with her words, and he was able to respond.

'That's okay,' he said, and then with a rush added, 'I'm sorry she always does that to you, she's such a bitch.'

Janet nodded, her hair barely moving. She'd been looking down for their entire conversation but finally looked up, looked straight ahead.

'It's fine,' she said, a steely determination in her voice. Alex could see her face now; he'd expected it to be swollen, or at least bruised, even though his own chest and face barely bore the marks of the kicking he'd taken the previous week. Janet's face was perfectly clear, as if she'd never been attacked at all.

'It's no–' he began, but Janet cut him off with a vehemence he'd never seen her display before.

'It's fine,' she said, slowly turning her head to look at him. They made eye contact again, and Alex's heart started beating in triple time. Her eyes, this close up, truly were beautiful. Alex had thought they were brown before, but now he saw they were blue, a clear, light blue, the colour of the summer sky. There were flecked with gold, something Alex had never seen before, and this only served to make them even more beautiful. He felt entranced, even if he'd wanted to look away he wouldn't have been able to. But he didn't want to look away; he never wanted to look anywhere else.

'I just wish she wouldn't always pick on you, though,' he said, pleading entering his voice. 'It's so unfair, just because she's pretty and popular…'

Alex stopped, afraid he'd said something stupid.

'Not that you're not…' he stuttered, but Janet cut him off again.

'It's fine,' she said, still looking at him, the steel in her voice much more pronounced. 'We've only got to get through this year, and then I never have to see her again. And besides,' she started to say, but at that moment Miss Klein entered the room, and Janet fell suddenly silent, her head dropping down, eye contact broken.

Miss Klein smiled at them both before sitting down and returning to her mountainous marking pile. Janet resumed reading, but Alex sat in disbelief. Had that conversation happened? Had Janet actually spoken to him, and he her, or had he imagined it?

The returning silence was so overwhelming he was just beginning to think he'd daydreamed the whole thing when he felt something nudge his leg. Looking down, Janet's hand was near him, and it in was a small wooden figurine. As he stared at it, once again completely nonplussed as to where she'd produced it from, she nudged him again, and slowly reaching out a shaking hand, he took it from her.

His fingers grazed hers and electricity shot into his hand and flew up his arm, nearly making him jump from his seat. For one brief second his entire body felt like it was on fire, but somehow it was a good feeling, a safe feeling. When he took the wooden figurine Janet's hand returned to her lap. Alex had a suspicion; he kept his hand below the desk and, slowly turning the figure over, was immediately vindicated; carved on the bottom were two letters: *JW*.

Chapter Fourteen

Janet didn't say another word for the rest of the day. The trio continued to work on their separate projects in silence, the only sounds the continued scraping of pens, the soft whooshing of pages being turned, the gentle ticking of the clock above the whiteboard counting down the seconds until the day ended. Alex glanced at Janet with a fair amount of regularity, but following Miss Klein's return to the classroom her head stayed firmly pointed downwards, her eyes focused only on the book she'd started reading upon completion of her maths work, her only movement the turning of the pages.

Eventually, after what felt like several lifetimes to Alex – although whether the time had dragged due to boredom, being left out, or because Janet was steadfast in her silence he had no idea – the bell rang to signal the end of the day. Miss Klein looked up from her marking.

'Right you two, you're finally free.' She smiled, looking relieved herself. 'Thanks for being so quiet, I've got through loads of this,' she indicated the pile of marking with her pen. 'There's still a million more books to mark, so looks like another night of working in front of the TV…'

She trailed off, and Alex looked at her, unable to decide if she'd finished talking, if he could go. He only moved when he realised Janet was standing up and he did so, too.

'Bye, Miss,' Janet said quietly, and Alex echoed her words. 'Bye,' he said, thrilled to be involved in the exchange which contained Janet.

'See you tomorrow for another fun day!' Miss Klein said with an enthusiasm that even Alex could tell was forced. He tried to smile at her, failed and, putting on his coat and throwing his bag over his shoulders, left the room.

Exiting the room and returning to the rest of the school was like waking up to Alex; the classroom had been peaceful, serene, wonderfully quiet. By contrast the school was like an explosion; all of a sudden there were people everywhere, a throng of bodies all pushing and shoving to be out of the building as soon as possible. The noise was deafening, the sound of it rushing into his ears; normally he'd be completely unaffected, be part of the mass himself, but today was different. He didn't know why, but his chest began to feel tight, his heart was beating faster than he'd ever felt it, and his breath was only coming in short, sharp gasps.

He extricated himself from the crowd and found solace leaning against the corridor wall. It's firmness against his shoulders was reassuring, and he clung on to the feel of it for dear life. People pushed their way past him, several bumped into him, but just being out of the crowd was enough for him to start to relax, for the pressure on his chest to ease and his respiration to become more free. Still, there was a tingling throughout his body, and his vision was blurring, the light fading. His head and shoulders suddenly felt incredibly heavy, and he could feel gravity winning the fight against his spine. His bag slipped from his shoulders and he began to slide down the wall, to the floor, when he felt a hand slip into his and pull him away.

The hand was small, soft, warm; it was dry, not in an unpleasant way but in a kind, caring way. He looked at it in amazement. He could feel the hand in his, but even as he looked at it, the seeing and feeling felt completely disconnected. His eyes travelled from the entwined hands up the arm attached to the mystery one, found a shoulder, and from there the back of a head. His vision was still blurred, and so he couldn't make out who it was; accepting his fate, he allowed himself to be pulled along.

It was funny, but despite the number of pupils still in the hall, their bodies almost forming one big mass, a lump moving in uniform towards the exit doors, the person pulling him along seemed to be moving through them. He looked down at his feet and saw they were moving much faster than the feet around them, finding space where there shouldn't have been any. When Alex had left the classroom there had been perhaps a hundred pupils between him and the door; mere seconds after the hand took his, he was outside, and looking back he saw he was in front of the other pupils, had somehow made it outside ahead of them.

The light struck his eyes and he winced, quickly closing them. The hand pulled him to one side before letting go, and he immediately felt lost; the hand hadn't just been his guide but his safety, it had been the difference between him falling over in the corridor, possibly being trampled by the crowd, and making it outside not only in one piece, but in record time. He stood for a moment with a disproportionate feeling of loss, his breathing returning to normal, the tingling feeling leaving him, his vision returning. His heart was still beating incredibly quickly, but he thought that had less to do with the other pupils and was entirely because of the hand that, until a few seconds previously, had been holding his.

Alex opened his eyes. Keeping them closed had had the two desired effects; not only was the blurriness gone, but the sunlight was less painful, more manageable. After standing and simply blinking for a few seconds, he looked around himself, trying to find the owner of the mystery hand. There was no one standing by him; the other pupils, now out of the building, were peeling off in various directions. No one was paying any attention to Alex as he stood there, looking around himself, confusion reigning over him. He looked from left to right, but all he saw was children laughing, running, jumping, pushing, and jostling each other, kicking footballs, showing each other things on their phones, singing the latest number one from the pop witch. No one was even glancing in his direction.

He continued to scan the crowd for a few seconds when something, or rather some*one*, caught his eye. To his left, walking slowly with her head down, was Janet. She too was completely unregarded; kids ran past her, around her, threw balls over her head. They didn't do it with malice, they didn't ignore her on purpose. Instead, Alex thought, it was simply as if she wasn't there. As if she was choosing to not be there. As he watched her walk, her head down, no part of her body but her feet moving, a familiarity came back to him. He remembered looking at the person pulling him through the corridor; even though his vision had been blurred, there had been a hundred other kids around, it couldn't have been...

'Janet!' he shouted, unable to stop himself, not even aware he was going to make a noise until he did.

Now a few kids looked at him, but only for a second before carrying on with their lives. He was far from the only kid shouting.

Janet didn't look at him; whether she hadn't heard him or had ignored him he didn't know. He was tempted to shout again but decided against it, instead jogging in her direction.

Despite the fact she only appeared to be walking at a casual speed, and Alex was jogging, he wasn't closing the gap on her at all. After ten or so frustrating seconds he picked up his pace, breaking into a light run. Again people looked at him, but only briefly; much like the shouting, he wasn't the only person running.

As Janet and Alex both got further away from school the number of pupils slowly dwindled; Janet lived – and

Alex could only assume that was where she was going – on the west end of the village, the opposite end to the school. Most kids lived near the school, on the east end. Lots of them travelled in from Hull and the other surrounding villages, taking the bus there each morning and home each afternoon. By the time Alex finally caught up with Janet, only two or three minutes since the mystery person had pulled him outside, there was no one else around. Janet lived at the end of a long track road, technically outside the village boundaries he'd heard his dad tell his mum once. All the other buildings had ended a hundred metres or so previously, and now the world was comprised of tall, green hedges, many overgrown; fields stretched to the left and right all the way to the horizon. It was only looking forward and back that there were signs of civilisation; behind him the village proper, and in front he could just see Janet's small house in the far distance.

He was just reaching out to tap Janet on the shoulder to get her attention; he was out of breath from running to catch up with her, so saying her name was out of the question. A bird was chirping in a nearby tree, and a fox suddenly darted across the path ahead of them. Alex's hand was mere inches from Janet when she suddenly stopped and whirled around, her hair flying in a solid mass, and looked at Alex. She moved so quickly he actually jumped back a few paces, flinching away from her.

'What?' she said, her voice firm and tough sounding. Alex didn't know if it was because he'd been chasing her, been about to touch her, or because no one else was around, but she said it at a regular volume, a volume he'd never heard her speak at before, far above her usual quiet whisper.

'I…' he said, faltering. He'd dropped his bag to the floor and was bent, his hands on his knees, struggling to recover his breath. 'Was that you?' he asked, gesturing vaguely behind him in the direction of the school.

'Was what me?' Janet asked; either she had no idea what he was talking about or she was a very good actor, Alex thought.

'In school,' he said, his voice still coming in bursts between deep lungfuls of air. 'Did you,' and he hesitated, wondering what the right word was. 'Did you rescue me?'

He felt stupid using that word, but it was the only one that seemed appropriate. Because whoever it was, Janet or someone else, *had* rescued him. He had no idea what had been happening, only that it was something bad, and whoever had got him out of school had saved him from it.

Janet didn't say anything, just looked at him, although Alex thought there was some amusement on her face. His breath finally caught, he stood up; he was taller than her by several inches, and as he looked down at her she looked up. Once again their eyes met. A fire burned in Alex with fresh vigour.

'Well thank you,' he said, deciding to take her silence as a yes. 'I don't know what was happening but it was bad, so thank you.'

'You're welcome,' Janet replied quietly, her voice no

longer confident but once again small, shy.

Alex waited but she didn't say anything else, so he picked up his bag and, opening it, pulled out the wooden figure Tom had given him the previous week. Dropping his bag again, he held it out to her like an offering.

'Did you leave this for me last week?'

Janet continued her silent vigil, so Alex turned the figure over and pointed the bottom at her.

'These are your initials. JW. Janet Willerby. It was you, right?'

Janet still remained silent, but Alex thought a bit of colour had come into her cheeks. Was it possible, was she blushing? The thought made Alex blush as well, and he wondered how they must look, two silent teenagers, standing at the mouth of a dirt track road, both turning red.

'It's the same as the one you gave me today,' he said, taking that one from his backpack, which he once again dropped to the ground so he could hold one figure in each hand, displaying them side by side. Janet's vow of silence continued.

'Well, whatever, thank you,' he said, picking up his bag once again and turning to go.

He stood for a moment, half turned away from Janet, and was about to walk away when her voice stopped him.

'Thank you,' she said. And then her words tumbled out in a torrent Alex hadn't expected at all. 'Thank you for trying to stop Emma, and for History a few weeks ago, and for talking to me today, and…' she hesitated, before finishing speaking. 'Thank you for treating me like a person.'

Alex was stunned; of all the things he'd expected her to say, if she said anything at all, that was not it. He had no reply, so was relieved when she spoke again.

'Do you want to…' she trailed off, indicating the track with her head. Alex wasn't fully sure what she was asking but nodded his head regardless. Janet set off walking and Alex turned back towards her and followed.

They walked in silence for a few moments, the only sounds birds frittering in the bushes and trees, the distant roar of a tractor, a light breeze rustling leaves. Alex wanted to talk to Janet; it was just the two of them, so far from the village that they might have been the only two people in the world. He wanted to ask her about herself, learn everything about her, but his courage failed him, and so he simply walked in silence, matching her stride.

As they walked a dazzlingly white cat dashed out from the bushes to the left, and was about to dive into the bushes on the right when it saw Janet and paused mid-step before running up to her. Alex had never seen a white cat before, and for a moment he thought of a story they'd been taught in English last year, *The White Cat of Drumgunniol*. He hesitated for a second, remembering in the story the white cat had been an omen of death. But that was just a story, he told himself. This cat, whiter than pure snow, miaowed at Janet and she bent down and scooped it up. The cat was rubbing its face all over Janet's, and Alex could hear it purring.

'Is this your cat?' he asked, half reaching out a hand to stroke it before changing his mind and letting his hand hang limply at his side.

'This is Lisheen,' she said, not looking at Alex, her eyes focused intensely on the cat. 'We live together.'

'So she is your cat?' Alex asked, confused.

'We live together,' was all Janet said, and Alex didn't reply, simply watched them. Lisheen stopped rubbing her face on Janet's and the pair looked at each other, looking deeply into each other's eyes. The cat had the greenest eyes Alex had ever seen, and if he hadn't known better, he would have sworn they were communicating, although he quickly dismissed the thought. How would that even be possible?

The three of them stayed where they were for a few more moments before Lisheen jumped out of Janet's arms and finally dived back into the bushes. Once it was gone, Janet started walking again and Alex followed.

'Do you have any other pets?' Alex asked.

'Oh no.' Janet said, 'I don't have any pets.'

'But…' Alex said, confused. 'What about Lisheen? You said you live together, so she must be your pet?'

'We live together,' Janet repeated simply, and said no more.

As they walked on in silence, a pair of small, brown birds flew towards Janet. Holding out her hand, they landed on her finger. One groomed itself, putting its head under its wing, flicking it from side to side. The other look at Janet for a moment, then at Alex, before looking back to Janet. Alex saw Janet give a small shrug, before the birds both took flight once again.

Soon, rounding a corner bordered by high hedges,

taller even than Alex, they came to Janet's house. It was a small cottage, made of old grey bricks. The roof was thatched, and the entire thing had a look that if a particularly strong wind blew, it'd collapse. There was no wall or fence of any kind, instead the high hedges simply stopped and the lane opened up into a small patch of land. Threadbare grass grew in patches, vividly green where it sprung up, and between these were small plots of soil with various plants growing from them. Janet walked confidently towards the front door but Alex stopped where the hedges ended. He couldn't quite put his finger on it but he suddenly felt an overwhelming sense of not being wanted; he felt he was in the wrong place, and if he tried to advance further something terrible would happen. Janet stopped walking when she was nearly across what was plainly her front garden and turned to face him. Alex's breath caught in his throat.

As she stood there, just outside her front door, Alex barely recognised her. Her hair, normally so lank and limp, looked soft, fresh, as if it'd just been washed by a professional stylist. Her school uniform was nowhere to be seen; Alex rubbed his eyes, confusion hitting him in waves. It had only been a matter of seconds, nowhere near enough time for her to get changed – and even if she'd had the time, where had she got the clothes from, when had she changed? Alex had been right there and had seen nothing – but she was unmistakably wearing different clothes.

Where all day in school, and for the entire walk home, Janet had been wearing her usual dirty, ragged school uniform of frayed grey skirt, dark grey shirt, and bobbled, faded grey jumper, she was now wearing a clean, flawless black dress. It looked like it might have been made of lace or something; it covered almost her entire body, from her shoulders down to just above her knees. It was cut low on her chest and Alex had to force himself not to stare at that spot specifically, but to look at Janet and her beautiful black dress as a whole. Above the dress her eyes shone from her face, which was also clean, almost sparkling. Alex didn't have much by way of comparison, but he thought Janet was the most beautiful girl he'd ever seen.

His heart, as it so often did in those days, began to pound in his chest. He wanted to go to her, to look at her close up, make sure what he was seeing wasn't just a trick of the light or an optical illusion or something. A few years before his parents had taken him to Edinburgh, and there they'd visited something called the Camera Obscura; it had been a museum, but a fun one. They had all these illusions, one where you put your head through a hole in a table so you looked headless, and another with funny cameras that played with perspective. His mum, who even then Alex had been taller than, had towered over him and made him look tiny.

He felt like he was back there, although he couldn't be. They were outside, there were no cameras or mirrors or anything around. He wanted to go to Janet, to hold her hand again – because by now he was certain it was her hand that had held his, had saved him – and tell her how pretty she was.

But he was still flooded with that feeling of doom, of threat, of being unwelcome. He felt that if he took even a single step forward, his heart would stop beating and he'd simply collapse and die. So he remained where he stood, unable to even call out to Janet. He looked at her in all her beauty and his heart ached. He finally accepted what he'd been suspecting all along; he fancied her.

He was snapped from his reverie when Janet called out to him.

'See you tomorrow,' she said, her voice light, lilting in a way he'd never heard before. For the first time, she both looked and sounded like the carefree young girl she should have been.

With that, she turned, her dress flowing out around her like a flamenco dancer, and disappeared into her house.

Chapter Fifteen

For days, Alex couldn't get the image of Janet transformed out of his head. She was always there, a constant presence in his mind; flouncing around it in her black dress, hair fresh and clean, shining like metal in the sun; her clean face, piercing eyes, the change in her voice, not just its volume but pitch and cadence too, a confidence within it unlike anything he'd ever heard; the way she'd moved, with an airy lightness, a freedom he'd never seen her possess before. Of course, Alex couldn't name all these things. In his mind she was just incredibly pretty, maybe even beautiful, although, aged 15, he still wasn't completely sure what that really meant.

Tom and Mo regaled him with stories of their trip to Brontë country; the sweets their mums had given them for the two hour bus ride, the special lunch they had at a cafe near the parsonage – which, they told Alex, was what the house the Brontës had lived in was called – the sweetshop in Haworth that had walls and walls of glass jars containing every sweet you could imagine, from gobstoppers to jelly babies to pear drops to fudge…on and on they went. Alex asked if anything had happened that wasn't related to food, and for a moment Tom and Mo looked at each other, puzzled, as if they forgot there were other things, before all three burst into peals of laughter.

The best bit, Tom and Mo both agreed, wasn't food related at all; it was the fact that Emma wasn't there. Jason wasn't either, but this was common for school trips; on the rare occasions he wasn't suspended when a school trip came around, he'd simply not bother getting his permission slip signed. He'd then spend the day twagging, doing whatever it was he did when he wasn't at school. Torture small animals, the boys would half joke, before falling silent, hoping they weren't correct.

'Because Emma wasn't there,' Mo said, 'it was so chill.'

'Yeah,' Tom echoed. 'Even Barnett was in a good mood.'

'Bullshit,' Alex said, with a wry smile on his face. That'd be the day, he thought.

'I'm telling you!' Mo insisted. 'He was smiling and everything, joking around with Miss Miller. At one point he even, like, poked her, I guess playfully, in her ribs, and she shoved him, but, like, they both looked really happy.'

Alex still didn't quite believe what Mo was saying, but he could almost imagine it. His day at school with no one but Janet around had been so relaxing, so calming. Not having to be on your guard, not having to be watching your back, afraid that a stray word or comment would be misinterpreted, that you'd bump into Emma completely by accident and get a slap in return. Even just not having to be scared that she'd choose you, for no other reason than she wanted to, and then you were in for it. Emma was a nightmare, both waking and sleeping, and Alex supposed that even old Barnett might be a nice person when she wasn't around.

'How was your day?' Tom asked some time later, his voice brimming with timidness, finally taking the plunge.

'It was fine,' Alex said. The pair looked at him for elaboration, their eyes wide and interested. 'I mean, it was boring, I just sat and did homework all day.'

'That's well shit,' Mo said.

'Yeah, but at least I didn't have to do any after school. And I was home by half four, not real late like you.'

'Half four?' Tom asked, cocking his head to one side. 'How come so late?'

Alex panicked; even though he treasured the time with Janet, walking her home and seeing her changed, he didn't want anyone to know. He had a crush on her, of that he had no doubt, but he desperately hoped no one would find out. He was already dreading Emma returning to school, making his life a living hell; if anyone else found out he'd been hanging out with Janet, his life would become hell even in Emma's absence.

'Oh, yeah,' Alex said, stumbling over his words, trying to make up a convincing story on the spot. 'I… erm… I bumped into my dad in the village doing some, erm, shopping, and he dragged me in to help him out.'

Tom and Mo were still looking at him suspiciously;

the story itself wasn't too outlandish, Alex didn't think, but the way he'd delivered it was definitely not convincing. Tom and Mo exchanged another look, before Tom changed the subject. Alex sighed to himself; he'd gotten away with it.

'You both coming round to watch City tonight?'

The conversation moved on to lighter things and the week slowly passed without incident, the days fading into one another, life continuing as it's wont to do.

Janet was back to her old self. She turned up to school on the Tuesday wearing her usual poorly cared for uniform, her hair back to its poorly tended condition, her head perennially down. Although, Alex realised, as he watched her more and more, her head wasn't actually always down. During morning break and at lunch, when the students were all outside, Janet's head would be held high, her gaze on the sky. Alex would see her following birds with her eyes, and often looking like she was searching for other things. What these things might have been, he had no idea.

Alex was desperate to talk to her; he wanted to ask if what he'd seen was real or some sort of trick. He wanted to ask her about her dress, her hair, all of it. Most of all, he wanted to see her like that again.

But there was no opportunity; every time he saw Janet there were other people around, and he didn't dare just go up and speak to her. He was desperate to, dying to, but he couldn't bring himself to. He knew he was being a coward, being an idiot, being a total piece of shit, but no amount of self-flagellation could move him to be brave in front of his peers, to take a risk, to put a target on his back. He'd spent so long blending into the background, avoiding any and all attention, either good or bad, that he had no idea how to act in any other way.

Luckily for him, Janet seemed to have no interest in speaking to him; she attended school without fail, sat quietly in lessons, spent her breaks alone, and went home again. It made Alex sad, but he was also relieved. Their day in school, their walk home, her show, was for them and them only. He'd treasure it forever, and maybe next year, when they'd left school, he could talk to her. He had no idea if she was going to college or anything; he was planning to go to the closest sixth form in Hull, the one nearest to Deerborn. He had no idea what he was going to study, he'd figure that out later. He wondered about Janet; she seemed really interested in plants and animals, from what little he'd garnered about her, both through rumours and observation. Maybe she'd go to the college in the city centre, the technical one that taught agriculture and stuff. Maybe she'd get a job working on a farm or in a garden centre or a vets or something. Maybe she'd do whatever it was that her mum did, which had always brought in money until recently, according to his dad. Alex didn't know, no one seemed to know, quite what that was. Alex didn't really care; he cared about Janet, not her mum. If he wasn't bothered by his own parents, why would he be by someone else's? Besides, he didn't believe the rumours. They might have held water hundreds of years ago, before science and electricity and the internet and stuff, but not now, surely? It was 2024 for fuck's sake, who could believe that?

The week remained perfectly ordinary until Friday morning; Alex's parents didn't get newspapers, they'd had to cut back on all unnecessary spending when his dad lost his job, and so Alex walked to school with Tom and Mo blissfully unaware. If Tom and Mo knew anything, they didn't say. The walk was normal; they talked about the previous night's football scores, what they thought would happen at the weekend. Hull were doing well, and the boys were on the verge of getting excited; they'd been let down one too many times already in their short lives to get truly carried away, but each carried within them a quiet fire of optimism.

Miss Naveed had greeted the class with a grimace and taken the register faster than normal, as if rushing through it. She'd had little resistance; the class had been strangely subdued, and when she'd stood up after completing the register to speak to the class, she hadn't had to raise her voice at all.

'Right, year eleven,' she'd said at her normal volume, the class in a weird hush, hanging on her every word as if they knew what was coming. Alex was left even more bemused. 'It's a short form this morning, we're all going to go to a special assembly put on by Mr Gullis.'

Murmurs rolled across the class, people whispered to each other behind their hands, some shook their heads. Alex even thought he saw a tear or two in some of the girls' eyes, and his confusion only grew. He looked around and tried to catch someone's eye, anyone's, but that morning he was in a class full of Janets. 30 children with their heads down, not speaking, seemingly just waiting for the day to be over.

'Get your things and let's go. I don't know what time it'll finish, how long it'll take, so grab your stuff because you'll probably go straight to first period afterwards.' Miss Naveed had been rubbing a piece of cloth between her fingers as she spoke, and she clutched it as she stood up and moved out from behind her desk.

Still oddly subdued, the class gathered their things and walked to assembly slowly, in silence. Alex had no idea what was going on.

'What's happening?' he asked Tom, who simply shook his head in reply.

'Keep moving, class,' Miss Naveed said, and Alex couldn't help but feel it was her polite way of telling him to be quiet.

Soon they were filing into the assembly hall, sitting in the back rows due to the fact they were part of the final year. The entire school was in the hall, they were the last to enter, and yet there wasn't a single sound coming from a single pupil. Normally, no matter the activity, the hall would be a hurricane of noise. It was large, perhaps a hundred feet across each side, with an incredibly high roof. The smallest of noises didn't so much fade away as ricochet from wall to wall, floor to ceiling, seeming to echo forever. The only sounds that morning, however, were hundreds of feet trudging across the floor, and the huge clock that stood above the doors marking each passing second with a loud *tick*.

Alex's unease grew; he looked around and saw Janet

at the end of their row. He tried to catch her eye but her head, as always, was down, her eyes downcast. He didn't know why, but he was afraid for her. He suddenly felt cold all over, and wrapped his arms around himself with a shiver.

As soon as their class was seated, Mr Gullis, who'd been standing at the stag's head-clad lectern watching them file in, began to talk. He was a tall man, imposing in his black suit and well-polished shoes. His hair was short, not a buzzcut but not far from it, and he hadn't even a hint of beard. Alex's dad had told him once that Mr Gullis had been a soldier before becoming a teacher, and Alex could see it in the man. Behind Mr Gullis, sitting in a row of small, red plastic chairs, Alex was surprised to see Emma and her parents, Mr and Mrs Sullivan. Even more surprising was the fact they were all crying. Alongside them was another stiff man, looking very uncomfortable in a suit; Alex didn't recognise this person.

'Good morning, everyone,' Mr Gullis said. Normally this would have been echoed by the hall, returned with a chorus of 'Good morning Mr Gullis,' but not today. Mr Gullis didn't seem to notice, simply carried on speaking.

'As you've probably seen on the news this morning, something terrible has happened. Joseph Sullivan has gone missing.'

As he said this a wail went up from Emma's mum, who looked a nervous wreck. Her husband was holding one of her hands, and in the other she was clutching a handkerchief, frantically alternating between wiping the tears streaming from her eyes and blowing the snot streaming from her nose.

'This gentleman,' Mr Gullis gestured to the unknown man behind him, 'is from Hull police. He's going to speak to you now, and I expect you all to listen. Any noise from anyone and you'll be immediately suspended.' From the look on his face, Alex knew it wasn't an empty threat.

With that said, he took a step back and exchanged places with the officer; Mr Gullis sat in his seat and the policeman stood at the lectern. If he was a policeman, Alex wondered why he was just in an ordinary brown suit and not in a policeman's uniform.

'Good morning, Deerborn Secondary,' the officer began, his voice deep and booming. It was like he was using a microphone, even though the lectern wasn't equipped with one. He looked more comfortable standing at the microphone than he'd done sitting down behind it. 'My name is Detective Abernathy, and I'm in charge of the investigation into the disappearance of Joseph Sullivan.'

Another wail from Mrs Sullivan pierced the room, causing a shudder to ripple across the assembled students; Alex's heart broke at the noise, and he wished she'd stop making it. Her husband and her daughter might have been bad people, both bullies who used their status and power to hurt those they thought were beneath them – namely Janet and Alex's dad – but that didn't mean Mrs Sullivan deserved to lose her son. He was only five, Alex knew; too young to be a bad kid, in fact barely a kid at all, basically still a baby.

'Joseph was last seen at approximately 7pm yesterday evening, on the playground next to Deerborn Junior School. He was playing with several other children, who were being supervised by Mrs Sullivan.' Another wail wrenched the air and Alex felt his bones shiver. He glanced down the row to Janet, but she wasn't moving, wasn't showing anything in her body language. 'One of the children fell and hurt himself. Mrs Sullivan, like the kind, caring mother she is,' the detective looked at her as he said this, as if his kind words could ease some of her grief, 'ran straight over to help them. After tending to the boy, she returned to the bench she'd been sitting on, which is when she noticed Joseph was no longer in the playground.'

Alex understood the power of her wails then; not only was her son missing, but it was her own fault. She was supposed to be watching him, and hadn't, and he'd run away or been taken or something. Alex still felt sorry for her, but less than he had a moment previously. He wondered, too: the playground was next to Hagan's Field, and the circle of tall, grey stones that stood within it. But stones were just stones, surely? Even if they stood upright in a circle and kids were warned from going near them? Stones couldn't hurt you, right? Alex thought of the white cat, Lisheen: had Joseph seen it? He shuddered despite the warmth of the hall.

'Mrs Sullivan immediately called the police, which is what you should always do in any bad situation.' Detective Abernathy said this firmly, as if, instead of praising Mrs Sullivan, he was criticising the students for doing something wrong. 'A team was sent out, and spent the night looking for Joseph, but he wasn't found. The team went home early this morning, and at the same time another team was sent out, who are still looking now.'

The assembly hall, with the exception of the Detective's voice, Mrs Sullivan's wails, and the loud *tick, tick, tick* of the clock, was still silent. If it wasn't because of such a horrible reason, Alex would have marvelled at this.

'There are three things I need from you,' Detective Abernathy continued. 'Firstly,' he said, counting on his fingers, 'I need you to think back to last night, especially those of you who live here in Deerborn, and think if you can remember anything strange. It could be anything at all; was there a car parked on the street you've never seen before, a man or woman walking around you didn't recognise? Did you hear a strange sound when you were getting ready for bed, or watching TV? Anything at all out of the ordinary, let your parents or one of your teachers know.

'Secondly, I need you to be on the lookout, again for anything out of the ordinary. If you see anyone hanging around that you don't know or see a strange car driving past. If anyone approaches you and you don't know them, again absolutely anything at all, tell your parents or a teacher.

'Thirdly and finally, I need you to be vigilant. What I mean by that is, be careful. Don't take any unnecessary risks, don't do anything stupid. Stay close to home, stay with your usual friends; don't talk to anyone you don't know, don't take any gifts from anyone you don't know, don't even go near anyone you don't recognise. If anything happens that you're not sure about, no matter how small it may seem, tell your parents or a teacher. No matter how small: if you see a pencil in a bush that wasn't there yesterday, *let someone know.* Anything could be a clue.'

A soft murmur made its way across the pupils, like a breeze rippling across the sea. It didn't last long; Mr Gullis stood up and boomed 'silence!' The effect was immediate.

'Thank you, Mr Gullis,' the Detective said, unruffled. 'There will be a policeman in the school until Joseph is found. And believe me,' Abernathy said, his voice once again seeming to turn on the students, as if accusing them of something. 'We will find Joseph, mark my words. We always find missing children, and as well as that, *we always find, arrest, and lock up the people that took them.*'

'Bullshit!' shouted a voice from the crowd. Mr Gullis was on his feet again in an instant.

'Who said that?' he roared. When no one answered, he shouted again. 'Do you think this is funny? Does anyone think this is a laughing matter?' Silence answered him. 'A five-year-old child is missing, this is anything but funny.'

Mrs Sullivan wailed again, and with that the assembly was over.

'Thank you, Detective,' Mr Gullis said. 'You can all go to your lessons now. Mr and Mrs Sullivan, Emma, if you'd like to follow me.'

The students stood up and began to file out. Now the assembly was over, now that Mr Gullis was leading the Sullivan family away and the Detective was going back to the police station or to join the search, the spell that had taken over the students seemed to break.

Everyone was speaking to each other; the fire of speculation had been lit, and the embers immediately threatened to burn out of control. Such was the excitement – because that's what it was amongst the students, most too young to have a proper understanding of the gravity of the situation – that the students spoke not to just their usual friends but to others they wouldn't normally even realise existed. It seemed all the rules were out the window when it came to cliques and groups, and Alex thought that maybe something good might come of Joseph going missing – assuming he was found soon and was okay, of course.

Alex's good feeling didn't even last until he was out of the assembly hall; he'd thought the entire school was leaving, but one person stayed still, remained in their seat. Janet didn't move, didn't stand up, showed no sign of going to History, which had about 15 minutes left. For reasons he couldn't quite put his finger on, Alex was suddenly, incredibly worried for Janet.

Chapter Sixteen

As if it knew about the events happening in Deerborn, the weather turned foul over the weekend. As September ticked over into October, the blue skies and brilliant, blinding sunshine were replaced by a covering of grey clouds, unbroken in any direction. The temperature began to fall, slowly at first; this was perhaps the only consolation the weather gave the villagers, not to change from mid-twenties to single figures overnight. As well as this it rained sporadically, downpours interspersed with hours of drought. But even when it was dry the clouds hovered, threatening; every villager who passed another in the street turned half an eye on the sky and commented on it.

Many did so because it's the British way, to keep a fastidious watch on the sky and compare notes when you meet someone who'll no doubt have been doing the same. But really, the reason the people of Deerborn talked about the weather so much was because it allowed them not to talk about the other thing, the only other topic that was on everyone's minds.

Besides, the village had changed dramatically over that weekend, and so the number of impromptu conversations on the street plummeted. Where previously everyone would stop and speak to everyone else, whether they were a friend, neighbour, or simply a face they recognised from around the village, everyone made the time of day. Following the disappearance of Joseph, all of that changed. People had become suspicious; on the rare occasions they went outside, when there was absolutely no other choice, they hurried to their destinations, quickly completed their tasks, and hurried home. Parents, who once would have slowly and languidly browsed the aisles of the supermarket Alex's mum worked in, now moved about like individual military units; they got in, got what they wanted, and got out again in the shortest possible amount of time. Commerce was hit in the few small shops on the high street because no one was browsing in them, either. If people had a need they'd enter, but really most people stayed at home, drew the curtains, and waited for the boy to be found, and for the person or persons who'd taken him – because everyone agreed that he had been taken, he hadn't simply wandered off or run away – to be arrested. They waited for the streets to be safe to walk through again.

After much persuading, Alex's parents let him join Mo and Tom and a few other kids playing football on the Saturday afternoon. His parents had naturally been reluctant at first, not wanting Alex to fall victim to the same predator – that was the word his parents were using – who'd preyed – also their word – on poor little Joseph.

Alex did his best to make them see reason.

'But I'm fifteen,' he pleaded, desperation etched into his voice. 'Joseph is five, surely they'll leave me alone?'

'Who knows, son, we just can't take the risk,' his dad had said, looking downcast. His black hair had become peppered with grey over the preceding few weeks and there were bags under his eyes. The village closing in on itself was not helping his job hunt; people were much less likely to openly welcome him into their shops and businesses. Everyone, no matter who they were, was being viewed with suspicion.

'I'm sorry, darling,' his mum had echoed. 'We'd be beyond ourselves if anything happened to you.'

'There's going to be loads of us, though, like twenty or something.'

Alex's parents had exchanged a look, and he thought he maybe might be allowed to go out after all. Without hesitation he pushed the point, exploiting his parents' momentary doubt.

'It isn't just me, Tom and Mo. Half the year is going; everyone in my year is sick of being locked inside, it's like, I dunno, almost like a protest or something.'

'A protest?' His dad had looked unconvinced.

'Yeah, like, I dunno, like we're sending a message that we're not scared or something.'

Alex's mum still looked worried, but his dad's features began to soften.

'Are there really going to be that many people?'

'Yeah.'

'You promise? You swear you're not just telling fibs

because you want to go and play?'

Alex grunted in frustration.

'I promise. There's going to be loads of us; if anyone comes, if anything happens, we'll kick the shit out of them.'

'Alex!' his mum had said, shocked by his language. His dad smiled, however.

'I bet you would and all,' he said, looking suddenly proud of his son.

'It'll be good,' Alex continued, pressing the point. 'Imagine if someone tries something and we're all there; we don't have to beat him up, we could grab him and wait for the police.'

Neither of his parents said anything, so Alex persisted.

'Anyway, I'm sure nothing will happen. If some freak did take Joseph, one five-year-old is a bit different to a bunch of year elevens.'

'That's true,' his dad murmured. He turned to his wife. 'What do you say?'

Alex smiled for a brief second before wiping it off his face; he'd won over his dad, but he didn't want to assume anything whilst his mum was still reluctant.

'I don't know,' she replied, wringing her hands. 'It's close to Hagan's field, and what if she–' Alex's mum had begun, but Alex's dad silenced her with a look, before he reached out and took her hands in his, both to stop her wringing them but also to comfort her, hold her, reassure her.

'Alex is right; kidnapping a five-year-old is different

than taking a fifteen-year-old. And there's going to be loads of them there, so anyone would be absolutely stupid to try anything. What do you think?'

Alex's mum still hadn't looked convinced, but the effect of both her husband and her son looking at her with doe eyes worked.

'Oh go on, then,' she said, still not sounding happy. 'But you're not to be alone at any point.'

Alex was delighted and no longer tried to hide his smile, which beamed from his face, lighting it up. He'd missed all the previous weekend with his injuries and then had been in school all week. He was looking forward to being outside for a bit, running around and forgetting everything, even if only for a couple of hours.

'Thanks, Mum!' he nearly shouted, already turning and running out of the living room, hastily putting on his shoes. His parents followed him into the hallway.

'Be back by six at the very latest,' his mum said. 'And come home as soon as Tom and Mo do, if they leave sooner.'

'Yes, Mum,' Alex replied, barely listening to her.

'Don't go anywhere alone, and don't talk to anyone you don't know.'

'I won't, Mum,' he said, opening the front door.

'Have you got your mobile?'

'Yes, Mum!'

'Alex,' his dad said firmly, stopping him in his tracks. He turned to look at his parents. 'Listen to your mum. Back by six, and no messing around. Got it?'

'Yes, Dad,' he said sombrely, feeling the mood and

not wanting to cause his parents to have a last-minute change of heart. 'I'll be careful, I promise.'

He was about to run out the door when his mum dashed forward and gave him a hug, squeezing him tighter than he could remember her doing for a long time. He hugged her back, wrapping his arms around her small figure. He was much taller than her, but still, she was his mum.

'I love you, son,' she whispered to his chest.

'We both do,' his dad echoed from further down the hall.

'I love you, too,' Alex mumbled under his breath. This seemed to do the trick, and his mum let go of him; he hesitated for a second, but when neither of his parents moved or said anything, he ran.

'Bye!' he shouted over his shoulder without looking back, and soon was through the gate and running up his street. He turned left at the end of his road, running up the main street and to the park, where the football match was already in full swing.

The match was a roaring success for Alex; as soon as he arrived he joined Tom's team, Mo on the other side, and was put up front. He scored a hattrick, including a header, something he normally tried to avoid doing, so scared was he he'd hurt himself or get hit in the face and look stupid.

The game went on for around 90 minutes; the fact it ran for the same length as an actual football match was completely coincidental, and it only ended when enough people had drifted away that it wasn't worth continuing any more.

'See you later, boys,' said Luke Schilling, walking past where Alex, Tom, and Mo stood in a small circle, in the middle of one of the goals.

'In a bit.' 'Bye.' 'See ya,' they chorused in return.

This went on for a little while, people slowly slipping away, most of them going home, offering apologies that their parents wanted them back. No one left alone, they went in twos and threes, lots of them to congregate at one person's house. Soon it was only the trio left on the pitch; Alex looked at his phone and saw it was half past five.

'Shit, I have to go soon, I have to be home for six.'

'Yeah me, too,' said Mo. 'My parents are freaking out about it.'

'Same,' said Alex and Tom simultaneously, and they both laughed, although it was quiet, subdued.

'No, but, like, my parents are *really* freaking out about this. My brother Abdul is in Joseph's class, they were kinda friends.'

'Oh, shit,' Alex said.

'Yeah.'

'What do you mean *kinda* friends?' Tom asked.

'Well, you know what Mr Sullivan is like,' Mo said.

'How do you mean?'

'Come on,' Mo replied, half a laugh in his voice. 'You know what I mean.'

Tom and Alex looked nonplussed.

'For fuck's sake, guys!' Mo said loudly, throwing his hands up in exasperation. 'Mr Sullivan hates my parents because we're not white. He won't let Joseph hang out with Abdul outside school because we're not white. Fucking hell.'

Alex and Tom looked at each other, unsure what to do. They obviously knew Mo wasn't white, and that at some point his family had been immigrants, but it had never been a thing until that moment. Mo was their friend, he was in their lessons, he liked football and films and hanging out; he was just a kid.

'Sorry, mate,' Alex mumbled.

'Yeah,' Tom added, equally quiet. 'Sorry.'

'It's okay,' Mo said, although from his tone it was clear it wasn't. 'This thing with Joseph has actually helped a little bit, to be honest.'

'How do you mean?' Alex asked.

'Well,' Mo replied, hesitating, before seeming to make a decision and ploughing on. 'Normally Mr Sullivan is always giving Dad shit, you know? Mr Sullivan owns the warehouse my dad's business runs from, and he's always being a dick, sending people from the building society round, saying he's had complaints of noise, mess, stuff like that.'

Neither Tom nor Alex said anything; Alex was looking firmly at his shoes, and he could just see Tom from the corner of his eye suddenly very interested in a spot far off in the distance. Neither boy looked at Mo, nor said anything, as Mo continued.

'It's obviously all made up. My dad says that Mr Sullivan wants rid of him; my dad signed the lease with the person who owned the warehouse before Mr

Sullivan, and there was something in it that said he couldn't be kicked out if someone else bought the place. Dad says Mr Sullivan wants him out because he hates him, hates all of us, because we're not white.'

'He's such a dickhead,' Alex muttered. Tom and Mo both nodded.

'He hates us 'cos we're Sikh, too. I asked my dad once, I told him I thought Christians like Mr Sullivan were supposed to love their neighbours or something, but my dad just sighed. But anyway, for the last couple of days, there's been nothing,' Mo said. 'My dad was worried because he's late with the rent – only by a couple of days,' he hastily added, as if not wanting to bring any negative attention to his dad. 'Normally Mr Sullivan phones up days before the rent's due, claiming it's late and if my dad doesn't pay soon he'll kick him out. But this month,' Mo said, with a small look of triumph on his face, 'nothing.

'My dad has paid it now obviously,' Mo hastily added.

As he stopped talking, Alex looked at him. Mo looked relieved, as if he'd been released of a great burden.

'What do you think happened to Joseph?' Tom asked, changing the subject slightly.

'I have no idea,' Alex said, genuinely – he hadn't really thought about it, and now he did, even if only briefly, he didn't have the slightest clue.

'My dad thinks…' Mo began, before stopping, as if unsure as to whether he should continue.

'Yeah?' Tom asked. Alex stayed silent, fearing what

Mo was going to say.

'My dad thinks – he didn't tell me this, I heard him and my mum talking last night – that it's something to do with Janet's mum.'

He fell silent after saying this, as if having dropped a huge bombshell on his friends. None of the three said anything for a few moments, as if absorbing the knowledge. Alex spoke first.

'Why?'

'Because… well… you know, because!' Tom and Alex must have looked confused, because Mo continued. 'You know the rumours. My dad's really superstitious, I think it's because he's religious or whatever. He's terrified of wit–' Mo caught himself before he said the full word, changed tack. 'Also because of everything that happened last week, you know, the shit even you were involved with.' Mo looked at Alex.

'Yeah, but…' Alex said, unable to properly articulate his confusion.

Tom scoffed, ignoring the first part of Mo's answer. 'That's nothing, Emma beats up Janet every other week.' Alex and Mo nodded sadly. 'Why would Janet's mum kidnap Mr Sullivan's kid, how would that help?'

'My dad said,' Mo repeated, 'it's because Mrs Willerby – that's Janet's mum – is a…' he trailed off.

'Yeah?' Alex asked, an edge to his voice now.

'It's because she's a witch,' Mo almost whispered, as if afraid by saying it he'd make it true and he'd be Mrs Willerby's next victim.

'Fuck off,' Tom said, laughing.

Alex didn't say anything; he thought about what Mo said. It was so stupid; Mo's dad was a grown man, there was no way he could believe in witches. Even so…

Alex's mind cast back to Janet and her black dress, the one he'd swore he'd seen her in only a couple of days prior. Witches didn't exist, one side of his mind told him. But then, the other side said, how do you explain the dress? And her hair? And the cat she was talking to even though she didn't say anything. And the time Alex had seen her seemingly talking to a spider or something in the snicket, and she'd just disappeared.

But witches aren't real, the first half of his mind insisted.

But then where did she pull the wooden figurine from on the day of the school trip? The other half countered. And what about when she pulled you out of school, through the crowd? And when you jogged after her, but even though she was only walking you couldn't catch up until you ran?

But, but, the first half faltered. But witches aren't real, it said, almost pleaded.

There was a rumble of thunder, low, distant, but ominous. Whilst the boys had been talking the clouds had darkened and were now an aggressive shade of very dark grey.

But, the second half of Alex's mind said, What if they are?

Chapter Seventeen

Alex forced himself to act normally as he walked towards his house with Tom and Mo. Their conversation about Mo's dad and Mr Sullivan and Janet and her mum finished, they moved back to regular topics; Hull City still doing pretty well in the table, the new Bond film that was supposed to be coming out at some point, whether they thought Margot Robbie would ever get naked in a film again. Alex smiled, laughed, joked, although all of it was an act, none of it was real. He was deeply relieved when they reached the top of the street both Mo and Tom lived on.

'What you doing tomorrow?' Tom asked them both.

'Family shit,' Mo said, and Alex nodded. He told himself it wasn't actually lying if he didn't say anything.

'Yeah me, too,' Tom said. 'My parents want the family together now, as much as possible, because of…'

He trailed off, but Alex and Mo both knew to what he was referring without the need for Tom to say it. They said their goodbyes, and Alex set off along the main road to his own street. As soon as he was a few metres beyond the top of Tom and Mo's road, sure they couldn't see him, he broke into a run. He ran all the way home, barely paying attention to the fact the street was completely empty. Thunder rumbled again as he entered the front garden, and he'd just got inside the front door, slamming it behind him, when the heavens opened and huge drops of rain fell from the sky.

His mum came rushing out of the kitchen and into the hallway, knife in one hand and half chopped onion in the other. Between the door slamming and Alex's panting, she was in a panic.

'Alex, Alex are you okay?' she said, not moving, just staring at him from the length of the hall.

'I'm fine,' he replied, and although he wasn't telling the truth, he was anything but fine, he was fine with regards to what his mother meant. He was alive and uninjured, in other words.

'I heard the door slam, and you standing there…' his mum said, leaving the sentence hanging in the air open ended.

'Oh, yeah,' Alex said, hesitating, before a thought struck him. 'Have you seen the rain? It's chucking it down.'

'Really?' his mum replied, the spell on her breaking, allowing her to walk down the hallway. Standing next to Alex, she balanced the onion and knife in one hand and with the other pulled back the curtain that covered the floor to ceiling window to the left side of the front door.

'Wow,' she said. 'It's really coming down out there.'

'Told you.' Alex knelt down to untie his shoelaces.

He looked up and his mum had an odd expression on her face as she watched him.

'You're not wet?' she murmured.

'What?'

'I said,' Alex's mum said, a bit more volume in her voice the second time around. 'You're not wet?'

She phrased it like a question, and Alex panicked for a second, though he didn't know why.

'Yeah,' he said, smiling, doing his best to look triumphant. 'Just beat it. I got through the door like one second before it started.'

Even though this was true it didn't move the confused expression from his mum's face. She continued to look at him, and after a moment he broke eye contact, untying the other shoe before taking both off and standing up.

'When's tea?' he asked.

This seemed to snap his mum out of her trance and she looked at him properly.

'Oh, about half an hour. I'll shout you.'

'Thanks, Mum,' Alex said, running up the stairs. He could feel his mum's eyes on him, watching him, but he didn't look back, didn't want to engage her.

The evening passed like so many Saturday evenings had in the house over the years. After a dinner of spaghetti bolognese, eaten on knees in the living room in front of the TV watching the reboot of Gladiators, which his mum and dad kept reassuring each other was not a patch on the original, Alex headed up to his room while his parents watched a film.

His head had been buzzing all evening, ever since Mo had mentioned what his dad said. There was no way Mrs Willerby and Janet were witches, surely? Yeah, he'd seen some odd stuff, but that's all it was, odd stuff. It was 2024, he told himself for the second time in the space of a few days, there was no such thing as magic.

He grabbed his laptop, an old, battered piece of tech he was desperate to replace but knew he wouldn't get to, not least until his dad got a job. He pressed the power button and the fan whirred to life like a jet engine. Eventually the computer awoke, and Alex went to Google and searched for 'witches'.

There were billions of answers, and after clicking on a few and skimming the resulting pages, he felt none the wiser. He went back to Google and changed his search to 'witches Hull', and bingo. Many fewer results, and based on the snippets on the page, much more relevant. He clicked on hullhistory.com and was presented with a crappy looking webpage, almost entirely text with a few low-resolution images.

The page was a wall of text, and rather than read it Alex pressed Control and F and typed 'witches'. He was rewarded with multiple results, and slowly began to read them.

In 1603, the website said, *King James 1st arrived from Scotland with a passion for witches. As such, lots of people who wanted to win his favour began focusing on witches, who were very feared at the time, because everyone believed in God so much. They were all terrified of the devil.*

Alex continued to read; in 1654, a woman called

Elizabeth Roberts was accused of witchcraft, but there was no record of what became of her. In 1650, Ann Hudson was also accused of witchcraft, but again there was no record of her fate. Alex read a handful more of these accounts of accusations and fates lost to the ages, before he came across something that stopped him in his tracks.

In 1604 – the website seemed to be in no particular order – Baron John Savile, desperate to look good in the new King's eyes, had presided over the trial and execution by hanging of five people accused of being witches. The five of them were a mixture of men and women. What stood out to Alex were the names. Two were called Roger Beadney and Mary Holland, but Alex ignored these. Two were called Janet Wrestle and Janet Butler, and Alex's heart began to pound. It was just a coincidence, surely? There must have been a million people called Janet throughout history, it was a pretty common name.

Not that common any more, Alex told himself, but still common. Still common enough for it to be a coincidence, anyway. He knew he was trying to convince himself of this fact, and might have won, had he not read the final name, which moved his reading firmly from coincidence and into the realms of fact. The fifth person hanged was a man by the name of John Willerby.

Chapter Eighteen

Alex spent the rest of the evening playing FIFA, sometimes online against Mo or his online friends, people he'd never met nor never would, but played regularly at online football, sometimes alone. His mind wasn't in it, though, and he performed poorly, losing almost all his games. He ended up playing against the computer on easy, just to score some goals and win. He was trying to distract himself, but it wasn't working. After all he'd read online, his mind was racing.

As well as attempting to distract himself, he was just passing the time. He'd been thinking all afternoon, all evening, ever since Mo had told him what his dad had said about Mrs Willerby, ever since he'd read the name 'Willerby' online, that he needed to go see Janet. Yes, he wanted to see her, he wanted to look at her and be in her presence and maybe hold her hand again and try and find some things out, speak to her and maybe ask her some questions. But mostly he felt he needed to warn her. He'd had that sinking feeling in the pit of his stomach since the assembly the day before and it had only grown; he was sure Mo's dad wouldn't be the only one thinking suspiciously about Mrs Willerby, and he felt he had a duty to warn Janet.

He went to bed earlier than normal; when he went downstairs to tell his parents and his mum queried the time with some concern, he said he was tired from playing football, and though he didn't think she believed him his dad said goodnight in such a way that it ended the conversation, allowed him to slip back upstairs. He set his alarm for seven the next morning; his parents slept in on Sundays, and he thought he could get to Janet's and back before they even knew he was gone.

He slept fitfully, and would have slept through his alarm if he hadn't stashed his phone under his pillow. It was the vibration that finally woke him, and after a couple of seconds of confusion he sat up, suddenly wide awake as he remembered why his phone had awoken him.

Moving as quietly as possible he put on the previous day's clothes, slowly opened his bedroom door, and padded down the stairs. Picking his shoes and coat up – he'd glanced through a gap in his curtains to see it was still pouring down – he slowly unlocked the front door, turned the key and twisted the latch as silently as possible.

He winced as the lock clicked, thinking it was so loud that Janet herself probably heard on the other side of the village, let alone his parents, and slowly eased it open. The door creaked slightly as he pulled it and he froze as he heard movement from directly above, the sound coming from his parents' bedroom. He stayed completely still, not daring to breathe; after a few seconds of silence he assumed one of his parents must have been rolling over in bed, and he slipped through the small gap in the doorway and pulled it closed behind him. He padded down the garden, stepping over the gate rather than opening it, and quickly moved a couple of paces to the right, hiding behind Mrs Mayberry's bushes. He squatted down; glancing up he was unable to see his parent's bedroom window, so he assumed they likewise wouldn't be able to see him if they got up. He put on his shoes and coat, wincing at the feel of his wet socks, and took off up the street at a run.

Even though it was so early on Sunday morning he still thought he might see some people, but the streets of Deerborn were completely and utterly deserted. Not a single soul, whether on foot or in a car, did he see on his journey. He'd been worried about what he might say if anyone stopped him, asked him where he was going, but no such thing happened. The weather probably helped; the air wasn't really cold, but the driving rain and biting wind had lowered the temperature an uncomfortable amount. Plus it was still quite dark, the heavy grey clouds not softening despite the amount of water they'd been throwing down since the previous evening. Alex thought most people who'd planned to go somewhere that early must have looked out of their curtains and changed their minds, and he was glad for it.

Not only this, but the village itself was quiet too. The church bells, which normally introduced every hour on a

Sunday, hadn't been ringing when Alex woke up, he realised. He stopped at the thought. It was as if the village itself were sleeping in or, and to Alex this thought felt more appropriate, was waiting. For what Alex couldn't have said, but he was sure waiting was what the village was doing. With a small shudder he resumed running.

It only took him fifteen minutes to run from one end of the village to the other, and soon he stood at the top of the track that led to Janet's house. He stood still, the village behind him, the Willerby's cottage in front. The track looked much the same as when he'd walked down it earlier that week with Janet; the tall, vibrantly green bushes on either side, fencing the path in, reaching for passing strangers; the trees in the fields behind them, leaves whispering to each other, birds singing from their branches in spite of the wet weather; he wondered if he might see the bright white cat with the piercing green eyes, whether it might chase him away. Because the more he thought about it, the more he decided that the feeling he'd had at the other end of the track the previous Monday, of doom and despair, hadn't been inside him, but had been coming from outside. Somehow, Mrs Willerby had done something that made people feel that way if they weren't invited, and so didn't come any closer. He had no basis for thinking this, but he did anyway. He was sure, if he told anyone, they'd say he was mad and cart him off to the closest mental hospital. Unless he told Mo's dad, who'd probably agree with him and say it was a spell Mrs Willerby cast. Alex shuddered.

After steeling himself for a few moments he slowly walked up the track. The rain had settled in shallow brown puddles, sometimes the entire width of the track, and Alex couldn't help but wish he'd come in wellies rather than his bright white Nike trainers. By the time he was halfway down his shoes were filthy and his feet completely soaked through; he persevered however, wanting to see his mission through. Wanting to see Janet.

About three quarters of the way down the track he stopped; the track curved to the right slightly, and directly ahead was a tall tree, bare of leaves, looking almost dead. In one of the lowest branches was a huge black bird that Alex thought might have been a crow. He also thought, and he felt stupid even as he did, that it was staring at him. Alex stood for a few moments staring right back; neither party moved until Alex, realising that time was of the essence if he wanted to be home before his parents got up and found him gone, made to take a step, and jumped out of his skin when the crow *cawed* at the top of its voice and took flight. The sound was deafening in the morning stillness, and as Alex watched the crow fly for a moment his heart stopped: he thought he'd seen some white on the crow's face, near its eyes. The sight was familiar to him, but he couldn't think why. He stood for a moment thinking about it before the wetness in his legs forced him to move again.

Alex walked the final few metres of the track, Janet's house coming into view, and for the second time jumped out of his skin when he reached the end of the path. The hedges ended and the ground opened up to the clearing in which the house stood; Alex, travelling in silence since the departure of the crow, nearly had a heart attack when Mrs Willerby stepped in front of him. She appeared as if from nowhere and, his heart pounding, Alex literally jumped off the floor, before landing with a splash and scrabbling back a few steps.

Mrs Willerby looked so much like her daughter – or, he thought, Janet looked so much like her mother – it was eerie. They were the same height, with the same colour hair and the same colour eyes. But where Janet was usually attired in her poorly conditioned school uniform, Alex couldn't really make out what Mrs Willerby was wearing. It looked like a cross between a dress and a tent; her head was sticking out of the top, her arms out of the sides, but otherwise it looked like she'd just draped a piece of cloth over herself. Her face was dirty, with marks of what Alex hoped were soil spotted here and there on her cheeks, forehead, nose. On one shoulder, Alex wasn't entirely surprised to see, was perched a large crow, its head turned away. Alex tried to see if there was white on its face and couldn't, but still, he'd have bet his entire football sticker collection it was the one from the tree moments earlier. The one that was from somewhere else he couldn't quite place.

He hadn't thought that, leaving so early to ensure his parents were asleep, Janet and her mother might also be sleeping, and so once his heartbeat slowed he was relieved to see Mrs Willerby. He hadn't thought how he'd knock on the door, or on a window, or even if he could make it past the point he hadn't last time. A lot of luck had fallen for him, and he was grateful for it. He was just thinking of what to say, how to begin, when Mrs Willerby spoke.

'Good morning, dear,' Mrs Willerby said, the cheeriness in her voice belying the raspiness of it. 'A bit early for a stroll, isn't it? And in such awful weather?'

She held her hand, palm upwards towards the sky, as if to let Alex know it was raining were he not previously aware. Something occurred to Alex then; although Mrs Willerby was standing in the same rain as him, and although he was soaking wet, water dripping off his entire body, Mrs Willerby appeared to be completely dry. Alex, however, didn't get chance to think about it before Mrs Willerby spoke again.

'I want to thank you for coming, I truly appreciate it.'

'But–' Alex began, before Mrs Willerby cut him off.

'I know who you are, and I know why you're here. Again, let me say thank you. You didn't have to come here today, you didn't have to warn me, but you have, and I'm very grateful.' She paused for a moment. 'As is my daughter.'

Alex stiffened at the last word and Mrs Willerby must have noticed, because she softly laughed to herself, a low, rasping sound, like tyres crossing a gravel driveway.

'I know all about *that,* too,' she said, a glint in her eye Alex couldn't look away from. 'I wanted to thank you for that too, for looking out for my daughter when you did.'

'It's okay,' Alex said in a very small voice, finally finding space – as well as courage – to speak in the conversation. 'What Emma does to her is–'

'Oh I know, dear, it's terrible,' Mrs Willerby said, and although she was saying it was terrible she spoke with a lightness in her voice that Alex felt undermined her words. 'What that girl does to her, and her father tries to do to me, it's unconscionable.'

Alex didn't know this last word, and it must have been clear from his face.

'It's not on, dear, is what I'm saying,' Mrs Willerby said.

'I just wanted to–'

'Let me know what your friend Mo's father said. And I thank ya for it,' Mrs Willerby said, and Alex was amazed and a little frightened she seemed to be able to read his mind, that she knew exactly what he was going to say before he said it. He was, he realised, having a full conversation whilst rarely saying anything. He felt like he should have been afraid, but there was something about Mrs Willerby he found oddly reassuring. She was what he thought a grandma must be like: kindly, approachable, but unknowable.

'Yes, it's happening again,' Mrs Willerby said with a sigh, looking first at the crow on her shoulder, then to the trees. She seemed to say it more to herself than Alex, so he stayed quiet and let her continue speaking.

'It's been a little while, oh since I was a girl, but it's happening again.' She fixed Alex with a firm eye; he felt he would have been unable to move even if he'd wanted to. 'Every generation, some little upstart thinks he – it's usually a he, at least now anyway, there used to be a lot of she's but not any more – can come for us, thinks he can put an end to us. The years move on, but nothing changes, it always comes back around. Life repeats itself; time is a flat circle.' She smiled, and for a second Alex thought he saw a flash of something, an anger, reveal itself. He also noticed that Mrs Willerby's teeth were perfectly straight and perfectly white, and they looked out of place with the rest of her. 'It'll happen soon,' she continued, 'in the next couple of weeks I'd imagine. But it won't be your friend's father, don't worry. It'll be *him*.'

Alex felt a warmth, not in him or around him, really he couldn't place it at all, but it was definitely there, defying the weather in which he stood. And he knew, without Mrs Willerby saying so, that she was talking about Mr Sullivan. He didn't know how he knew, the knowledge seemed to just come to him.

'He'll be here, and he'll try, but we'll be okay. We're always okay,' Mrs Willerby said, and she sounded wistful, almost sad. 'I'll be forced to do what I try to avoid doing, I just hope Janet won't have to. It'll be a sad day, but then it'll be over, at least until Janet's grown.'

'Sorry,' Alex said, finding his voice when Mrs Willerby stopped speaking. 'What's going to happen?'

Mrs Willerby startled slightly, as if in her monologuing she'd forgotten Alex was there. She looked at the crow again before turning back to Alex.

'You'll see, my dear,' she said, fixing her gaze upon him once more. 'You'll see.'

With that she abruptly turned around and began to walk back towards her house. With another loud *caw* the crow took flight. As if took off, Alex could see the white on its face, and suddenly it hit him where he'd seen it before: in his dream. The one that also had Mrs Willerby and the fire. Was that what she meant about it happening again? A fire?

Alex didn't get to think of this too much, because before she reached her front door Mrs Willerby turned back to face him. She was still bone dry, despite the fact Alex thought his very insides were soaked with rain.

'You're a good lad, and your dad's a good man. Your ma, well, far be it from me to judge a well-intentioned woman. You all want to be careful, though. There are some bad people about, and I don't mean whoever took that little boy.' Alex started at the reference to Joseph. The way she said it made it plain to him, if he hadn't been certain already, that she wasn't involved in his disappearance. 'There'll come a time when you have to choose between right and wrong. I have every faith in the world in you, but do your best to help your parents see reason. They're good people,' she sighed, 'but good people can be led astray under trying circumstances.'

With that, she entered her house; Alex hadn't seen her open the front door, but suddenly it was closing behind her with a loud *thunk*, and he was alone. He was about to turn around and quickly go home, get back into bed, when movement caught his eyes. Above the front door and to the left he saw a curtain twitch; peeking out from behind it was *her*. As Alex watched, Janet slowly raised a hand and softly waved. Alex waved back, and he thought Janet smiled before the curtain twitched again and she disappeared.

Chapter Nineteen

Alex stood for a moment, looking at the Willerby's house. He tried not to focus on what he assumed was Janet's bedroom window, instead trying to look at the house as a whole and just occasionally glancing towards the glass.

After a few minutes he realised she wasn't coming back; looking at his phone, he started at the time. It was nearly eight, the time his parents usually began to stir back into wakefulness, to leave the dream realm behind. He span around on the spot and ran, as fast as he could in the treacherous conditions, slipping several times on the track and nearly landing face down in a couple of huge, muddy puddles.

He passed a handful of people as he traced his path back to his house, but no one paid him any attention. The village was full of Janets that morning; people walking with their heads down, minding their own business, just trying to ride out the worst of it in the hope it'd soon end. Alex himself was one of them; the rain was driving to the point it stung his face, and he pulled his hood even tighter around his head as he pounded along the slippery streets, splashing through several large puddles and further soaking his already drenched feet and ankles.

Eight o'clock came and went as he endured his journey, but once again the church bells remained silent. Alex ignored the involuntary shudder he felt at this and continued to run, trying to put the silence out of his mind.

Soon he arrived behind the Mayberry's large bush, and was just bending to untie his shoes when he heard his mum calling his name. He stood up, freezing as he became completely erect, and panicked. *Shit*, he thought, he was caught. He edged to the end of the bush and peered around it and into his front garden. His mum was on the doorstep in her light blue dressing gown, hair dishevelled, calling his name. She looked terrified, her eyes wide, her skin pale, her mouth moving in time with the words coming from it, and the sight wrenched at Alex's heart. He briefly considered waiting for her to go back inside and trying to sneak in, but he knew, he just knew it was hopeless. Even if he did somehow manage to get back inside, how would he explain to his mum his soaking wet clothing, the fact he hadn't been in bed or the bathroom or downstairs watching TV when she got up? No, he knew he was fucked, and he realised, with a resignation that belied his 15 years, that his best course of action was to simply come clean.

Reluctantly, sheepishly, confirmed in his decision mentally if still hesitant in it physically, Alex leaned out fully from behind the bush. His mum stiffened when she saw him and ran down the garden, getting drenched herself in the process. She kicked up splashes of water as she moved but she was so angry and relieved she didn't even seem to notice the weather. She grabbed Alex and hugged him tighter than he could remember being hugged in a long time.

'Alex, oh my god, Alex, come here my boy,' she said, her words falling out of her mouth so fast they blended into one. 'I was so worried about you, oh my god,' she continued, starting to cry as she did. 'I thought he'd got you, I thought he'd got you too and we'd never see you again. What happened, where have you been? Come here,' and she hugged him even tighter with these last words.

Alex was about to answer when his dad came outside, similarly attired in a dressing gown – dark blue – and slippers. His ever more greying hair was soaking wet, plastered to his forehead, and there were lines of water running down his face. Alex guessed he'd been looking outside, though whether the water on his dad's face was rain or tears Alex couldn't have said. Alex's dad didn't seem to notice Alex at first, but when he did his eyes popped out of his head; Alex thought he looked like Bugs Bunny or something. His dad was clearly more angry than relieved and stayed in the doorway, perhaps mindful of getting any more wet, perhaps not trusting himself not to give Alex a clout on the side of the head. Alex's dad had never hit him, but Alex supposed if he did now Alex wouldn't blame him.

'Come in, come in,' his dad said, gesturing with his arms for Alex and his mum to come inside the house. Alex tried to move but his mum was still holding him so tightly he wasn't able. The rain was still falling on them in heavy, insistent drops, and all Alex could hear was that and his mum's sobs.

'Come on, Mum,' Alex said, his voice muffled against her chest. Hearing his voice seemed to break her paralysis and she released him, ever so slightly, enough that the pair could walk up the short, narrow path and into the house. Alex's dad stepped aside to let them pass, and once Alex and his mum were inside his dad closed the door gently, locking it as he did so, giving it a firm tug to make sure it was shut tight.

Alex braced himself; he had been right about his dad, the man was furious. Alex's mum let go of him and the three of them stood still, silent, for a moment. The only sounds were the ticking of the hall clock and the soft *drip, drip, drip* of water falling from Alex and his mum to the floor. Alex braced himself, looking at the deer antlers, the floor, anywhere but his father.

'Where the hell have you been?' His dad roared with such ferocity that both Alex and his mum jumped. 'We thought you were dead, you bloody idiot. Disappearing overnight, when there's a… a *killer* on the loose.'

'Dad,' Alex said, trying to keep his voice level. 'No one's dead.'

'What did you say?' He yelled at the top of his voice; Alex heard some china in the living room cabinet actually rattle. 'What did you say to me?'

Alex, realising it wasn't a rhetorical question, started to answer.

'I said–'

'I know what you bloody said,' his dad roared once more. 'No one's dead, he says,' looking at Alex's mum in disbelief, before turning back to Alex and pointing a finger at him. 'If you keep this up someone bloody will be.'

'Darling,' Alex's mum said to her husband, her voice wavering. 'It's okay, he's back now.' She put her hand on Alex's dad's arm but he immediately shook it off. He didn't say anything else, however, so Alex's mum continued. 'Where have you been, son? Tell us, we won't be mad, we promise.'

'I don't bloody promise,' Alex's dad muttered under his breath.

'*We* promise,' Alex's mum said again, frowning at her husband. He remained silent.

'I…' Alex began, stopped, not sure what to say. He'd thought he was going to tell the truth, but suddenly, standing there, water dripping off every part of him and pooling at his feet, his dad angrier than he'd even seen him, the truth felt insignificant, inadequate. 'I…' he said again, before stopping again.

'You can tell us son, it's okay,' his mum said, and his dad grunted in what Alex took to be agreement.

Alex's mum put her hand on his arm. He didn't shake it off; he could feel his mum's warmth, despite her being dripping wet, on his bare arm, and it reassured him. He realised he had to tell the truth, even if only because he had nothing else to say.

'I was at Janet's house,' he said, looking at the floor, not daring to look either of his parents in the eye. 'I went to...' he paused, before forcing himself to continue speaking. 'I went to warm Mrs Willerby and Janet. Mo said yesterday his dad thinks Mrs Willerby took Joseph but I know she didn't!'

He said these last four words with such vehemence, finding the courage to look his parents in the eye, each in turn, that now it was his father's turn to jump. He took a step back, looking a little shocked by his son. Alex continued.

'Mrs Willerby didn't do anything, neither did Janet, I know they didn't.'

'You went where!?' His mum now rounded on him, his dad's fury channelling through her. She was about to continue in this manner but Alex's dad silenced her with a look, and when she spoke again her voice was calm, level, though still it wavered.

'How,' his mum said hesitantly, as if she was about to ask a question she didn't want to know the answer to. 'How do you know, son? Is there something you need to tell us? You know you can tell us anything, can't he dear?'

She turned to look at Alex's dad and he nodded with a grunt. Alex's mum continued to look at his dad, and he realised she was waiting for him to say something, to back her up.

'Anything, son, you can tell us anything,' he said, arms crossed, fury slowly departing his features. 'Has Mrs Willerby–'

'I don't know anything about Joseph if that's what you're asking,' Alex said, and his mum visibly deflated with relief. His dad looked unmoved. 'But I know Janet and her mum didn't do it, I just know.'

'What do you mean, son?' his mum asked, concern written all over her face.

'I…' he said, pausing again, before releasing his words in a furious flood. 'I know Janet, I spent the day with her when I couldn't go on the school trip, we walked home together. She's not…' he faltered again, as if steeling himself, before pressing on. 'She's not what people say she is. She's just a kid.'

His speech complete, Alex's shoulders sagged. Now his mum was silent; Alex's dad spoke in a low voice, surprising them all.

'I know, son,' was all he said, keeping one arm folded across his chest and using the other to scratch his chin, the sound of his fingers in his stubble like a jet engine in the nearly silent hallway. All the fury had melted from his features and his face showed a mixture of concern and sadness.

'I know, son,' he said again. 'I know exactly what you mean. I don't know how you know, and I don't know how I know you know, but you do know, and so do I. The Willerby's didn't do this, but I'll be sure as hell surprised if they don't get the blame.'

'Exactly!' Alex shouted, straightening up again. 'Everyone's going to blame them and Janet's life will get even worse than it already is, and it's not fair. She's just a girl.'

'Is she a girl you…' Alex's mum said with a hint of fear in her voice, but his dad cut her off once again with a look that said it wasn't the time or the place.

'Why don't you go upstairs, have a shower and put on some dry clothes?' his dad suggested. 'We'll have breakfast, and then you can join me in the living room.'

Alex looked at his dad, his head cocked. What did his dad mean, join him in the living room?

'When we're all dry and warm and have full stomachs, you and I need to have a long talk about the Willerbys, son,' Alex's dad continued. 'There are some things you need to know about that family.'

Chapter Twenty

Half an hour later, feeling much more alive with dry clothes and a cooked breakfast inside him, Alex stood up from the table at the same time as his father and followed him out of the kitchen. Alex's mum made to follow but his dad stopped her with a look.

'I think this is one that's best between father and son,' he said to her, and Alex's mum, though she didn't look happy, didn't argue. Instead she began to clear the table, scurrying about the kitchen as if she were satisfied just to have something to do with herself.

Alex followed his father silently, who held the living room door open for him, letting him enter, and then closed it softly behind them. Alex's dad gestured to the couch, and once Alex was seated, sat in the worn armchair.

Alex looked at his dad who was looking around the room as if he'd never been there before, as if he'd never seen the pictures, the wallpaper, the view out of the window. Alex's dad looked out the window for so long Alex turned around and looked himself, to see if there was something he should see. All he could see was their front garden and the street beyond; the rain was still falling in sheets, and with a pang Alex realised that another summer was officially over. He started and turned back when his father started talking.

'I'm going to tell you some things now, Alex,' he said, his voice quiet, his tone soft, concerned, wary. 'You're not going to believe a lot of it, and I can't prove most of it, but you just have to trust me. Can you do that?'

Alex nodded, and knew he was nodding not because it would make his father continue speaking but because he knew he would believe his father. He couldn't explain why he knew Mrs Willerby and Janet had nothing to do with Joseph, he just did. He guessed his father was the same with whatever he was about to tell him. He guessed it was somehow in the same way as Mrs Willerby had known what he was going to say that morning before he'd said it.

'My father, your paternal grandfather,' Alex's dad began, glancing at a picture on the mantelpiece in which his parents stood side by side, smiling in black and white, on their wedding day. 'Was not a nice man. I loved him, but I'm under no illusions. He was not a nice man.'

Alex had never heard his dad talk about his father and he remained silent, not wanting to stop him saying more. Alex had asked both his dad and his mum about his grandfather on numerous occasions but both had just shooed him away. He was excited, if not a little nervous, to finally hear about the man.

'Your grandfather lived his entire life in this village.

He was born here, got married here, raised me here, worked all his life here, and died here. You know the house my former boss, Mr Sullivan, and his family live in?' Alex nodded. 'That used to be my house; my father used to own it, and I grew up in it.'

Alex's eyes widened in shock. The house his father was talking about was huge, it must have been five times as big as the one they lived in currently. It sat back from the road in acres of grounds, green lawns stretching halfway to the horizon. Alex couldn't believe it.

'I was also born in that house, but as you can see, I haven't lived in it my entire life, and I probably won't die in it. Unless something really odd happens,' he said with half a laugh, as though the thought wasn't actually that funny at all.

'You know the building society I used to work at?' he continued; Alex nodded. 'My father used to own it.

'He started it with Mr Sullivan's father, your classmate Emma's grandfather. Hugh, he was called, the one I knew as Mr Sullivan, the current Mr Sullivan's father. My father and Hugh were thick as thieves, they were; they met in year one at school, and stayed friends right until Hugh died, some fifty years later. They went to school together, did work experience in the same bank, and that was where they got the idea to start the building society.

'It used to be,' Alex's dad continued, 'that if you lived in the village, you had to go all the way into Hull if you wanted a bank account, or if you had one and needed to take some money from it. There were no banks out here, nothing. Until my grandfather and Hugh Sullivan started one.

'It was a roaring success from the off; people around here were begging for a local bank account, and my grandfather and Hugh Sullivan provided it. They got all the villagers to join, plus a lot of people from the surrounding villages; the bank wasn't happy at a new rival popping up, but as they were unwilling to open a branch out here there was nothing they could do.

'The pair were just twenty-two when they started the building society, and by the time they were thirty they were both rich.'

Alex couldn't help but glance around the living room when his father said this. His grandfather had been rich; why on earth did Alex and his family live in this crappy little house?

'As well as their bank accounts, most of the locals moved their mortgages to the building society when their contracts let them. My father and Mr Sullivan quickly became lenders to most of the properties in the village. Including the Willerbys.'

Alex sat up a little straighter hearing the Willerbys mentioned for the first time.

'Again, my father and Hugh Sullivan dealt with who I knew as Mrs Willerby, the mother of the woman you know as the current Mrs Willerby, the woman who was Janet's grandmother. My father hated dealing with her; he said women shouldn't get involved with money, and every time he saw Mrs Willerby he demanded to speak with her husband. She never said she didn't have one or anything, she always just replied with 'he's not available at the present time.' I remember my father thundering that phrase around the house; even if he was in the kitchen, and I was in my room two floors up, on the other side of the house with the door closed, I could hear him as if he was right next to me, saying it straight into my ear.

'He and Hugh Sullivan wanted rid of the Willerbys; at that time it was Mrs Willerby and her daughter, Janet's mother, and my father wanted them gone, not just from the house but from the village.

'They didn't want Mrs Willerby and her daughter gone just because they were women. There were some people sniffing around, buying up land in the area. You might not know it because the house is so small, but the Willerbys have hundreds of acres of land, all the fields you can see around it. Hugh Sullivan, as soon as he made it big, started buying up land around the village, buying the village itself. Rumour was he couldn't afford the Willerby's land, but the people sniffing around were willing to cut him in on a deal if he managed to get rid of Mrs Willerby.

'The rumours you've no doubt heard around the village' – Alex nodded – 'are nothing new. They weren't even new back then; my father had heard them from his father, who told them about the former Mrs Willerby. And his father had heard them about her mother, on and on, back for generations.

'People were much more religious back then, much more superstitious. I know Mr Sullivan claims to be a Christian, goes to church every Sunday in his best suit with his wife and daughter in their best dresses, his son in his,' Alex's dad hesitated for a moment, as if he'd forgotten that Joseph was missing, 'his son in his best suit. But his father actually was a god-fearing man. Where Mr Sullivan only wants rid of them now for the value of the land, as well as a deeply held grudge, back then my father and Hugh Sullivan wanted rid of them because they were scared of them. They wanted the land too, don't get me wrong, but I think my father and Hugh Sullivan were scared of that little old woman and her daughter.

'My father never admitted to being scared; even though everyone was, everyone believed the rumours about the Willerbys, as a businessman, a husband and father, my father would have been a laughing stock if he'd said it out loud. I thought I knew because he got this look in his eye whenever Mrs Willerby was mentioned; behind the anger and fury, I thought I could see some fear. I think he was scared she was going to destroy him, or even just that she had the power, and he wouldn't be able to stop her. I understand, to a point; the summer after my father and his partner started trying to take hold of the Willerby's land, several farms in the area which sat on land rented out by Hugh Sullivan had terrible years. Crops were destroyed by birds, rats got into barns and scared cows to the point they didn't provide milk, all manner of things happened. The families weren't able to pay their rent to Hugh Sullivan, and he assumed it was the work of Mrs Willerby.

'A normal man might have left her alone, live and let

live and all that, but not my father, oh no. When he wanted something, he was determined to get it. From the moment he decided he wanted the land Mrs Willerby's house sat on, he couldn't rest until it was his, or he was dead. Well,' Alex's dad said with an entirely humourless laugh, 'that bargain was certainly fulfilled.'

Alex's dad paused for a moment, scratched his chin once more. The only sound in the room was the soft ticking of the clock gently drifting in from the hall. Alex glanced out the window, thought he saw a flash of black, but when he looked again there was nothing there. He wondered where his mum was, what she was doing, but was distracted from thoughts of her when his dad stood up and moved to the picture of his parents, picked it up, looked at it tenderly. He continued to look at it for a moment before placing it back down gently and moving back to his seat, facing Alex once more.

'One day my father came home in great spirits. 'What is it?' my mother asked, and he shouted at her with delight. 'It's happening, it's finally happening,' he said. I was only a lad, maybe ten or eleven, sitting on the kitchen floor rolling a wooden truck back and forth whilst my mother observed the kitchen staff.

'What's happening?' she asked my father, and he grabbed her in both his hands and planted a kiss firmly on her lips. It was so unlike him, he wasn't an affectionate man at all. I think my mum was a little scared then; what he said next only frightened her further.

'I've finally got the bloody Willerby woman!' he roared, so loudly that I jumped and began to cry in spite of my age. My mother hugged me and bade my father to continue, though much quieter. I should say,' Alex's dad quickly added, 'I don't really remember any of this, just bits and pieces. The rest I've put together from what my mother told me many years later.

'Today was her deadline for payment, and she missed it. Tomorrow I'm going with the boys to get her out. I'll finally have the blasted land; I can demolish that hovel she calls a house and sell the land to someone who won't run it as an eyesore.

'The boys were the Ricketts twins, I think their grandsons go to your school? My father and Hugh Sullivan used their services occasionally; they had not a single brain cell between them, but they were both amateur boxing champions and always ready for a fight. My father and Hugh Sullivan called on them when they had to evict someone; people often kick and scream, my father told me once, but the Ricketts soon put a stop to that. The kicking anyway.

'So the next morning my father was up and away early, like normal. Only instead of heading into Hull, he headed into the village. He met the Ricketts boys at the top of the track that leads to the Willerby house and the three of them marched down it like an invading army.

'What happened next is a mystery; as I say, I know all of this from my mum, but she said he never told anyone what happened at the Willerby house that morning. The Ricketts boys never told anyone, either; they actually left the village, moved away the very next day; it was only when one of their sons moved back about twenty years ago that there was a Ricketts presence in the village again, the father to the twins you're at school with.

'Whatever happened at that house, my father never spoke of to anyone. In fact, he never spoke again. He returned home a few hours after he left, hung up his coat as usual, took off his shoes, accepted a cup of tea from the housekeeper, and never opened his mouth. He never said a word until he died of a heart attack a year or so later.

'Hugh Sullivan was furious. I remember him coming round the next day demanding to know what had happened, why the Willerby woman was still in her house. He also wanted to know why my father wouldn't say anything, and where the Ricketts boys had gone, but I don't think he actually cared about either of those things, not really. I don't think he even cared too much about old Mrs Willerby, or all the money he was missing out on. I think what he truly cared about was being beaten.

'He came to our house to yell at my father perhaps ten or so times over the next month; my father never said a single word to him, my mother said; she'd sit in the room, holding her husband's hand, encouraging him to talk whilst Hugh Sullivan yelled, but he never uttered a peep.

'After a month of this, Mr Sullivan had had enough; he took the eviction notice from my father and marched from our house directly to the Willerbys. My father, though he never spoke again, was still well in every other way. When he realised what his partner meant to do he followed him, and my mother followed her husband.

They followed Hugh to the top of the track; my father stopped there, would go no further. Mr Sullivan marched straight down it, and soon disappeared around the curve. My father and mother waited, hand in hand, and before long Mr Sullivan emerged, but he wasn't alone. Mrs Willerby was with him, and my mother couldn't believe what she was seeing: the pair were talking and laughing like old friends.

'They walked up the track, Hugh Sullivan and Mrs Willerby; Hugh had his arm out, and Mrs Willerby held onto his elbow. As they got closer, my mother said, she realised it wasn't a conversation per se; Mrs Willerby was muttering to Hugh Sullivan, and he was vacantly smiling and nodding, his face blank to all feeling. They stopped just out of earshot, and for a moment stood still whilst Mrs Willerby muttered into Hugh's ear some more. Eventually she released her grip on his arm, and whilst he remained still for a moment, she turned and walked home without so much as a glance backwards towards Hugh or my parents.

'After standing still for another moment, Mr Sullivan smiled at my parents like it was the first time he was seeing them. And then he bent into one of the bushes at the side of the road, rustled around for a moment or two, before standing back up holding a jerry can.

'My mother said she didn't recognise it at first, she just assumed Hugh had seen some rubbish and was doing his civic duty in picking it up for proper disposal. It was only when he opened it and she smelled the petrol, she said, that she realised what it was.

'Mr Sullivan, she said, held it above his head before turning it upside down and emptying it on himself. The clear liquid rained down on him, on the bushes and ground around him. Both my mother and father moved towards him, wanting to stop him, but they couldn't get close. My mother never truly said why, but she said they couldn't get onto the track. I pressed her as to why and she shouted 'I just couldn't' before bursting into deep, wrenching sobs.

'Unable to reach him, to stop him, my father and mother could only watch as Hugh Sullivan soaked himself in petrol. They watched as he reached into his pocket and removed his tin of cigarettes. They watched as he put a cigarette into his mouth, lit it, and in the process set himself on fire.'

Chapter Twenty-One

School remained hushed for several days, as if operating under a shroud. Even though Emma's suspension had finished she was kept off school by her parents. No one had seen Jason since he was suspended, but that was fine as far as everyone was concerned, no one missed him. Not at least Alex; his bruises had long since healed, but that didn't mean he was in a rush to see the cause of them again any time soon.

Alex had spent the days after his father's story thinking hard about it all; the Willerbys, the Sullivans, his own family, their places in all of this, not just in Deerborn but back in the past, and now in the present; he wondered what would happen in the future to Mrs Willerby – the current Mrs Willerby – and her words echoed in his ear.

He'll try…we'll be okay…we're always okay…

Alex thought about these words a lot, and wondered exactly what they meant. Who was *he*? And what would he try? Try as he might, Alex couldn't make sense of the riddle, no matter how much time he devoted to solving it.

He also thought about something he'd heard his dad say, later that Sunday morning once Alex had been dismissed. Alex had gone upstairs to play on his PlayStation, but after a few hours he'd been thirsty and had ventured downstairs for a drink. He'd been halfway back up the stairs, glass of orange juice in hand, when he'd heard his parents talking in the living room. He was going to ignore it until he heard his mother say, 'Maybe you should have done what Mr Sullivan wanted and kicked her out, then we wouldn't be in this mess.'

Alex had stopped, stood perfectly still and remained as silent as possible to overhear. He cursed the ticking of the clock, which in the still afternoon air sound louder than a thousand bombs.

'No dear,' his dad had said. 'Don't say that. I did the right thing.'

'But Joseph–' she'd started, but Alex's dad had interrupted.

'No, I won't hear any of that.' Alex heard shuffling sounds, like his dad had stood up and was walking around the living room as he spoke. 'You and I both know Alex is right, neither she nor her daughter have anything to do with the disappearance of that poor little boy.'

'But–'

'But nothing,' his dad said, his voice loud and firm. 'You're a good woman, and I love you, but you've got to stop with this nonsense.'

There was silence for a moment, before Alex's dad

started speaking again, more calmly this time.

'I know what you think, but it's bullshit. It's absolutely bullshit.'

'But–'

'But nothing,' his dad said again. There was more silence for a moment before Alex heard his dad say, 'I love you.' After another moment of silence his mum replied.

'I love you too.'

The conversation had moved on to other things and Alex had gone back upstairs, but rather than picking up his game again he turned it off and lay on his bed, his head spinning. Something else Mrs Willerby had said floated back to him.

They're good people...but even good people can easily be led astray under trying circumstances...

Alex had thought until his head hurt, before falling asleep, sleeping right through the rest of the day and waking on Monday morning.

School continued to happen around Alex; even though he was there he didn't feel much a part of it. Though the whole school had been subdued immediately following the assembly and breaking news of Joseph's disappearance, soon things were back to pretty much normal. Students were disruptive in lessons, didn't do their homework, ran and jumped and screamed and played at lunch. The teachers, Alex thought, seemed happier that things had a bit of normality to them. He thought they'd probably be even happier when Joseph was found and the whole thing forgotten about, but he wasn't sure if that would ever happen. Whilst he was sure the Willerbys had no involvement, he had no idea what had happened, just like everyone else, and whilst he hoped Joseph was fine, that he was found and returned home, Alex was more concerned about Janet and her mother than anyone. Even though Mrs Willerby had assured him they'd be fine, he couldn't help but worry. They were two women, how could they stand up to Mr Sullivan? Especially if he came back with the police or something?

The week following Alex's absconding to the Willerbys and back passed without incident until Thursday lunchtime; the weather was foul, summer was well and truly in the past and though autumn was present, it felt like it was barely clinging on in the face of an insistent winter. The days were grey, the skies darkening in mid-afternoon, long before the sun actually went down. They were the kind of bleak English days when it feels like the sun hasn't even come up at all, the night hasn't actually given way to day but instead has simply lightened itself slightly in imitation. The kind of days when you just want to stay in bed, to write it off as a bad job and try again the next day.

Thursday lunchtime brought yet more dark grey clouds but they hadn't broken; it was chilly but not cold, windy but not blowing a gale. Alex, Tom, and Mo sat in their usual spot on the low wall separating the playground and the playing field, eating their sandwiches. What happened next might have surprised Tom and Mo, but to Alex, even though he'd had no idea of it until it started, it felt inevitable.

The trio were eating, talking, minding their own business, when Tom stopped and looked up. Alex and Mo, realising he wasn't taking part in the conversation, looked at him and saw him looking up. Their gazes followed his and what they saw was very strange.

Alex later thought it was like a disaster movie, *2012* or *The Day After Tomorrow* or something; students were running, all of them running in the same direction. From where the boys were sitting, the pupils were running from the field, behind them and to their right, and running across the front of them, heading left from their vantage point, towards the science building. In the sky above clouds of birds were flying too, black masses undulating together; they moved as if following the children, flocks of them travelling in the same direction as the crowds of feet. Alex felt a dread start to rise within him.

The trio watched for a moment before Alex stood up with a realisation of what was happening. His lunchbox, previously resting on his lap, fell to the floor, his apple, crisps, and chocolate bar spilling everywhere, but he didn't notice. Without a word he started running too, joining the crowd as they moved quickly behind the science blocks. Alex heard one of his friends, perhaps Mo, shout after him but he wasn't listening. His ears were focused on another sound, one coming from in front of him. It sounded like the sea at first, low and murmuring. The closer he got, the more he realised it was exactly what he'd feared; it was an excited crowd.

Emma's not here, he thought, it'll be something else, Janet won't even be involved.

How wrong he was.

Rounding the science block, using his hand on the corner of the building to steady himself, cutting his palm on jagged brick in the process but not even noticing, he saw the familiar shape of a crowd. He didn't hesitate this time; he pushed his way through, throwing other kids out of the way, shoving them left and right with no regard for who they were, how hard they were supposed to be, how much he might regret it later. It got warmer the closer he was to the centre of the mass, but even as he realised this he dismissed the thought and fought his way through the crowd in a matter of seconds. What he saw was both entirely new, but also something he'd seen a thousand times before.

Janet was on her hands and knees, head down. The only difference to the previous scenes of this respect was that Emma was nowhere to be seen and it was Jenna hitting her. It was Jenna, tall, spindly Jenna, with her long ginger hair flowing down her back, stopping just above her waist. Jenna, who if you ever spoke to her alone seemed like she was actually a nice, normal girl, one who was too easily led astray by Emma and her violent delights. Jenna who, although she was always near, was rarely involved. Jenna standing there, a clump of Janet's hair in one fist, beating Janet's head with the other.

Francesca and Aliyah stood behind her, egging her on. Behind them, and all around the scene, the rest of the school was egging Jenna on, too. The crowd was baying for blood in a way he'd never seen them do before. Alex's worries that Mo's father wasn't alone in his thoughts seemed to be coming true, and as he moved into the middle of the hole at the centre of the doughnut, he heard Jenna talking and knew he was right.

'Where *is* he?' she said, the 'is' being emphasised with a fresh hit on the top of Janet's head.

Janet said nothing, didn't respond in any way, other than to whimper with each connection.

'Where is he?' *Whack*. 'Where is he?' *Whack*. 'Where is he?' *Whack*.

It was clear Jenna was talking about Joseph. Alex stood, frozen, only a few metres away from the pair; neither seemed to notice him, Jenna too intent on apparently torturing some sort of confession out of Janet, Janet simply doing her utmost to survive the latest attack on her person. What happened next filled Alex with delight even as it terrified him even more so for the future.

His frustration began to get the better of him; he wanted to stop Jenna, but after the kicking he'd gotten last time he'd intervened, he didn't want to physically touch her. It was all he could do to plead with Janet, and hope she could hear him over the noise of the crowd.

'Janet,' he said, unable to keep the desperation out of his voice. 'Janet, please, you have to fight back.'

Janet didn't look at him, or make any movement to show she'd even heard him speaking. He was hot now, standing so close to her; it was as if she was emanating heat, there on her hands and knees. Alex had no idea how such a thing could be possible. He stood still for a moment before pleading again, this time louder.

'Janet, it's not going to stop unless you stop it. She won't stop hitting you unless you make her.'

Jenna seemed to notice him now and paused for a second, looking at him through narrowed eyes.

'The fuck do you want?' she said to Alex, but he ignored her.

'Janet, please.' And a thought hit Alex from nowhere, was out of his mouth before he even realised what he was saying. 'Think of the flames.'

Now Janet moved. Alex didn't know why he'd said those words, where they'd come from, but they had the desired effect. Jenna was still standing still; whilst she still had a fistful of Janet's hair, her energy was all focused on Alex, and Janet used this opportunity to pounce.

She jumped to her feet, cat-like, Jenna's hand rising far above her heard as she did so. Jenna turned to Janet, a look of shock on her face, just in time to see Janet's fist connect with her face. The crowd gasped, both in shock and horror. They'd been quite happily watching Jenna beat up Janet, but they hadn't expect Janet to fight back. Alex was delighted, and clenched his fists with the thrill.

'Yes, Janet,' he whispered quietly to himself, silently praying she'd hit her again.

Jenna had let go of Janet's hair when Janet's fist collided with her face, and now she stood still, hands hanging limply at her sides, looking dazed; whether it was the pain or the shock and surprise of the punch, Alex didn't know. He didn't care, he was just so happy Janet had fought back.

The crowd, which had grown quiet in its shock, seemed to wake up. Slowly the volume rose once again; it grew even higher than it had been previously, as if the assembled pupils, shocked at first at the idea of the fight, now seemed to relish it. Alex even heard someone shout, "hit her again" and a ripple of laughter made its way through the crowd.

The two girls were now standing in the middle of the circle, staring at each other. Janets lips were moving ever so slightly as if she was saying something, but over the noise of the crowd baying for blood Alex couldn't make out any words. What he could see was a small wisp of smoke start to rise from Jenna's shoes. Jenna didn't seem to have noticed; she didn't take her eyes off Janet for a second, plainly wary of receiving a second punch.

Janet looked filled with a confidence Alex had only seen once before, for a moment, held entirely within the twirl Janet had done in her black dress. Alex felt his heart swell, felt his feelings rush in on himself. He fancied her so much, he really did, and he wanted to tell her. He wanted to scream it, let everyone hear. Instead he stood, part of the watching crowd, wondering what was going to happen next.

Jenna was the first to move; her hands, which had been limp by her sides, formed into fists again. She moved towards Janet and, with an animal roar, a primal sound, swung her fist towards Janet's face. Janets lips stopped moving as she dodged the punch with the practiced ease of a pro boxer, simply leaning to one side and letting it pass. The crowd cheered. Alex cheered.

Jenna swung again, and this time Janet didn't move quite quickly enough; Jenna's fist glanced off her ear and Janet moaned in pain. The crowd made an "oooooh" sound; it was like being at back at that first Harvest Festival boxing match. Only this time, rather than being disturbed by it all, Alex was among the people baying for blood. But unlike the crowd, he definitely cared from which fighter it came.

Sensing an advantage Jenna swung again; this time Janet not only dodged properly, but moved her entire body. She left one foot dangling out, however, and Jenna tripped over it and fell, throwing her arms out in front of her but not unballing her fists quickly enough. She landed on her face with an audible *thud.* The crowd broke into peals of laughter; Janet looked at the assembled faces then, as if noticing them for the first time, before quickly looking back at Jenna. It was a good thing she did, because in the split-second Janet had looked away Jenna was back on her feet and taking aim once again.

Jenna was clearly not a practiced fighter because the exact same thing happened: she swung, she missed, she tripped. Only this time she was able to unfurl her hands but it didn't help. As her outstretched palms collided with the playground a sickening scream wrenched the air. The crowd, sensing something was really wrong, that this had gone beyond what any of them expected, immediately fell silent. Janet knew something was wrong too, because she instantly moved towards Jenna, falling to one knee beside her.

'Are you okay?' Janet asked frantically, her voice high and fast.

'Get away from me,' Jenna screamed through her tears. She rolled into a sitting position and cradled her left forearm in her right hand close to her body. Even from where Alex was standing it was clear from the angle of it that the arm was broken. Aliyah and Francesca rushed to her side and squatted down, pushing Janet out of the way.

Janet's face was a picture of remorse; she tried to speak to Jenna again, but was again rebuked.

'I'm sorry, Jenna, I'm so sorry,' she said.

'Fuck off,' Aliyah said, and Francesca added, 'haven't you done enough?'

'I can help,' Janet said, reaching out for Jenna's arm with both her hands.

'Get the fuck away from me!' Jenna screamed with a ferocity Alex couldn't believe, more animal than woman. He was about to move towards Janet, pull her away, afraid of what Jenna could do with such a temper, even with a broken arm, when someone beat him to it.

At some point during the carnival a handful of teachers had arrived. The crowd quickly dispersed and soon it was just five pupils and three teachers. Mr Farridge and Miss Naveed were squatting down alongside Francesca and Aliyah next to Jenna, speaking to her. Miss Klein stood with Janet, speaking in a low voice Alex couldn't make out.

'It wasn't her fault,' Alex said, to no one in particular. No one so much as glanced at him.

Mr Farridge eased Jenna to her feet and then he, Miss Naveed, and the three girls set off towards the school building. Miss Naveed had already taken out her phone and was presumably calling Jenna's mum as they walked.

A moment later Miss Klein started walking Janet in the opposite direction, towards a different school building. Alex, assuming Janet was being taken to Mr Gullis' office, shouted at the backs of Janet and Miss Klein.

'It wasn't her fault, Miss, Janet didn't do anything wrong.'

'Be quiet, Alex,' Miss Klein hissed at him over her shoulder, before turning back around.

Alex stood still, feeling helpless. He was about to walk away when Janet turned and looked at him over her shoulder; her eyes, normally hidden, were plain for him to see. They were as blue as the summer sky and brimming with tears. As they looked at each other, a single drop rolled slowly Janet's left cheek. Alex touched his own cheek and his fingers came away wet.

The sight of Janet, innocent Janet, once again beaten, and now in trouble for it, broke Alex's heart. It also steeled him into action. Without running back to Tom and Mo to get his bag, without telling any of the teachers, he ran across the playground, through the gates and onto the street. Instead of running home he ran the opposite way, towards the dirt track that led to the Willerbys' house.

If the previous weekend he'd felt the need to warn Mrs Willerby, now it was more important than ever. He didn't know what was going to come from this whole sorry episode, but he knew it would be nothing good. Nothing good at all. He thought the Willerbys might be lucky to escape alive.

Chapter Twenty-Two

Alex ran as fast as he could; he heard distant rumbles of thunder, closely followed by a bright flash of lightning and then more thunder. Other than a brief thought that the storm must be very close he paid it no mind; he kept his head bowed, pushing his legs up and down as fast as they would go.

His heart was pounding, not just from the exercise but from everything that had happened. He knew he should go to Miss Klein, Mr Farridge, Naveed, Gullis, anyone, rather than Mrs Willerby, but still he ran. He knew he should go to them and explain what had happened, what Jenna had done, explain the fact that Janet hadn't actually done anything herself. All she'd done was dodge an incoming blow, and Jenna had fallen and broken her own arm. If Janet got in trouble for it he'd, he'd…

He stopped: what would he do? And more so than that, what *could* he do? Standing in the middle of Deerborn, the raining starting to fall in light drops on and around him, Alex realised something, something most people only learn when they're much older, and through a great deal of trial and error: he was completely and utterly powerless.

Even as he felt it the realisation, at the same time as being devastating, was also freeing. He was powerless to do anything at all to protect Janet, Mrs Willerby, to stop Jenna or Emma or Mr Sullivan or whoever. And as he thought this, he had another realisation: *that's what Mrs Willerby meant!*

Her riddle hadn't been a riddle after all; she'd been telling him plain and true, he was just too stupid to notice it. Much like his grandfather and Hugh Sullivan had tried to stop Mrs Willerby senior, Janet's grandmother, so indeed would the current Mr Sullivan try and stop the current Mrs Willerby.

But where the seniors had simply tried to remove the Willerbys and sell their land, he worried Mr Sullivan would do something worse. Even though Alex was only fifteen and couldn't comprehend what it felt like, he'd seen enough cop shows on TV and in the cinema to know that people did funny things when their kids were involved. He'd seen this story once about a woman whose kid had been hit by a car, which had then rolled on top of the child. The mother, just a normal woman, had lifted the car off her child and saved his life. Just a normal woman, and she'd managed to lift an entire car! What would someone like Mr Sullivan, already very powerful, do to save his kid? Or think he was saving his kid anyway? Alex also knew that, when it came to kids, a lot of parents didn't see reason. *Just look at Emma*, he thought. There was no reason there, and yet her dad defended her constantly. None of it made any sense to Alex.

He was just about to start running again, one final push to get to the dirt track, when something caught his eye. Looking up and to the left he saw a bird looking at him from a tree, black as obsidian except for circles of white surrounding its eyes. He was in the middle of putting it out of his mind when he realised he'd seen the bird before; it was the same crow as his last trip to Mrs Willerby's house. He and the crow looked at each other for a moment, then with a caw the black bird jumped off its perch, flew over to Alex, and dropped something in his hand.

Alex looked down and realised it was a piece of paper, folded into a tiny little square. He slowly unfolded it and saw a handwritten note; he looked up to thank the crow but it was nowhere to be seen. It hadn't returned to the tree, instead flying away.

Alex was hesitant to read the note; he knew pigeons carried messages for people but he didn't think any other birds did. Unbidden, images of the crow on Mrs Willerby's shoulder and Janet exchanging looks with the white cat entered his mind. He dismissed them, flattening the note in his hand, and read it:

Alex, thank you kindly for once again coming to warn me. I know what's happened; Janet will be home soon to tell me, but I already know. You needn't worry; I told you it was coming, and it is, but not just yet. Soon, but not yet. It'll be him, and he won't come alone. Others will leave, some will remain, but he'll not go. He'll not let go. *He's not like his father, who though he was a bad man would at least listen to reason. It's just a shame my dear old mother used bad reasoning as well as good. Go home my boy, and take care of yourself. You're a good lad, and I thank you for everything you've done today for Janet. Our kind aren't liked around here, but some people, like you, like your father, make us think that one day we might be. If only I'd live to see it. It's almost funny; every year at the Harvest Festival the people of this village get together to celebrate icons they don't believe in. Yet when I celebrate them, it's… well, never mind what it is. Go home and spend the evening with your family, because you never know when you might lose them. Don't worry about Janet and me, this will all be over in a little while. If Janet comes to you, please continue to be kind to her. Thank you.*

Alex read the note twice; both times he turned it over afterwards looking for more, or to see if it was signed, but the unsigned front page was all there was to it. Alex had more questions than answers; how did Mrs Willerby know about Janet? How did she know he was coming to warn her? And what did she mean, *you never know when you might lose your family?* Was she talking about Janet, or Joseph, or did she know something about Alex's future? He folded and put the note in his pocket with a shudder, and headed home.

Chapter Twenty-Three

As Alex walked through the village, head still bowed, neck still bent at an angle only the youth can achieve, his brain wouldn't stop turning over and over the thought that something bad was going to happen to Janet. He'd only just realised how special she was, how much he wanted to spend time with her, and now she might be taken from him. What was he supposed to do? Once more he felt powerless, but this time it was less freeing, and a lot more devastating.

By the time he arrived home tears were streaming down his face, and as he pushed open the front door and stepped inside, his mum poked her head out of the kitchen door to see who it was. She had a mixing bowl under one arm and had been stirring its contents using a wooden spoon with the other; she now stood still, looking at Alex, confusion on her face. She glanced at the clock.

'Are you okay, son? Why are you home at this time?'

As she said this, Alex realised he had no idea what time it actually was. He took his phone out of his pocket and glanced at it; as well as several messages and missed calls from Mo and Tom, which he ignored, his phone informed him that it was just after 2pm. It had only been half an hour since he ran away from school; he couldn't believe it, it felt like it'd been days.

'I…' he began, before breaking into tears completely. He sagged where he stood, his body seeming to collapse in on itself, visibly deflating. His mum popped back into the kitchen for a second and when she re-emerged she'd put down the bowl and wooden spoon and was wiping her hands on her stained red and white checkered pinafore.

'Come here, dear, oh it's okay,' she said, moving to him down the hallway. When she reached him she wrapped him in a gigantic hug and Alex fell into her, gave himself to her without holding anything back. He felt like he was five years old again but didn't care, he welcomed the idea of giving himself up to his mother completely.

He sobbed openly, the sounds wrenching the still air of the house. The sobs bounced back at Alex from the walls and ceiling; they felt like a taunt, like the house was laughing at him. The pair stood quietly for several minutes, Alex's mum doing nothing but holding him, Alex eventually moving from sobs to whimpers before he was able to control himself.

'What is it, dear?' Alex's mum asked him, but even though he'd finished crying he was unable to speak and simply shook his head. 'It's okay, son,' she said in a soft coo, trying her best to reassure him. 'Go upstairs and lie down, and I'll come up soon and check on you. Do you want anything?'

Alex snivelled, wiped his nose with the back of his hand, wiped his eyes, shook his head.

'Okay, dear.'

She didn't say anything more, and after a moment of hesitation Alex trudged up the stairs. Halfway up he heard his mum say quietly, 'I love you, son,' but he didn't stop, didn't turn, didn't reply. He simply carried on moving slowly to his room.

The next thing Alex knew his mum was sitting on the edge of his bed, gently shaking him awake.

'Alex, Alex,' she repeatedly softly, her voice like a warm hug. Alex rubbed his eyes as he slowly came to; he was on top of his duvet, still in his school uniform. He looked at his mum, bleary eyed, and tried to smile but was unable. There was no part of him that felt like smiling.

'What time is it?' he mumbled quietly.

'It's just after half seven.'

'Wow, I slept late,' he said, stretching. 'What's for dinner?'

Alex's mum paused for a second before responding.

'No son,' she said. 'It's half seven *in the morning*. You slept all night.'

'What?' Alex said, not understanding.

'After you went up yesterday afternoon I left you for a while. When I came to check you were fast asleep and looked so peaceful I didn't want to disturb you. I kept checking throughout the evening, but it was the same every time, so your dad and I decided to just leave you to it.'

Alex looked at her, still not fully comprehending. He'd slept all night? It was morning, time for school again? It couldn't be?

'What do you mean? Is it time for school?' Alex asked.

'I'm afraid so, son,' his dad boomed. Alex looked up and saw him standing in the doorway, tying a tie around his neck with some difficulty. 'I thought we should wake you, I didn't want you to sleep from school right through until school again, but your mum insisted.'

Alex's mum nodded, a look of concern etched into her features.

'You've had a rough few weeks, son, and by the looks of it the sleep has done you the world of good,' his dad said. Alex said nothing, simply listened to his parents speak.

'Why don't you jump in the shower and I'll make you some breakfast?' his mum offered. Remaining quiet Alex nodded, stretched, and stood up. His legs wobbled slightly, but he managed to make it to the bathroom in one piece. His parents watched him go, and the more they looked at Alex the more uncomfortable he felt. He did his best to hide it; his parents seemed genuinely pleased he'd slept all night and he didn't want to dispel their concern, reject it, seem ungrateful.

An hour later, clean, wearing fresh clothes, and with a hot breakfast in his stomach, Alex felt a lot better. He still felt less than human, thoughts of Janet and her potentially impending doom, fear for what might happen to her, still dominated his thoughts, but he at least felt physically better, even if he didn't emotionally or mentally.

His dad had left whilst he was in the shower; 'Job interview,' his mum said, optimism lacing her voice for the first time in a while. 'A good one, with a bank. We're hopeful. If he can get this one, with the Harvest Festival coming up…' Alex thought she did indeed look hopeful, it was carved on her face. Alex also hoped it worked out for his dad, but only in a cursory way; really he didn't care too much. He could only think of Janet.

His mum asked if he wanted to skip school, take a day off, but Alex said no, told her he wanted to go, get back to normal. The school had rung, his mum said, but she'd told them he was unwell, made excuses so he wasn't in any trouble. Alex thanked his mum, but didn't care: the only trouble he was concerned with was any that Janet might be in. She was the reason he wanted to go to school.

He was standing in the hallway, shoes on, looking confused, when he remembered why he couldn't find his coat and bag. One of the messages Mo had sent – after his excitement had died down and he stopped saying teachers were freaking about his absence, they were fuming, he was in so much shit – said that Mo had his bag and coat and would take them to school for him. Alex had replied saying *thanks*, ignoring all the other messages. Whatever happened, despite what his mum said about him not being in trouble, would happen.

He opened the door, his mum watching from the living room doorway, and stepped outside.

'Bye, Mum, see you later,' he yelled over his shoulder, before pulling the door closed behind him. He walked down the path and was about to open the small white gate separating his garden from the street when he froze, one hand on the gate, the other in his pocket.

On the other side of the gate, staring at him, stood Janet.

Chapter Twenty-Four

They stood in silence facing each other. Alex kept one hand on the gate, unmoving; Janet was standing with her arms straight by her sides, her school uniform as limp and uninspiring as ever, her hair matted, clumped with – Alex now saw – bits of dirt and leaves. Even as his heart pounded at seeing her, he felt a dart of revulsion at her appearance. But, he also realised, he didn't actually care. He didn't care how she looked, or indeed how he did, a kid who'd slept most of the previous day, outside in October without a coat. He only cared that she was there, and so was he.

'Hi,' he said eventually, forcing himself to speak, to acknowledge her.

'Hi,' she whispered back, so quietly he barely heard her.

'How are you?' Alex asked timidly, his own voice barely above a whisper.

'I'm fine,' she replied, and Alex believed her. Her face, that once again should have been a constellation of bruises, was completely clear. There wasn't a single sign she'd been attacked the previous day; there weren't even any marks on her clothing or anything. Alex wanted to ask how, why, but didn't dare, because he thought he knew the answer.

'How are you?' Janet asked him.

'I'm fine,' he said, genuinely. Just being in her presence for a few moments had made him forget anything else. Being near her was the only thing that mattered.

'Are you going to school?' Alex asked, gesturing in its direction with his head, his hands still on the gate and in his pocket respectively.

'No,' she replied. 'I'm suspended.'

'What?' Alex said, his eyes wide, incredulous. 'What do you mean?'

'One week suspension for fighting,' Janet replied simply, no inflection in her voice, as if the concept of being banned from school didn't move her at all.

'But you weren't fighting!' Alex said, the unfairness of it coursing through his veins and arteries. 'All you did was move, Jenna fell over and broke her own arm.'

'I also punched her in the face.'

'Well yeah, but–' Alex began, but Janet cut him off.

'It's okay, Alex,' she said, and any response he'd been about to make was silenced by hearing his name in her voice. Alex. *Alex*. She'd said it, she'd just said it, using her actual mouth and her actual words. Alex thought he'd never heard anything so magical.

'But–' he began again, but she cut him off again.

'I promise, it's okay,' Janet said, and then she did

something that changed Alex's life forever. Her left hand twitched, seemed to want to move then stop, before slowly rising. Alex noticed it and watched it as it rose as if in slow motion, moving towards him, and came to rest gently on top of his hand. He held the gate, and Janet held him, and Alex thought he'd never felt anything more wonderful. Her hand was warm, soft, and he felt safe and comforted; he felt at home. He recognised the feeling from when she'd helped him escape school a few weeks previously, and he savoured it once more. Nothing bad could happen when Janet was touching him.

He realised he was staring at her hand on his and forced himself to look at her. Her eyes were down too, but she slowly raised them to meet his.

'It's okay, I only go to school so my mum doesn't get in trouble. There's nothing anyone there can teach me.'

Alex didn't understand this so didn't respond. Instead he simply looked into her eyes, stared into them deeply, lost himself. They were a burning orange, a beautiful colour, one he'd never seen in the human eye, one he didn't even think was possible. Plus, hadn't they been blue before? He was shocked from this train of thought when Janet spoke once more.

'Will you come with me? I want to show you something.'

'But I have to go to school,' he said, realising how lame it sounded as the words left his mouth. Why on earth would he go to school? Why would he do anything other than what Janet wanted?

'Please–' Janet began, but now Alex cut her off.

'Yes,' he said, firmly, as if to convince himself more than her.

Janet's face lit up; her eyes glowed even brighter, to the point Alex nearly had to look away. He could feel her retinas scorching his. But he couldn't look away, he realised; Janet was holding on to him somehow, she had him in her spell. He shuddered at the word, its implications, but really it was the only one that fit. He was under Janet's spell, and he couldn't be happier about it.

'Really?' she asked, as if she didn't believe him.

'Of course. I'll go anywhere with you.'

He hadn't known he was going to say these words until they were out of his mouth, but as he did he instantly knew they were true; he would go anywhere, do anything for Janet. If she asked him to walk off a cliff, he'd do so happily. He'd fall into the sea and drown with a smile, knowing his last actions had been to obey her.

'Are you sure? It's–'

'I'm sure,' he said, and he was. He'd never been so sure of anything else in his life.

Janet smiled, and even through her lank hair, the dirt on her face, her scruffy uniform, Alex thought she was beautiful.

Chapter Twenty-Five

Alex nervously followed Janet towards the end of the street; Main Street was teeming with kids heading to school, adults fastidiously walking younger children to the primary school clinging to their hands all the while, adults heading to work. In such a small village everyone knew everyone, and Alex had no idea how he was going to get away with skipping school, to pass unnoticed. Janet was fine, she was suspended; besides, no one cared about her anyway, Alex thought with a pang in his stomach. He wasn't suspended, people did care about him – at least to an extent – and his absence would be commented on, the fact he was walking away from school rather than to it would be noted. He gave voice to these concerns, the first words the pair had exchanged since they started walking.

'Janet,' Alex whispered to her, a few feet away from the top of his street, 'we have to wait.'

'Why?' she asked, turning to look at him and mirroring his whisper.

'People will see me, they'll wonder where I'm going.

You're okay, you've been suspended, but I'm supposed to be in school.'

Janet looked at him for a moment, her face nearly neutral; she had a small amount of concern and confusion, but that was all. She was regarding Alex as if what he was saying was very stupid.

'You'll be fine,' she said to him softly, gently, reassuring him. 'Just take my hand.'

Alex looked down and saw she'd stretched her arm out, holding her hand out to him, palm up, waiting. Alex moved his arm slowly, hoping Janet didn't notice how much he was shaking. It was anticipation, he told himself, excitement and anticipation, not fear. He wasn't scared at all, he told himself. Tried to convince himself.

He put his hand in hers, and instantly all his concerns vanished. It was like he'd drunk liquid confidence; standing at the top of his street, holding Janet's hand, Alex felt invincible. No longer was he scared of being spotted and called out, told on. In fact, he found, he wasn't scared of anything. He wasn't scared of Janet, and what he almost definitely knew to be true about her. He wasn't scared of Mr Sullivan, what he might try and do to Mrs Willerby and the house she shared with her daughter. He wasn't scared that he'd fail all his exams at the end of the year, that his dad would never find a job, or that whoever had taken Joseph would take more children; all Alex felt was alive, truly alive. There was fire inside Janet, he knew that now, and holding her hand allowed him to feel it.

And it warmed his soul.

'Are you ready to go?'

Alex turned and saw Janet was looking at him, and he smiled at her, a genuine smile he could feel lighting up his face, transforming him from scared boy to confident young man. He nodded and they set off, hand in hand, up Main Street, the school at their backs and the world opening up in front of them.

It was a warm morning, an Indian Summer morning, and people were walking without coats, without hats and scarves and umbrellas. Even as they hurried, Joseph's disappearance no doubt on their minds, they were walking with their heads held high, embracing the sun much like plants, tilting their faces towards it knowing it might not come back until next year.

Alex was amazed; despite the fact everyone was walking with their faces turned up, no one looked at Janet and him as they passed. Not a single person: he tried to avoid looking at people at first, still feeling confident but not wanting to push his luck. Soon after he realised people weren't looking at them, he started staring intensely into every face he passed, almost willing them to look his way. No one did. Alex knew he wasn't invisible, knew it wasn't possible, but still…

'Janet,' Alex said, and she turned her face up to his. Even though it was only a small movement, not one that could even be considered a gesture, Janet turning her face to his unlocked something in Alex, and he felt his heart level up. He didn't know exactly what that meant, nor how he would have described it if anyone had asked, but that was the only way he could explain how Janet looking at him like that made him feel. He was no longer the Alex that had left his house that morning, had run away from school the previous day, had been sleep walking through his life for so long. He was a new and better Alex, an improved version. Alex 2.0.

Janet didn't say anything, but her face was so inviting Alex continued regardless; he was rapt by her rapture.

'How come no one can see us?' he asked, deciding directness was the best course of action. He'd decided this because it felt right, and following his feelings, at least whilst he was holding Janet's hand and was completely invincible, seemed the best way to proceed.

'They can,' was Janet's simple reply.

'What do you mean? Everyone is looking right past us, it's as if we're not here,' Alex said, before adding: 'y'know, not visible.'

'Don't worry,' Janet said, a smile creasing her features, causing her cheeks to bunch, small dimples appearing either side of her mouth. Alex wanted to scream at the top of his lungs, start a fire, do something that would draw the world's attention to what he was seeing, how beautiful she was. 'We're both here, and visible.'

'But they're not seeing us at all?' Alex asked, reassured by Janet's smile but still curious.

'They're choosing not to,' Janet said simply. Alex found her short, clipped replies more confusing than illuminating.

'What do you mean?'

Janet stopped; they'd travelled most of the village,

and with a start Alex saw they were nearing the top of the track that led to Janet's house. Was that where she was taking him? Would he be allowed inside, be able to pass the invisible barrier that had held him back before? Once they were inside, would they…

He forced himself to stop wondering. Whatever happened would happen; he felt safe with Janet, and knew she'd allow no harm to come to him. He'd go anywhere she wished; everywhere would be heaven as long as she was by his side.

'People see what they want to see,' Janet said, her face now turned away from Alex's, back into that old familiar pose of being downcast. Alex wanted to grab her chin, have her look at him again, but he didn't know how.

There was a sadness to Janet's words that permeated through the good feeling that had enveloped Alex; it was a thread he wanted to pull, to unravel, but before he could ask any more Janet started walking again. Alex matched her stride.

They did indeed head down the track, through the tall hedges; the white cat appeared once again but didn't stop, simply glanced at Janet and whispered a soft miaow as it dashed from the bushes to their left and flew into the undergrowth on their right.

'Morning, Lisheen,' Janet said happily, and Alex couldn't help but say 'morning' too. Why he was talking to a cat he didn't know, it just felt right.

They continued down the track, following the now familiar curve to the right, and Janet's house came into view. Alex hesitated as they approached the end of the path, anticipating having to stop, but Janet continued walking without breaking a step, and Alex walked with her.

Passing into the clearing, Alex stopped and looked around. Janet's hand slipped from his as he did so, but it was okay, Alex thought, the feeling of comfort and safety remained. Alex was looking for two reasons; firstly, because the area looked completely different from the inside than it had from the out, and secondly, because it was the most incredible place he'd ever seen.

From where from the track ended, the area surrounding the house looked ragged, the grass patchy, soil and flowerbeds overgrown, in need of repair. The small shed was missing planks, the door hung off its hinges. From beyond the boundary, however, it was perfect.

The lawn was complete and even, no patches, and it was a glorious, deep green. Alex longed to take off his shoes and socks and walk on it barefoot; he thought it'd be like walking in caramel. The flowerbeds were well kept too, neatly bordered with no soil spilling out. The plants, which from the outside looked dead and in need of removing, were thriving. There were glorious red roses, tulips of every colour, great purple shoots of lavender, and a million other flowers Alex didn't know the names of. They were in full bloom, and Alex thought they were incredible. Not just the vibrant colours but the smells too; the heavy scents hit his nostrils and he felt alive with their power, he felt at one with them.

The shed was in perfect condition, as if it had been

erected that morning by a team of professionals with the utmost care. To his left, not visible from the track, was a swing set. The metal was a brilliant red, the paint unchipped. The chains showed no sign of rust; again, they looked brand new.

In fact, Alex realised, the only thing that didn't look different was the house itself. And that was just fine, Alex thought; someone like Mr Sullivan would never understand, but the house was beautiful. And somehow, standing where it did surrounded by the beauty of nature, instead of looking shabby in comparison, it only looked more impressive. Alex was suddenly envious of Janet and where she lived. It was the garden of Eden, he thought, and although he wasn't completely sure what that meant, he knew it was true.

'Janet,' he began, and he tried to say more but his words caught in his throat. He'd been so busy looking at the garden, he hadn't looked at her. If the garden was a thing of beauty, Janet was transcendent.

Alex didn't know if it was because he'd passed into the garden, or if she'd nipped off and changed, but it didn't matter. What did matter was that he was seeing Janet as he'd seen her only once before, the last time he'd been present when she was in the garden. Her hair was shining in the morning sunlight, beautiful and straight, framing her face, which itself was a sight to behold. Her skin was clean and clear, her cheeks shining too, with a radiance that took Alex aback.

Her eyes were open, the orange of them also shining in the morning light. Their colour tempted Alex, he was drawn to it. He wanted to be enveloped by it, become one with it.

Most importantly, in Alex's eyes, her clothes had changed too. Gone was her shabby school uniform with its black marks, frayed threads, and loose hems. Back was the black dress Alex had seen her wear only for a few moments previously. Up close, it was even more beautiful than he remembered.

It had long sleeves that opened out at the wrists violently, changing from snug to incredibly flowing. The body was tight, cut into a V-shape just above her… breasts. Alex was taken aback again as he saw the tops of them, he swallowed hard as he noticed how smooth the skin looked. He forced himself to look away; Janet was looking at him, and he didn't want to ruin it by being a little pervert.

The dress was short, stopping mid-thigh like a ballerina's skirt. Below it Janet was wearing black tights, and on her feet simple black pumps. Alex couldn't take his eyes off her, the transformation was incredible; Janet was incredible. He was lost for words, lost for actions, lost for anything. If his body didn't do it automatically, he thought he might forget to breathe.

Janet watched him watching her for a moment, before turning, once again the lower part of her dress flowing outwards, and bounded off. With a skip of his heartbeat, Alex thought she was going into her house, but at the last minute she turned left and moved along the front of it, trailing a hand on the lumpy brickwork. She turned at the end of the house and traced its side, and was about to disappear from view when she stopped and turned to Alex.

'Are you coming?' she said. 'There's something I need to show you.'

Chapter Twenty-Six

Alex followed Janet without hesitation; as he moved closer to the house he felt a pulse, although whether it was emanating from within the house or himself he couldn't tell. He thought it might have been both: he thought the pulse might have originated from the house, but his body had taken it up as he drew closer, drawn in by the pulse itself, by the promise it held.

He followed the same route as Janet; he passed a small window and glanced in but couldn't see anything; the sun was too bright, the room too dim, to allow for visibility. Up close, the house was in an even greater state of disrepair than it had looked from the end of the track; the bricks it was made of were crumbling, many with large pockmarks in them. They were balanced unevenly; the wall he was traversing reminded him of the dry-stone walls that separated the fields behind his house. They were haphazardly put together, looked like they were in danger of falling at any moment, but yet, as his mum had told him when he asked, they'd stood for hundreds of years, and would stand for hundreds more. Though covered with moss and lichen they persevered through the years, through the seasons, and Alex thought this house was the same.

Alex felt that idea strongly as he walked along the front of the house: no matter what happened on this land, no matter what fate befell the Willerbys, no matter what anyone tried to do with them or to them or impose on them, the house would survive. It would survive, Alex knew without knowing how, because it was alive. And because it always did. He was slowly beginning to understand what Mrs Willerby had said about time repeating itself, it being a flat circle. The house would survive because it had survived before; it would survive because it would survive again. He knew this made no sense, and yet it made perfect sense to him.

Alex soon reached the corner and turned, still retracing Janet's steps. She was at the end of the side wall at the back of the house, facing him; one hand was resting on the wall, slowly moving up and down, as if stroking the house, petting it like it was a living creature. The other was on her hip, in a gesture that Alex would come to understand later in life signified impatience, although that morning he had no idea.

The land on the side of the house was shaded and cool; they were in the house's shadow, and the temperature had dropped slightly. But only slightly; although October was drawing to a close it was a warm morning, fresh and clear. There was moisture in the air, and dew on the ground, but otherwise it could have been any morning in June or July, the start of a beautiful summer's day.

Janet watched Alex as he approached; the closer he got to her, the faster his heart was beating and the warmer he felt. He longed to be by her side, to hold her hand again, to be led by her. His hand, the one that had enveloped Janet's – or been enveloped by it, he wasn't sure – was still warm, the trace of Janet still lingered there, the shadow of her touch. He remembered an old episode of *The Simpsons* his dad had shown him, when Bart had touched the hand of the girl he had a crush on and had vowed never to wash it again; Alex wasn't going to go that far, but he completely understood Bart's impulse. He wanted to bring his hand close to his face, smell it, rub it along his cheek and imagine it was Janet's hand touching him. But she was watching him, looking at him with her head cocked as if enjoying his movements, and so he did nothing other than focus everything he had on walking normally, on not stumbling, on not making an idiot of himself.

As he neared Janet she turned, her skirt once again flowing outwards, and bounded off ahead of him, behind the back of the house. Alex was frustrated; it felt like chasing someone in a dream, always so close yet always out of reach, always on the verge of being grasped by his fingertips but always slipping away at the last moment. Mixed in with the frustration was anticipation, which was reaching a level he'd never felt before. He'd had crushes on other girls, there was no denying that – he still remembered the months he'd pined after Laura Green, watching her in lessons, on the playground at break and lunch – but what he felt for Janet eclipsed that entirely. If that had been a schoolboy crush, Alex thought, then this was love. He didn't know what love was, but he thought he felt it all the same.

Alex emerged at the back of the house and his breath caught in his throat. The view was spectacular. From the street, because of the high hedges, you could only see the track leading to the house, as well as the top of the house, the roof and chimney. From the end of the track your vision was still narrowed, you could see a bit of the garden, the front of the house, and that was it. It was like wearing blinkers. From any vantage point, no matter where you stood, there were no clues whatsoever about this secret, hidden vista that was the Willerbys' back garden.

The land opened up into a beautiful valley; the ground ran away beneath his feet, a small dirt path leading towards a collection of trees that Alex thought was probably too small to be called a forest, was perhaps just a wood or a copse. He'd read that word in a book recently then looked it up in the dictionary; it felt right here.

The collection of trees was directly in front of where he stood, on the valley floor; to its left was a small pond, or at least it looked small from where he stood, but he was too far away to really know. The water shimmered in the morning sun, impossibly blue and impossibly still.

To the right of the trees were fields full of the most wonderful colours Alex could imagine, reds and greens and blues and yellows, all shining vibrantly in the morning sun. It looked like a picture he'd once seen of tulip fields in the Netherlands, a rainbow of colours stretching from here to eternity. The fields glowed, for the valley behind the house was bathed in sunlight; the surrounding fields were in semi-shadow, not completely dark but nowhere near as bright as the valley Janet had presented Alex. It was like, he thought, the sun shone just for Janet. And in that moment, standing there, he knew that to be true.

Between the house and the trees, the pond, the fields, was empty grass, broken only by the small dirt track, perhaps no more than two or three feet wide. Alex came to stand beside Janet, who was no longer moving; she stood with her back to the house, facing the valley, and as Alex turned and looked at her he saw a supreme calmness on her face. The beauty of it nearly made his legs turn to jelly, he nearly fell to the floor.

It was only in that moment Alex realised Janet's usual facial expression was one of extreme pain. He knew she suffered and struggled daily, perennially with her head bowed, not saying anything, with her dirty skin and hair, her dirty clothes. School was an unforgiving place, and Janet ticked pretty much all the boxes bullies like Emma looked for. But standing here, Alex thought he was seeing the true Janet, the *real* Janet.

Her face was blank, but not empty. Her eyes were wide, their brilliant orange reflecting the morning sun, giving it a fire as it touched the land. Her mouth was open, and Alex thought her lips might have been moving, as if she was whispering something. He tried to listen but couldn't hear anything other than far away birds chattering, leaves rustling in a slight breeze, the sound of a bee buzzing nearby. Alex was about to ask her what she was saying, stopped himself, then asked anyway; it was just Janet and him, and he might never have the opportunity again.

'Janet,' he said softly, for she looked like she was in a trance and he didn't want to startle her. Not, he realised as he thought this, that he could scare her if he tried. He could feel her, standing there beside him. He could feel her power.

Janet didn't respond for a moment, instead continuing to stare ahead, unblinking, lips slightly moving. Alex didn't repeat himself; after another minute or so Janet's lips came to rest, she blinked rapidly as if just waking up, and a smile showed on her lips. She turned her head to look at Alex.

'Hello,' she said to him, as if only just noticing he was there. She smiled as she said it, her voice a soft lilt, and Alex's heart broke and was repaired and broke all over again. He was definitely in love.

'Were you,' he began, hesitating, not sure how to phrase the question. He opted for simplicity. 'Did you just say something?'

Janet nodded, keeping her eyes focused on Alex's, the smile still sitting on her face. When she didn't say anything, Alex continued.

'What were you saying?' asked Alex, keeping his voice low, not wanting to be overheard. The fact there was no one for miles around, that he could have shouted and his words remained private, didn't occur to Alex.

'I was saying hello, and giving my thanks.'

She said it was if it made perfect sense, although to Alex it gave him no answers, only more questions.

'To who?' he asked, his voice now barely above a whisper. His heart was still pounding, and he realised again that mingled into the excitement and pleasure of being with Janet, he was scared. Scared of her. Scared of where she was taking him. Scared of what it all would mean. Scared it might end.

'You'll see,' she said, and with that she skipped off down the dirt path, laughing as she did so. Alex didn't move; he stood stunned, still looking at the spot Janet had occupied until only a moment ago. With a wrench he turned his head and saw Janet had stopped a few metres down the path and was looking back over her shoulder at him.

'Come on,' she said, the smile on her face echoed in her voice. 'We're nearly there.'

With that she bounded off down the path once more, her skirt and hair flying wildly behind her as she skipped gaily. Alex watched for another moment before he managed to force his feet into action and began running after her. He was scared, yes, but also more excited than he'd ever been in his life. Janet was going to take him into the woods, he knew, and show him something, reveal part of herself to him. He couldn't wait, he was hungry for the knowledge.

He was ready to know Janet as her true self.

Chapter Twenty-Seven

Even though the field separating the house and the wooded area had looked huge to Alex from the vantage point of the house, he and Janet covered it in a matter of minutes. Janet was well ahead of him the entire way, her hair flying out behind her, a trail of beauty and joy Alex tried his hardest to join up with. No matter how fast he ran, how hard he pushed his legs up and down, no matter how much of himself he put into that sprint, he wasn't even close to matching Janet. Although she barely seemed to be trying, her speed was infinitely faster than his, and so she was waiting at the edge of the wood when he finally arrived.

Alex stopped, bent at the waist, hands on his knees, desperately sucking up air like a drowning man. Janet stood once again with her hand on her hip, on her face a look of amused scorn.

'Took your time, eh?' she said to Alex. She said it with a lightness in her voice, making it clear she was only winding him up.

Alex tried to respond, but he was still too out of

breath; it was everything he had in himself to stay as upright as he was, and not simply lay down at Janet's feet. That was actually something he thought he might end up doing one day, if he was lucky, but that was another conversation for another time.

Janet left him alone for a moment, turning to face the wood, looking inside it. When it became clear that Alex still needed more time to recover, Janet looked frustrated. Turning around, she placed her hand on Alex's bare arm, closed her eyes and whispered under her breath.

Alex suddenly felt an incredible power rush through him; if asked, he would have described it like how Popeye looked in the cartoons when he ate spinach. Alex felt the power running up and down his arms and legs, through his chest; he was no longer short of breath, he was able to stand up straight and talk properly.

'What was that?' were the only words he could find. Janet smiled at him but didn't reply, instead turning back to the woods.

'Shall we?' she offered, and stepped across the tree line and inside.

Like a faithful hound, Alex once again followed her. It was much cooler in the woods, the air shaded from the sun, which by that time was beating down a blistering heat. Alex hadn't realised how much the heat had affected him until he was basking in its absence.

Everything was much cooler and chiller in the woods; the tree cover was thick, meaning it was dimmer too than the field he'd just run across, but there was still more than enough light to see everything. It reminded Alex of the forests he ran through when he was playing Zelda, running around as the main character, Link, dashing between trees and avoiding prickly bushes.

Janet was moving ahead of him with a confidence he couldn't help but admire, and longed to replicate. There was no discernible path, but Janet moved as if there was, as if she knew exactly where she was going. Alex did his best to follow but it was rough going; the forest was thick, the trees and bushes growing wildly in every direction, no sense of any sort of order was at all present.

But where Alex had to move slowly, cautiously, dodging tree branches and bushes that almost seemed to be reaching for him, desperate to grab him in their wooden fingers to never let go, Janet moved as if they were still in the field and there were no obstacles at all. Where Alex had to look before placing his feet down for every step, cautious not to stand on any of the bright plants or gloomy-coloured but hopeful looking mushrooms, Janet walked at a normal place, seeming to somehow just know where to put her feet down without asking.

As well as the trees, bushes, plants and other natural flora, the forest, at least based on what Alex could hear, was teeming with animal life. Birdsong came from every direction, and even though Alex knew nothing about birds, he could make out myriad separate tunes that meant there must have been scores of birds hidden away in the branches above his head. It was a cacophony, a symphony; the songs were disparate, clashing with each other, and yet somehow the sound was still pleasant to

Alex's ears.

It was complemented by the hooting of owls, which confused Alex; he was sure owls were nocturnal, he'd seen *Planet Earth*. The wood was dark, sure, but not dark enough that anyone, especially an animal with their inbuilt sense of time, would confuse it for night. Even under the heavy canopy of the trees, it was very clearly still a bright and sunny day, anyone – or any*thing* – could see that.

Crickets chirping, grasshoppers rubbing their legs together, frogs croaking; Alex thought he could hear all the varieties of insect you might find in a giant forest, condensed down into this small wood. It wasn't big, at least it didn't look it from the outside, and yet somehow from the inside it seemed vast, endless. Alex felt he could have walked for hours, days even, and not reach the other side.

The thought suddenly threatened to overwhelm him; he'd been so invested in looking at the trees and bushes to his sides, the branches above him, so interested in trying to spot even one animal which was contributing to the music that wasn't so much hitting his ears as completely enveloping his entire person, that he realised he couldn't see Janet.

He stopped moving and scanned the area he'd last seen her, directly in front of him; she was long gone. Again, he thought, though she was wearing all black, and the wood was dark, it was nowhere near dark enough to be camouflaged. The forest was awash with greens, yellows, reds, browns. Even in the low light he should have been able to see her easily, and was alarmed he couldn't. He looked left and right, searching as best as he could, trying to pick his way through the tangled branches and plants, bushes and grass.

When he couldn't see her on either side of himself he spun quickly on the spot, wondering if maybe he'd accidentally turned himself around and she was behind him, where she'd always been. There was no sign of her behind him, or indeed in any direction. He continued to turn on the spot, looking up and down, all around, but there was nothing. He was completely alone.

Where before, when he was with Janet, the wood had seemed beautiful, welcoming, the disorderliness of it quaint and charming, it now began to feel sinister. The branches and bushes seemed to be reaching for him as if they wished to do him harm, as if they wanted to grasp him and never let go until he became one of them. The mushrooms, which were so numerous all around his feet, suddenly seemed like they were very poisonous, and all Alex would have to do would be to brush one gently and he'd die. The branches overhead no longer seemed like they were protecting him from the harsh sunlight; it now seemed like the wooden canopy was keeping him trapped inside, preventing him from ever leaving.

Alex's breath sped up, his heartbeat increased in pace. He kept turning on the spot, but this only made him more afraid. Since he'd begun turning, he no longer knew from which direction he'd come, so he couldn't even retrace his path. The woods looked identical in every direction, every tree looking exactly like its neighbour, and Alex suddenly began to panic that he was trapped, that he'd never make it out. He began to fear everything everyone had said about Janet and her family was correct, and his belief in her had been stupid, naive, and that he was now going to be punished for thinking he knew better.

And then he felt a hand slip into his, felt its warmth, and every bad feeling vanished instantly, replaced by the incredible serenity that only holding Janet's hand could provide. Because he knew it was Janet's hand without even looking. In some ways, he was now used to it, its size and shape and warmth, but as well as this, he just knew.

When he did finally look he was confirmed to be correct; he had no idea where she'd gone, where she'd come from, but he didn't care. All that mattered was that she was back.

He turned to face her, and they stood only a few inches apart. Their eyes met; once more Alex was completely in the thrall of the bright orange of her retinas and the way they almost seemed to be on fire. Their colour was even more pronounced in the darkness of the wood, and Alex was entranced. He could feel her breath on his face, warm and somehow floral, and he could smell her. Despite all the smells of the wood, Janet's rose above it and made its way into Alex's nostrils. It was earthy, like soil. She smelled like a flowerbed without the flowers, but with the promise of beautiful buds soon to bloom. Roses, peonies, tulips, other flowers he'd seen but couldn't name; they all comprised Janet, and yet she was so much more.

Alex's heart, which had slowed when Janet rescued him, began to beat quickly again. She wasn't saying anything, just looking at him, and Alex got the sense she was waiting. And he thought he knew what she was waiting for.

He closed his eyes, like he'd seen people do on TV, and slowly began to lean towards her. He could sense Janet's face right there, her lips so close to his. This is it, he thought, this is the moment I get everything I've ever wanted.

And then he felt Janet's hand leave his and he heard her pad away. He opened his eyes to see her ahead of him, looking back over her shoulder.

'Come on,' she said, the playful glint in her eyes once more. 'We're nearly there.'

Chapter Twenty-Eight

Alex followed Janet for perhaps 30 seconds before she turned a corner – if there can be said to be such things in a wood – and vanished from sight. His panic threatening to return, Alex dashed after her, and after turning the corner his breath was taken away.

The wood opened up into a clearing; it was a circle, perhaps ten feet in diameter, formed of trees. The ground was a perfect covering of bright green grass, and there were no flowers, no fallen leaves; it was as if it had just been cleaned and tidied. From where Alex was standing at the edge, it looked like a perfect circle, like it had been measured and built that way. But Alex knew, somehow he just knew – it was like the wood itself was telling him – that no man had been involved in its making. It had made itself, the wood told him, and took care of itself.

Janet stood in the middle of the clearing; exactly in the centre was a tree stump, old and gnarled. Alex could tell, could sense it in the air in the clearing, that the tree had died naturally, it hadn't been cut down. The stump was perhaps two feet tall, barely halfway up Janet's thighs; its wood was dark, much darker than the trees that bordered the clearing. The stump was almost black, despite the brightness that surrounded it. In fact, the clearing was so bright that Alex wrenched his eyes from the stump and looked up. Unlike the rest of the woods, there was no canopy covering of branches and leaves here. The sun shone down uninterrupted, lighting the area like a spotlight. Alex realised the wood the stump was made of must have been even darker than he first thought, to look so dark in such light.

Janet was standing facing it; Alex was behind her so couldn't see what she was doing, but he thought she might have been praying, or at least doing something like praying. He thought he could hear her whispering; unlike the rest of the wood, which was alive with the sounds of nature, the clearing was silent, deathly so. It was still, too; as well as there being no animal song, there wasn't the sound of branches moving, leaves rustling, none of it. Alex thought in that moment it might just have been himself, Janet, and the tree stump alone in the world.

He stayed where he was; if Janet was praying, or doing whatever it was she did that other people called praying, he didn't want to interrupt. Besides, he was happy just being near her, happy to be with her whilst she did it. Janet clearly felt differently, however, because she spoke to him then. She didn't turn her head or her body, look at him in any way; instead she simply spoke loud enough that he could hear.

'You can come, it's okay.' Her voice was soft, almost a whisper, but in the silence of the clearing its sound carried perfectly to Alex's ears.

He stepped forward as if compelled; he didn't know if he was walking, being pushed by the trees behind him, or being pulled by Janet herself. He didn't dwell on it, because whatever the reason the end result was the same. He moved across the thick, spongy grass, almost bouncing, and soon was at Janet's side.

The tree stump was even smaller and darker up close. And standing in front of it, Alex could see that it wasn't completely dead; there were leaves growing from it, protruding from various parts of its circular body. There didn't seem to be any rhyme or reason to their appearance, they just were. Some of the leaves were small, barely bigger than his little finger. Others were huge, bigger than his head, and he wondered why they didn't fall down under their own weight. Regardless of their size, the leaves were all uniform in colour; they were a rich, deep green, nearly black themselves. But the colour wasn't sinister or malign, Alex didn't think; it was beautiful.

They stood in silence, side by side, for a moment, before Janet spoke.

'What do you think?'

'It's beautiful,' was Alex's reply, and he wasn't just saying it to be nice to Janet, he meant it. In fact, he thought the tree stump might be the most beautiful thing he'd ever seen. Aside from Janet, obviously.

'It is, isn't it?' Janet said, a smile growing across her face. Though both were looking at the stump, Alex could see her from the corner of his eye. The smile made her look even more beautiful than she already was.

'What…' Alex said, plucking up the courage to ask. 'What is it?'

'It's my family,' Janet said simply, her voice light and airy, without further explanation, as if her answer made perfect sense.

'What do you mean?' Alex asked, puzzled. How could a tree stump be her family?

'This tree is my family,' she repeated. 'The leaves,' she pointed to one, 'represent a woman in my family who has gone home.'

The leaves were her family? And they'd gone home? Alex only grew more confused with every word Janet said. And yet the confusion didn't upset him like it might have; standing with Janet, he knew it'd all make sense eventually. He didn't say anything, just waited for her continue.

'When a member of my family dies, we bury them here in this clearing. We return them to the earth which gave them to us, return them back to Mother Nature who allowed us to be with them for a few years. She only lends women to our family, though, and we always return to her when we pass.

'This leaf here,' she bent and lifted one up gently in her palm, careful not to break the stem, holding it towards Alex, 'is my grandmother.' Alex's heart skipped a beat remembering what his father had told him about Janet's Grandmother, and what she'd done to Hugh Sullivan. 'Mother Nature let us have her for 154 years before claiming her back. I miss her, of course I miss her every day, but I know she's happy and healthy, back once again mingled with the roots of the tree, the wood, a part of everything that surrounds us. Besides, I know I'll see her again soon.'

Janet looked around as she said this, as if to illustrate her point. Alex saw her eyes as they passed over his, and for a second he thought they might have been green, dark green like the leaves she was holding, but her gaze passed so quickly he couldn't tell.

Her eyes soon rested back on the tree, and she let the leaf fall from her palm, bounce up and down on its stalk before resuming its natural position. She was silent for several minutes, giving Alex time to gather the courage to ask the question he knew he had to then, or he never would.

'Janet…' he said, his voice shaking with nervous tension. He realised he just had to say it. 'Are you a witch?'

He didn't know what he expected her to do or say, whether to nod and reveal her powers, or look at him and die laughing at his stupidity, or something else entirely. As it was, she simply responded with one word, before falling silent again.

'Yes.'

Chapter Twenty-Nine

Alex's mind was racing. *Janet was a witch.* He realised, as she confirmed it, that he'd always known, really. The things he'd seen, the rumours and third-hand gossip and conversations between his parents he'd overheard, it all made sense to Alex. And yet, it didn't make sense at all. How could Janet be a witch? *Witches aren't real.*

'How… I mean… what… I mean…' Alex spluttered, unable to form his thoughts into coherent sentences. 'What do you mean?'

Janet had turned back to the tree stump, and when she spoke her voice was low, edged with suspicion, nearly a growl; she was back in her usual defensive posture.

'You already knew that,' she said.

'I mean…' Alex said. 'I thought… some stuff I've… but… I mean… like…' he sighed, stopped, started, paused, faltered. 'You're a witch?'

He said it with such incredulity that Janet flinched. Alex's heart broke. Even though she'd admitted she was a witch, even though his worst fear had come true, he realised it hadn't changed how he felt about her. Standing next to her, looking at her now, her small, delicate, powerful body encased in the beautiful black dress, her hair long and shimmering in the sunlight beating down through the gap in the trees. Even her eyes, though he couldn't see them in that moment he could picture them, orange as the sun, a million times more alive, more power contained in those two small spheres than in a thousand nuclear bombs.

When he next spoke, his voice was lower, softer; he tried to be understanding.

'How can you be a witch?' he asked, and Janet said nothing for a moment.

'How–' Alex repeated, but Janet cut him off.

'I heard you,' she snapped, impatience in her voice. 'I'm a witch because I'm a witch,' she said, and although Alex didn't know what she meant, he also understood completely.

'My mother is a witch, and her mother was a witch, and her mother, on and on and on back to, I dunno, I guess the beginning of time.' She stopped, started to move her head up as if she was going to look at Alex before letting it fall again. 'We're witches. I don't know how else to describe it to you, Alex.'

Hearing her say his name distracted him for a moment; he thought it was his favourite sound in the whole world.

'I saw you once…' Alex started, trailed off.

'In the alley by your street?' Janet finished for him, phrasing it like a question but Alex knew she knew. Alex thought Janet probably knew a lot of things she had no right knowing.

'Yeah.'

'Yeah,' Janet echoed.

'What were you doing?' Alex asked, wondering if his suspicions were going to be confirmed. 'I thought you were talking to–'

'A spider?' Janet barked out an entirely humourless laugh. 'You were right.'

'But, like,' Alex said, exasperation permeating every facet of his voice. His words were coming out as desperate pleas. 'How can you talk to spiders?'

'I just can,' was Janet's short reply.

'But, like,' Alex stopped, changing tack slightly. 'The cat we saw on the track near your house?'

'Lisheen?'

'Yeah.'

'What about her?'

'When we saw her,' Alex said, 'you picked her up, and I swear.' He stopped, lapsed into silence.

'Yes?' Janet prompted.

'I swear,' Alex said, 'even though you didn't say anything, I swear you and that cat were,' Alex paused, searching for the right word. 'Communicating?'

Janet turned to face him, taking her eyes off the tree stump and placing them on Alex. Alex turned to face her, and they stood for a moment in silence like a couple about to be wed.

'Alex,' Janet began, steeling herself. 'You're correct, we were communicating. Lisheen and I can share our thoughts. It's not like talking telepathically or anything, I can't ask her questions nor she me, but we can share information, we can commune. When we look into each other's eyes, like you are I are doing now, I can tell her things and she can tell me things.'

Alex flinched, broke eye contact and looked away. He didn't really know what Janet meant, but the thing she'd said about eye contact made him very aware they were sharing it in that moment, and he had to break it. He looked at the floor, and the carpet of brilliant green grass that surrounded their feet. He wanted to go home; he never wanted to leave.

'I don't understand,' Alex said desperately, pleading with Janet. He looked at her again. 'How can you talk to a cat? And a spider? *How!?*'

Janet sighed. Alex forced himself to look into her eyes; he thought she was thinking, organising her thoughts. She looked distracted, taking a moment to compose herself before continuing.

'Nature,' she began with a violent exhalation, before composing herself and continuing. 'People talk about nature as if it's something separate from us, as if we're apart from it.' She looked around as she spoke, her eyes moving from Alex to the trees, the branches, the tree stump, back to Alex. 'Even people who like nature, they speak of it as this separate entity, this separate thing. *But they're wrong.*'

She said these last words with such force that Alex jumped.

'We *are* nature. Nature is *us.* Just because we walk on two legs and speak in words and use our thumbs to create tools, we humans think we're something different, something special, something *better*. But we're not better. We're not special. We're not even different.

'We are nature,' she said again, 'and nature is us. I'm a witch, and my mother is a witch, but do you know what that really means?'

She looked at Alex, but even if he could have made his mouth work, he had no words to respond with.

'All that means is that we accept our place in nature. Witches aren't like you see on TV and stuff,' she scoffed, looking like she'd just eaten something that tasted foul. 'We don't cast spells and hurt people, we don't destroy crops and take revenge on those who are suspicious of us.

'It's nothing like that stupid pop singer sings about, or says in interviews and stuff. I hate her so much, dancing around on stage telling everyone she's a witch. She isn't! If she really was a witch she wouldn't be parading it around, because she'd have grown up how I've grown up, and learned long ago to hide it. People don't like witches; they love the idea of witches, but they don't like the reality.

'People watch too much TV, they think witches are evil hags who cast spells on anyone, any time, for fun. We're not! We don't hurt people just because we want to, we try not to hurt people even when we really have to.'

She paused for a moment.

'And we didn't kidnap Joseph Sullivan just because his sister hates me and his dad hates my mother.'

Alex felt hot suddenly, like the temperature in the

clearing had risen by ten degrees. He pulled his shirt from his body where it was stuck with sweat, wiped his hand across his forehead, rubbing the sweat off it and onto his trouser leg. The temperature settled back to its previous, more bearable level as Janet calmed down.

'My mother and I had nothing to do with his disappearance,' Janet said, looking at Alex. She had tears in her eyes and he longed to comfort her, but knew she needed to finish what she was saying before he could offer any support.

'If anyone deserves pain it's those two, but Joseph is entirely innocent. He'll be found soon, though,' Janet said. 'I just hope my fears are wrong.'

Alex wanted to ask what she meant but she continued speaking before he could.

'The reason I can talk to cats is because we're both a part of nature. The reason I can talk to spiders is because we're both a part of nature.'

She stopped talking, looked down, scratched her nose with one finger, and looked back at Alex.

'Long ago, my ancestors made peace with everything around us; we live side by side with animals and plants, never consuming our brothers and sisters unless we have to. We don't eat meat, we don't drive or fly or anything like that. We live in harmony with the world. Over a long period of time, that has allowed us to communicate with nature. We, my mother and I and our family, exist on a different plane to you.'

Plane? What the hell did she mean? They weren't on a plane?

'We may be standing here, in the same world, but that's only on the surface. Because the problem is,' Janet said, reaching out and taking Alex's left hand in both of hers. 'The problem is, you can only see the surface.' Her hands were warm, and Alex felt safe with his inside them. 'We have sunk below. We have seen the other side.

'We are more.'

Alex felt a surge of heat passing into his hand, up his arm, around his body. Whilst the feeling scared him a little, he also realised it made him feel alive. He felt powerful, his usual feelings of helplessness and loss were gone. He felt like he could do anything, conquer any challenge that came his way. He felt, with Janet by his side, he could take over the world.

'It's nice, isn't it?'

'Huh?' Alex said, quickly withdrawing from his thoughts and returning to Janet.

'What you can feel right now. It's pleasant isn't it, the power?'

Alex was taken aback; how could she know what he was feeling? Then he realised, and wanted to smack himself for being so stupid. She knew what he was feeling because *she was making him feel it.* He knew this thought was right, he just knew: Janet was giving him a taste of her power, was proving to him everything she'd said. He'd believed her without question, but now, with this proof, he knew for certain.

'Is that how you feel all the time?' he asked.

'Yes,' Janet nodded, a soft smile growing across her lips.

'Wow, it's…' Alex said, searching for the words. 'Incredible.'

Janet's smile played out in full, and she even looked a little embarrassed, but didn't say anything.

'How do you, like, not just use it all the time?'

'What do you mean?'

'If I felt like that, I wouldn't let Emma Sullivan bully me. I'd… I'd kick the shit out of her.' These last words came out in a rush, and Alex felt a strange relief at having voiced them.

Janet looked at him for a moment, as if trying to decide how much to tell him. She looked amused, concerned, relieved, and excited, all at once. Her face was a picture, one Alex wanted to frame and hang above his bed so he could look at it all the time.

'That would be nice,' Janet said quietly, as if admitting something to herself. 'But we can't. It would be easy, and would solve the problem of the Sullivans, but would only make things much worse. Time is a flat circle, and we no longer make the mistakes our ancestors did.'

'How do you mean?'

'What do you feel right now?'

Alex hadn't been expecting the question, and it caught him by surprise.

'I don't understand,' he said, even though he thought he did.

'Just tell me, Alex,' Janet said, his name sounding like a waterfall in her mouth, a thunderstorm. There was power in the words, but it was latent. It wasn't making itself known, but Alex knew it had the potential to be deadly. 'Just tell me how you feel right now. Don't be shy,' she said, smiling at him encouragingly. 'Don't worry about saying anything that you think is stupid. I won't laugh; I understand.'

One of her thumbs was stroking the back of his hand, and the feeling of it moving tenderly back and forth gave him the strength to answer her question.

'I feel,' he began slowly, and then his words all tumbled out in a rush. 'I feel strong. Powerful. But it isn't just that. Like, I could beat 100 bad guys in a fight right now, but also I don't need to? Like, if they came at me I'd let them win, because my winning would be dreadful. I could kill them all with one look, but how could I do that and live my life? And what would happen next?'

Alex stopped, took a breath. Janet smiled once again.

'And there you have it,' she said simply. Alex understood completely.

'I'm sorry, Janet,' he said. 'I'm sorry for everything.'

'It's okay,' she replied, and he might have imagined it, but Alex was sure she took a step closer.

The pair were still maintaining eye contact, and Alex could once again feel her warm breath on his face, smell her beautiful scent. He knew what it was that she smelled like, it became blindingly obvious to him: nature. She didn't have one smell but hundreds, thousands, all mingled into one. She smelled of life, of love, of beauty and truth and peace. She smelled *right*, Alex thought, and he never wanted that scent to leave his nostrils.

This time it was Janet who leaned in, Janet who closed her eyes. Alex closed his too but didn't move, didn't need to. Alex could feel her breath getting hotter and heavier as it neared him, could sense her face moving closer and closer. It seemed to take an eternity, it felt like she was moving to him from a million miles away, from the surface of the sun, but then there she was.

Their lips met in a collision of ecstasy, and then Janet kissed Alex, Alex kissed her back, and everything was right.

Chapter Thirty

Alex floated home; not literally of course, although he did wonder if Janet had that ability. Probably not, he thought, that was just something people did on TV and in films, but still…

He'd wanted to ask Janet about her abilities, ask her even more about what it was like to be a witch, but he hadn't. In a fit of adulthood, something Alex didn't recognise in himself but which affected him nonetheless, he considered Janet's powers – if that was even the right word – the kind of thing where you can't ask. If the person ventures the information you can listen, gently inquire, that kind of thing. But you can't just straight up ask, it'd be incredibly rude. And as Janet hadn't offered any more information, Alex had to be content with what she'd told him.

They'd kissed for another minute, before Janet broke their connection. Afterwards neither of them said anything, they simply looked at each other. Alex felt changed in some ways; he felt older, more grown up, as if he'd just crossed an invisible barrier. He knew he wasn't a man yet, but he also knew he was no longer a boy. He was somewhere in between; but if that in between was where he would kiss Janet, he told himself, he was perfectly happy there.

Something had happened on the way back out of the woods that, though it wasn't necessary, had backed up everything Janet had said. She led him out, this time holding his fingers loosely in her own, guiding him with touch. At first he'd ducked and dodged the overhanging branches, the wooden fingers that were desperate to touch him, but he soon realised he didn't need to. It wasn't that they were moving out of his way, exactly, but something akin to that. He was receiving the same treatment as Janet, gifts given by nature, and he felt calm and serene.

Unfortunately, not all the trees had received the message; just as they were about to emerge from the woods and back into the field that separated it from Janet's house, a branch whipped across Alex's arm, cutting him. The pain was instant; the cut was shallow, only a few drops of blood peeked out from it, but it stung nonetheless. Alex sucked in his breath and Janet turned round to see why he'd done so. When she saw his arm she let his hand drop, and began scanning the ground with her eyes.

'Here we go,' she said, to herself more than Alex, gently bending down and plucking a handful of small green leaves that were hanging off a stalk amidst a multitude of purple flowers. The flowers were bell-shaped, tall, long, and thin; as Janet plucked the leaves and brought them towards Alex he could smell them, although to try and describe the scent would have been impossible.

'Close your eyes,' Janet said, sounding like a woman enthralled in her task. Alex obeyed her, and a moment later he felt something cool on his arm. It stung at first, but then the pain passed and it felt like he was running his arm under cool water. It was refreshing.

'Okay, open them,' Janet said, and again Alex obeyed. He looked at Janet, but she wasn't looking at his face but rather his arm. Glancing down, Alex was shocked – but not really, not any more – to see that his cut was gone. It wasn't healed, there wasn't a scab or even a faint trace to show it had ever been there. It was like nothing had ever happened.

'Hyssop,' Janet said. 'Normally you boil it and drink it to ward off fever spirits, but it also works as a balm.'

Alex turned his arm over, rolling it one way then the other. He was amazed, he didn't know what to say.

'Thank you,' he just about managed to stutter, and Janet looked him in the face and smiled. She'd then taken his fingers once again, and they were soon out of the woods and back in the brilliant sunshine. Any lingering doubts Alex had harboured, whether conscious or lower, about everything Janet had told him in the clearing had disappeared. He believed.

Now, halfway home and still flying – Alex and Janet having kissed once more at her front door before parting – Alex kept glancing at his arm, as if he half expected the cut to reappear, as if Janet had fooled him somehow, or even that her... magic – he hesitated to even think the word, but had no other idea what to call it – only worked when she was nearby. But no, his arm was still clean, still clear, still uncut. He marvelled at it.

He was so lost in his amazement that he almost didn't notice the crowds of people moving against him; it was only when the crowd became thick enough that he had to turn sideways and slip through small gaps that he truly became aware of it. He stopped and looked around; a wave of people were heading towards the edge of the village, he was very much swimming against the tide. There must have been 40 or 50 people he could see, and he wondered how many more had passed him when he hadn't been paying attention. The crowd reminded him of something, but he couldn't quite put his finger on what it was.

He stopped and looked around, eyes and mouth both wide open, doing his best impression of a fish. He could hear mutterings, murmurings, from the people who passed him. They were speaking in low voices, almost whispering to each other, conspiratorially, and he could only snatch a word here and there. He thought he heard 'body' and 'playground' and 'about time', but in isolation they didn't mean anything to him. If he hadn't still been floating from Janet's kisses, he might have been able to put two and two together. As it was, it was only bumping into his parents that enlightened him.

'Alex, where have you been?' his mum said. His dad silently nodded, not looking at Alex, instead gazing all around at the scores of people.

'At school,' Alex said, panicking and lying. His mum didn't even seem to notice.

'Come on, love,' his dad urged his mum. 'We have to go. We have to get there.'

His dad started walking away and his mum made to follow, but Alex grabbed her arm and stopped her.

'What's going on?' he asked, fear beginning to rise.

'Come on,' his dad urged his mum, taking her other arm. Father and son were using their mother as a rope in a tug of war; the pain of it was written all over her face.

'Mum,' Alex said, his voice louder and firmer. 'What's going on?'

He saw his parents exchange a look, a dark look, and he knew instantly what had happened.

'They found Joseph,' his mum said, and for a brief moment Alex allowed her phrasing to let him believe Joseph was alive and well. That idea was quickly dispelled by the pain in her eyes.

'Come on,' his dad urged again, and this time he won. Alex's parents started walking, marching really, towards the end of the village where Janet lived. Alex had to jog to keep up and raise his voice to be heard over the noise of the crowd that had now swallowed them. Alex's dad was moving faster than everyone else, pushing his way to the front. Alex and his mum struggled to keep up.

'They found the poor little boy's body,' Alex's mum said, sniffing back tears as she did so. 'In the playground where he was taken. The groundskeeper found it, him, this morning when he was doing his usual rounds. He called the police, and somehow the news got out.'

'He'll have leaked it himself,' Alex's dad said back over his shoulder. 'This is exactly what he'll have wanted.'

Alex could hardly see his dad over the heads of the crowd. He was standing on his toes, and his dad was just about visible a little ahead of them. The crowd still reminded Alex of something, but for all his life he couldn't think what.

'What does Dad mean?' Alex asked his mum. 'Who leaked what? Who wanted this?' Alex's voice turned pleading. 'Mum, *what is going on?*'

Alex's mum stopped, her arm falling out of her husband's grasp, but Alex's dad continued moving, weaving his way through the crowd. Alex and his mum stood still, facing each other like he and Janet had only a little while earlier; people moved around them, like stream around an island. They were occasionally jostled but mostly avoided. Alex almost wished they hadn't been, because what his mum told him filled him with a fear greater than any he'd ever previously experienced.

'Joseph's body was…' she began. Alex cut across her when she hesitated.

'Mum,' he urged. '*Just tell me.*'

'Joseph's body was found mutilated,' she said.

'What does that mean?'

'It was missing… parts, it wasn't entirely whole.'

'What was missing?' Alex's mum didn't say anything. 'Mum, *what was missing?*'

Alex's mum visibly shuddered before she answered, and when she did her voice quivered.

'His eyes. His fingers and toes. His tongue. His body

was there, but those bits weren't found.'

Alex knew then what had happened. He didn't know how, but he knew. He turned and ran to catch up with his father, because he knew what his dad was doing too. Suddenly, and with a dreadful clarity, Alex knew what the crowd of people reminded him of, and knew what was going to happen.

It was like being in school; the crowd was moving towards the source of the violence, desperate to be involved somehow. The source of the violence was going to be the Willerbys; it didn't need to be violent, but Alex knew it would be if Mr Sullivan got his way. *When* Mr Sullivan got his way. And it was Mr Sullivan, Alex knew, that had leaked the news about his son's body. It was Mr Sullivan, he knew, that had riled the crowd up. And it was Mr Sullivan, he knew, that would be at its head, leading the charge towards the Willerbys. Mr Sullivan was finally going to get his way, Alex realised with a fresh new terror. The crowd, or mob as Alex now realised it should more accurately be called, were going to kill Janet and her mother.

Chapter Thirty-One

Alex raced to catch up with his father. He had to elbow his way through the crowd, jostling people aside and squeezing through so many small gaps. It was different than fighting his way through his fellow students; the crowd was bigger, more compact, and people moved aside less easily. He could see his father's head and shoulders perhaps five feet in front of him, but it took Alex an age to reach him.

'Dad!' he yelled, his voice faltering. He was out of breath, the exertion taking its toll. His father seemed not to hear.

'Dad, Dad, wait!' Alex yelled as loud as his tired lungs would allow. His father still didn't stop, or turn, or show any acknowledgement he'd heard his son.

Alex redoubled his efforts, no longer politely sliding past people but finding the strength to shove them out of the way, using his elbows to dig into people's sides, violently throwing them aside. None of them seemed to notice; it was almost as if they were in a trance, not completely within their own minds or competence.

Eventually, Alex reached his father. He grabbed him by the arm of his coat, and finally his father looked at him.

'Dad, we have to stop them!'

His dad nodded grimly, his face a topographical map of frown lines.

'I know, son. Come with me.'

Alex's dad's voice was flat, and that only made the fear Alex felt triple in size. It was one thing for Alex to be scared, he was just a kid, lost in a scary situation; there was every chance he might be misunderstanding what was about to happen. But his dad being scared? That really terrified Alex. Adults know, Alex knew, they know what's happening. If my dad is scared, Alex thought, then this is a scary situation.

Alex's dad had adopted the same plan as Alex, throwing people aside in his efforts to reach the front of the crowd, or mob, or whatever it was called. Alex didn't think the name was too important, he was more concerned with what they were planning to do.

Alex's dad reached the front of the crowd just as the crowd reached the top of the track that led to the Willerby's house. Alex was only a fraction of a step behind him and, as they pushed out from the jostle of bodies and into the open air, Alex gulped down great mouthfuls of it, filling his lungs. Alex's dad turned to face the mob, holding up his hands in a position of supplication. Alex stood next to him, and though he was bent at the waist, his hands on his knees, doubled over with tiredness, he could still see the crowd.

He was in no way surprised to see the Sullivans at the

front. In the centre stood Mr Sullivan, with what Alex thought was murder etched on his face. His normally human features were twisted, grotesque; he looked like the gargoyles that clung onto the walls of the church in Hull that Alex's Geography class has visited the year before. His face was small, his eyes were narrowed, filled with suspicion and hatred, and he had a sneer on his face.

Alex was surprised, however, to see fire in Mr Sullivan's hand. He was holding what looked like a long piece of wood with some cloth at the end of it; the cloth, which was raised to the sky, was burning. Flames shimmered on it, flickering in the light afternoon breeze. Alex, though perhaps ten or fifteen feet ahead of the crowd, could feel the flames licking his cheeks. His fear, which he had thought at its maximum, was turned up another few notches. He knew then what Mr Sullivan planned to do to Janet and her mother. Alex was not going to let it happen, no matter what it took to stop the crowd.

Mr Sullivan had his wife and daughter with him, the former to his right and the latter to his left. The three stood at the head of the crowd, like generals in an invading army; behind them were scores of people, it looked to Alex like most of the village. There were also plenty of faces he didn't recognise, which he assumed must have been from Hull and the other surrounding villages. The extent of Mr Sullivan's influence terrified Alex.

Alex looked at Emma; though she was standing next to her father, she looked like she'd rather have been anywhere else. She looked awkward and uncomfortable; she wasn't holding a burning torch herself, her hands were in her trouser pockets. Her head was down, she was looking at the floor, from side to side, appeared to be avoiding any and all eye contact. One of her feet was worrying at the ground beneath her, toes down heel up, rotating slowly back and forth, back and forth. She was the picture of discomfort.

Her mother, on the other side of her father, looked somewhere between her husband and her daughter. Her face was a mixture of anger and astonishment, as if she hadn't expected things to get where they had so quickly, if at all. Her brow was furrowed but her eyes were wide, doe-like, and even as she looked furious she also looked lost.

The rest of the crowd had a singular emotion: hate. In the few seconds it took Alex's father to compose himself, Alex looked at the faces he could see. The two Sullivan women were the only ones who looked like they didn't like what was happening. The rest of the mob looked like they'd been waiting for that moment all their lives.

Then Alex dad's spoke, and everything changed.

Chapter Thirty-Two

'People, people, please,' he shouted, his hands still palms out, doing his best to be heard over the baying of the crowd. 'Listen to me, please, you have to stop this.'

No one said anything; the murmuring continued, a discordant jangle of voices loud against the afternoon stillness. People turned and whispered to each other, some hiding behind their hands, others pointing at Alex's father. The Sullivans remained silent, Mr Sullivan staring at Alex's dad as if trying to burn a hole in him.

'I know what you want, but please listen to me: *you're making a mistake.* What happened to Joseph,' and now there was movement from the front row. Mrs Sullivan let out a low moan, and Emma glanced at Alex's dad, at Alex himself, before looking back down. Mr Sullivan looked like he was about to speak, but quickly stopped himself. 'What happened to Joseph was a terrible tragedy, but the Willerbys had nothing to do with it!'

Hearing the name set the crowd off; there were yells, angry shouts, more torches were lit and thrust towards the sky. The tension, far from being relieved by what

Alex's dad was saying, only heightened. Alex's dad raised his arms, gestured for calm and quiet. He got some of the latter but none of the former.

'Mrs Willerby is innocent. Her daughter Janet is innocent. Burning their house, burning *them*, is not going to solve anything.'

Shouts came from the crowd, and a few objects were thrown at Alex's father. He dodged them deftly, an empty Coke can clattering to the ground behind him, the noise eerily normal amidst the clamour from the crowd.

'Please, I beg you to go home. No crime has been committed here by these women.'

Now Mr Sullivan spoke, and when he did the entire crowd fell silent. He spoke in his normal voice, but in the sudden silence his words were clearly heard by all.

'Go home, man, this doesn't concern you.'

'It does–'

'It does not. My son is dead!' Mr Sullivan shouted before faltering, his voice wavering. His wife reached for his hand but he shrugged her off. She looked heartbroken.

'My son is dead, and these women killed him. I demand revenge.'

'Revenge!?' Alex's dad said, incredulous. 'What the hell are you talking about? This isn't a film, this is real life.'

'I don't care!' Mr Sullivan thundered, causing the two women either side of him to jump in fright. 'My son is dead; I don't care about anything any more. Step aside and let us get on with it.'

Mr Sullivan lifted his foot, as if to step forward, but lowered it as Alex's dad spoke again.

'These women are innocent, and I cannot let you harm them.'

'Innocent?!' Mrs Sullivan screamed the word, her voice shrill, piercing the afternoon air, renting it. 'They killed my boy!' she screamed again, before breaking into loud, harsh sobs. Neither her husband nor her daughter moved to comfort her; Mr Sullivan was still glaring at Alex's dad with unmasked fury, and Emma was still looking uncomfortable, upset.

'Innocent,' Mr Sullivan echoed. 'These women are not innocent. Emma,' he said, turning to his daughter. 'Tell this foolish man what you told me this morning.'

Emma didn't say anything; she didn't look at her father, didn't open her mouth, instead continued to stare at her foot worrying the ground. Her father spoke again.

'Tell them, dammit!' he said, and Emma jumped and began speaking, keeping her eyes firmly on the floor. Her voice was low, but still it carried to all gathered.

'I saw them,' was all Emma said, but it was all that was needed. Her father took up the mantle.

'Did you hear that?' he shouted at Alex's dad, triumph drenching his voice. 'Emma saw the *ever so innocent* Mrs Willerby and her *completely innocent* daughter Janet take my son. She saw them!'

He shouted these last words at the top of his voice, and the crowd roared back its anger and commiseration. Alex stared at Emma, hating her. She was lying, it was so obvious she was lying. Emma hated Janet, and was making this up to get back at her because Janet had had her suspended from school. Alex wanted to burn Emma in that moment; she was more guilty than Janet could ever be.

'Emma,' Alex's dad said, addressing her for the first time. She didn't look at him.

'Don't you dare talk to my daughter!' Mr Sullivan roared, but Alex's dad ignored him.

'Emma,' he said again, his voice soft and calm. 'Is that true? Did you see Mrs Willerby and Janet take your brother?'

Emma continued to ignore Alex's father, continued to watch her own feet.

'I'm telling you she did, man!' Mr Sullivan shouted. 'She told me this morning. Are you calling her a liar?' he said, and then added with a sneer, 'Are you calling *me* a liar?'

Alex's dad was about to speak when a soft voice stopped him.

'It's okay, dear,' Mrs Willerby said. 'I'll take it from here.'

Chapter Thirty-Three

As if appearing from thin air, Mrs Willerby stood beside Alex's dad. Alex jumped with a start, and looking around saw Janet too, standing on her mother's shoulder, slightly behind her.

The air seemed to crackle with their presence, and a blanket of silence fell on all gathered. Alex, his father, Mr Sullivan: they all gaped at Mrs Willerby. Janet, Alex saw, was back to her usual self; dirty hair and skin, frayed and worn clothes. Mrs Willerby was wearing her long dress, soil dotting her appearance too, a motley collection of bright coloured leaves in her hair. Alex was thrilled to see Janet, and at the same time terrified about what was going to happen to her. And perhaps even more terrified about what she might do to prevent it. Mrs Willerby's words echoed in his head once more.

I'll be forced to do what I try to avoid doing…

Alex's heart began to beat very fast.

Janet will probably have to as well…

Suddenly his fear for Janet and her mother vanished. It was Mr Sullivan he was scared for now. The air continued to fizzle around him, and Mrs Willerby began speaking in earnest. Her voice wasn't raised, she didn't shout. Her tone was mild, reasonable, but firm. Alex was glad it wasn't aimed at him.

'Mr Sullivan, how nice to see you,' she said, and she sounded almost genuine.

'Don't talk to me you… you *witch*!' Mr Sullivan emphasised the final word, and more murmurs rippled through the mob. Mrs Willerby chuckled to herself.

'That word,' she said, her voice still calm but forceful. 'Such a small word that carries so much meaning. Do you know where it comes from?'

Mr Sullivan looked bemused. Mrs Willerby ignored him and continued.

'It's from the Old English word wiċċe, a word that came into being many hundreds of years ago, over a thousand, really.' Mrs Willerby was talking perfectly normally, as if she was answering a question in the living room of her home, sharing a cup of tea with an interested stranger.

'Right from the beginning it was a term loaded with malice. From its very first utterance it's been said with hate. With spite. With malevolence.'

Mrs Willerby looked at Alex; he could feel the full force of her spirit in him as she paused briefly to regard him, before continuing. Janet was silent, but Alex could feel her presence like a threat.

'My people,' she said, gesturing to herself and Janet, 'have lived on this land for over 500 years. We plan, Mr Sullivan,' she said, his name sounding like a threat in her voice, 'to live here at least 500 more.'

'You killed my son!' Mr Sullivan screamed. Mrs Willerby, much to Alex's surprise, chuckled to herself.

'You and I both know that isn't true,' Mrs Willerby said, her voice the epitome of reasonableness.

'Emma told me she saw–'

'I know what she told you,' Mrs Willerby interrupted, and for the first time she sounded angry. Clouds appeared overheard, the sun went behind them and the afternoon became overcast. The air, previously electric, seemed to shimmer and ripple, and the temperature rose a few degrees. Alex's heart began to beat faster. He looked at Janet, who was in turn looking at her mum. Neither of them were saying anything; no one said anything, every single person gathered was silently waiting for Mrs Willerby to continue.

'Your daughter is a liar, Mr Sullivan,' Mrs Willerby said, and when Mr Sullivan moved to speak she held up a hand and he remained silent. 'But you know that already, don't you? My daughter's cat is called Lisheen, but in name only. Your daughter acts as her. Your daughter, for reasons that aren't very clear – one can only assume it's because you and your wife are unkind, neglectful, spiteful parents – hates my daughter.' Mr Sullivan blanched, but Mrs Willerby continued unheeded. 'Your daughter regularly attacks my daughter, physically beating her.

'I've told my daughter to stand up to yours, but she refuses. Whilst I wish she would defend herself, I'm also very proud of her. Are you proud of your daughter, Mr Sullivan?'

He didn't say anything.

'Are you proud of the woman she's becoming? Are you pleased with the young woman you've raised?'

A sob wrenched the air; Mrs Willerby stopped speaking, and looked at Emma. Alex, his eyes focused on Mrs Willerby, followed her gaze. Emma was crying. Neither of her parents moved.

'You see!' Mrs Willerby shouted, a sad triumph in her voice. 'Even now, you don't so much as move a hair to comfort her, when she openly weeps in front of you.'

'Emma–' Mr Sullivan began.

'She's right!' Emma shouted, her voice surprising everyone. 'She's right, I lied, I made it up.' Emma collapsed to the floor in floods of tears. Her mother moved to comfort her, pushing her husband out of the way. Husband and wife exchanged a look before Mrs Sullivan squatted down and put her arms around her sobbing child.

'That doesn't… it… I… I mean,' Mr Sullivan blustered. 'I don't care what she says, or what anyone says. You killed my son! You must pay. You and that evil daughter of yours.'

Janet looked up for the first time at the mention of her. She fixed her gaze on Mr Sullivan, and Alex could see her orange eyes burning with a fury he couldn't even begin to comprehend. Mr Sullivan wilted under her gaze, unable to hold it.

'Therein lies your problem, Mr Sullivan,' Mrs Willerby said. 'You'd much rather hurt my daughter than help your own.'

That seemed to be enough for Mr Sullivan; with a glance at his wife and daughter, he lifted one foot, took a step forward, and turned to face the mob.

'We do this now!' he shouted, and the crowd roared back. 'Who's with me?'

Shouts went up, the sound of feet shuffling impatiently where they stood, murmurs of anticipation. The charge that had been fizzling and crackling in the air became an almost audible buzzing, and Alex felt the hairs on his arms and the back of his neck stand up. The temperature continued to rise despite the sun being hidden behind clouds.

Alex had been looking at the crowd, watching the mass of bodies begin to undulate with frustration. He turned his gaze back to Mrs Willerby, but it was Janet who drew his attention. She'd silently slipped to his side and was tugging at his sleeve.

'You have to come with me,' she whispered to him.

'But–'

'There's no time. Come, now,' she urged him, before moving away, retreating a short distance up the track that led to her house.

Alex similarly tugged at his father's arm and, locating his mum on the edge of the crowd, used his hands to gesture for her to approach. She came hesitantly, and when he had both his parents' attention he said, 'come with me' and moved to where Janet stood. His parents followed him, and soon the four stood twenty feet behind Mrs Willerby, their faces to the crowd. What Alex thought was a safe distance for what he knew was about to happen.

'Janet, are you–' he began, but she cut him off.

'It'll be okay,' she said, her voice low and flat. 'Everything's going to be okay.'

Her eyes were fixed on her mother, and Alex followed her gaze. Mrs Willerby was standing still, and though Alex couldn't be sure without being able to see her face, he thought he could hear her murmuring. A sound caught his attention, and turning to look at Janet he could see she was whispering. She was also giving off an incredible heat; Alex felt like he was standing next to a hundred-foot-high bonfire.

No one said anything for a moment, before Mr Sullivan shouted to the mob.

'Come on, let's end this once and for all.' He raised his torch like a general, and the crowd raised theirs in return, mixed cries of anger and hatred emanating from the mass of bodies.

Mr Sullivan turned back to face Mrs Willerby, and took a step forward, thrusting his flaming torch as he did so. Mrs Willerby didn't flinch, and though this caused him to hesitate for a fraction of a second, Mr Sullivan took another step. The crowd moved behind him, stepping in time, and Alex cried out, screamed desperately for someone to do something. The only movement came from Mr Sullivan and the mob, until they all stopped suddenly as if no longer under their own volition.

Janet's murmurs had become louder and louder until Alex could hear her chanting:

Belenus I come to thee
Wander in of will freely
Offer all the names of he
Send them back unhappily

The words were familiar to Alex, and with a start he realised where he'd heard them before: in his dream of Mrs Willerby. His heart started to be beat in triple time, and his whole body began to shake with anticipation and fear.

Alex felt something invisible flash past him like a strong gust of wind. Then Mrs Willerby spoke, and everything fell apart.

'Fire, flame, it's always the same. Time ever repeats itself.' She sounded almost sad as she said this, looking at the crowd before shouting: 'Can't one of you bastards ever have an original idea?' There was unguarded fury in her voice, and Alex, even from where he stood several feet behind her, nearly lost control of his bladder. When Mrs Willerby spoke again her voice was quiet once more.

'Every generation it's the same, you ungodly monsters come for us, claiming it's us who are the monsters. Us, who mind our own business, who live in peace with Mother Nature and all of her glory. Us,' she scoffed then, 'who are the monsters.'

She stood silent for a moment, the crowd transfixed before her.

'You seem so desperate, so I ask you all: do you want to see a monster?' she asked, her voice quiet but powerful. 'Look to the man who actually killed your son. *He's* a monster. The police have all the evidence they need, they just haven't put all the pieces of the jigsaw together yet. And before anyone thinks it, it's nothing to do with those stones in that field; superstitious nonsense.

'But you needn't worry about the investigation, or any of that, Mr Sullivan,' she continued, smiling a terrible smile. 'You'll be seeing your son before you see his killer. You're going to the other place, though, so it'll only be for a moment. Be sure to savour it.'

She looked at the blazing torch in Mr Sullivan's hand, the flames whipping in the breeze. The fire licked at the air, flashing this way and that. Mrs Willerby looked at it silently for another moment, before fixing her gaze on Mr Sullivan's face. She looked deeply into his eyes, and then spoke the words that both started and ended it all.

'You don't burn us,' she said, her voice carrying the power of a thousand old gods.

'We burn you.'

Mr Sullivan began to scream.

Author's Note

Many of the names in this book have been borrowed from real people who suffered real tragedies.

Spurious accusations have cost humans their lives since the dawn of time.

I hope to one day live in a world where justice is more than just a word.

SRL Publishing don't just publish books, we also do our best in keeping this world sustainable. In the UK alone, over 77 million books are destroyed each year, unsold and unread, due to overproduction and bigger profit margins.

Our business model is inherently sustainable by only printing what we sell. While this means our cost price is much higher, it means we have minimum waste and zero returns. We made a public promise in 2020 to never overprint our books for the sake of profit.

We give back to our planet by calculating the number of trees used for our products so we can then replace them. We also calculate our carbon emissions and support projects which reduce C02. These same projects also support the United Nations Sustainable Development Goals.

The way we operate means we knowingly waive our profit margins for the sake of the environment. Every book sold via the SRL website plants at least one tree.

To find out more, please visit
www.srlpublishing.co.uk/responsibility

www.ingramcontent.com/pod-product-compliance
Ingram Content Group UK Ltd.
Pitfield, Milton Keynes, MK11 3LW, UK
UKHW040106280226
468530UK00005B/192

9 781915 073600